UNBRIDLED REIGN

DOLCE OBSURITÀ #3

UNBRIDLED REIGN

CHELSEA BURTON DUNN

4 Horsemen
Publications, Inc.

DEDICATION

If you are related to me, I suggest you either put this book down or agree that we never discuss it.

For every strong woman who felt like maybe one man wasn't enough to handle you, I got you. And for all the people who have hidden their true feelings for someone away.

TRIGGER WARNINGS:

Mentions/threats of sex trafficking
Descriptions of torture and body mutilation
Graphic death
Graphic violence
Mentions of domestic violence
Mentions of alcohol abuse
Mentions/threats of rape
Instances of misogyny
Graphic sex
Serious dive into anxiety, depression

NON-ENGLISH WORDS/PHRASES:

Tatuś: Daddy (Polish)

Nipote: Nephew (Italian)

Sì, parlo italiano. Per te farei di tutto: Yes, I speak Italian. I would do anything for you

Bravate: shenanigans

Incazzato: I'm pissed

Mimmo: my little boy/my son

Mio figlio: my son

Cazzo!: Fuck!

CONTENTS

CHAPTER 1

ADRIAN

The room was loud. The only light was from the cell phone screens in the crowd, cherries of cigarettes and cigars, and the bright spotlights that illuminated the ring at the center of the dingy warehouse I was in. It reeked of filth: smoke, booze, sweat, and blood. I sat at the makeshift booth that had been set up on a cement platform. It gave us a good view of the matches as they happened, while also setting us apart from the ravenous crowds of degenerates below. Most of them weren't in the life, not truly. Gambling addicts, drug dealers, and other petty criminals were usually the ones who came to these illegal fights. They were on the fringe, but most of them were still good citizens.

Fights were an easy way to make or exchange money. It was also a convenient place to discuss business.

That night, Sal and I had been sent by his father, Salvatore, to discuss an upcoming shipment of weapons we were supposed to be securing. Our men at the railroad had been threatened a time or two by some of the

Polish. They were testing our patience with their games; we both knew who the real power in Missouri was.

Marek Lewandowski sat slightly to my left, where I could still eye him and see what was happening in the ring. He was nervous, that much was clear, with the way sweat was beading at his temples, and his carefully slicked back hair was starting to come out of its gelled confines with each swipe of his hand over it. It hadn't taken much to find out some interesting information about Marek's boss, who also happened to be his father. Piotr Lewandowski, though he may have been the Polish boss in the area, was little more than a petty criminal who liked to pretend he could play in the big leagues.

Enzo, Sal's brother, and a computer genius, had done very little digging before he discovered exactly what type of manpower they had. Not much. There was another set of Polish that were based in the Chicago area that might back them, but mostly they were left on their own to grow or to dwindle. It didn't really seem to matter to the rest of their organization what happened, since they were such a small faction of the bigger machine.

Knowing this, Sal and I needed to make sure they understood who they were messing with each time they threatened us or stole from our shipments. Of course, we had already ramped up our men on the railroad site, but we also had to be careful to not increase so much that we'd garner police attention. That would mean larger payoffs, something Salvatore wanted us to avoid.

And so, we were here, to subtly let Marek and his father know if they stepped on our toes once more, they might get squashed like the pests they were.

"So, Marek," Sal started, turning to look at the sweating man and trying not to smirk when he flinched.

Most people didn't see the subtle flashes in Sal's face that I did, only noticing his calm and stoic outer demeanor, but I saw the amused glint in his eyes. "Did you place any bets on the matches?"

Sal was enjoying this a great deal. There were few aspects of our life in the Mafia under his father that either of us enjoyed, but watching someone squirm under our assumed power was always rather entertaining. It helped that in this particular case, we wouldn't really need to threaten much. Just the idea that we'd be doubling our efforts to protect what was ours should have been enough, but we had additional things we could threaten as well. He certainly wouldn't like it if we decided to take over his business in the heroin trade. Their connection was loose anyway, and their structure for dealing was weak.

We could easily take it from them. We didn't want to, but Marek, as well as his father back home in St. Louis, both knew it wouldn't even be a fight.

"I did," he said, his eyes darting to his men just a few paces from him. One of them held the little betting slip.

"Which matches?" Sal asked, drawing his whiskey glass to his lips.

"Two and four," Marek said, this time smiling to himself; I could see the predatory gleam in his eyes, despite the low lighting.

Matches two and four were women.

Most of the fighters that were pulled for these games were people who were already doing legitimate fighting but needed extra cash. Any martial art was hard on the body of the fighter, but not really lucrative enough to be someone's full-time job, not unless they made it to the big leagues. For everyone else, it was either find regular gigs, work in crime, or do some illegal fighting as well.

Women martial artists in the Underground were far less prevalent and far more prone to injury because matches sometimes were held between giant hulks of men and the unsuspecting women. We never allowed those sorts of matches within our territory and under our umbrella, but that didn't mean other places had those same rules.

Just as I was about to ask why Marek only placed bets on the female matches, the referee stepped into the ring and the loud sounds of the crowd died down a little.

"Tonight, there's a change of plans," the ref said when the mic was handed to him.

I glanced at Sal, whose brow furrowed, gesturing for Paolo to go find out what had happened.

"Match one has changed to Match five. Match two will be our starting fight. All bets are still valid," the ref said, before handing the mic over to someone on the other side of the ropes and stepping back.

"I guess The Tank already got a bloody nose from someone in the back. Elio requested the changeup," Travis told us after discussing with the young boy who ran up to our platform during the announcement.

We nodded, understanding, though how The Tank, our best fighter, had gotten that bloody nose would be questioned later. Now, it didn't matter. I wasn't here to watch the fights; I was here to intimidate and get Marek to back down before he and his father were squashed beneath us. Only a moment later, I hoped he'd fight back so we could.

Marek's whole body seemed to light up with a strange sort of charge as soon as the two fighters were announced and brought out into the ring. It was a big enough reaction that it made me both feel repulsed by him, and curious what could have made him react that way. My eyes darted to the ring, watching as the two women squared up to face one another. The ref was shouting over the commotion of the crowd to them as they nodded their heads at his instructions, and then he waved the flag, and the clock started.

At first, I didn't understand what Marek's problem was. Maybe he was just a disgusting pervert, enjoying watching women beat the shit out of one another (I still wasn't ruling that out), but then I saw her.

Her hair was pulled back, but the long shimmering locks of blue ranging from deep to so pale it could have been white flashed out with each movement of her lithe body. Her skin was tan—either she spent a lot of time in the sun, or she naturally had that complexion, I wasn't sure. But beyond how much I felt oddly drawn to her body, it was how she fought that really made me question everything within myself. This woman was a machine. Each attack was well executed, perfectly timed. There was not a movement that hadn't been calculated. No blow landed that she hadn't intended, no hit she took was not anticipated and used to step into her next move.

She was beautiful and deadly.

I needed to know who she was.

And apparently so did Marek.

Round three was starting. If Ash—as I heard the ref call her when he declared her the winner of the first two rounds—won this one, the match would end. If the match ended, I would be able to find her. We ran this outfit after all, and perhaps…

"That bitch will be fighting me off if she doesn't do as she's told," Marek practically growled. His voice was low, as if he was only talking to himself, but I was close enough to hear him. Apparently, Marek didn't need to know her. His excitement was more because he already did.

"And what was she told, Marek?" Sal asked.

For the first time since my eyes hit that ring and saw Ash, I finally looked at Sal. He looked like the Devil himself, or maybe his father, which was close enough. His dark eyes looked nearly black, sharp jaw tense with clenched teeth. Rage was potent, as it seemed to come off him in waves. Out of the two of us, I was usually the more volatile, but something about the way Marek had talked about Ash had set him off. He felt that zing, that connection, that desire the same way I did. Not surprising, given how close we were to each other, but still a little frustrating.

Marek balked at Sal's words, outright cringing as soon as he saw Sal's face in all its menacing Italian glory.

"I-I only—"

"Put a plant in one of our fights?" I asked, leaning forward just slightly, making Marek flinch a bit more. The two of us, Sal and I, were not a team to be trifled with. In all the years we had been friends, having grown up together, there was no other duo that seemed to strike as much fear as us. Or at least that's the impression we got.

A lot of illegal gambling involved cheating. Of course it did, but our fights weren't thrown; our games weren't rigged. It was well known that if you got involved in Kansas City's scene and you cheated, you'd be facing a world of pain or worse. Marek looked at me like I'd shot his favorite puppy in front of him.

"I didn't! I just told her—"

"Which girl?" Sal asked, nodding toward the fight as the next round began.

"Blue," he said quickly. Of course, the girl I couldn't keep my eyes from was the one he had in his clutches. It was just a matter of how desperate she was. She was working for Marek, or under his thumb. I didn't like either situation, but as I watched her, the fierce look on that face, the grace with which she moved, I wasn't sure someone *could* have her under their thumb, at least not for long.

"What did you tell her?" I asked, not taking my eyes off her as she whipped her blue locks side to side with a headshake.

"She's been doing these fights in St. Louis to pay off her father's debt. She inherited it after he *unfortunately* passed," Marek said, his voice turning less than sympathetic at the end. "She needed to lose this fight. She's mine, so I wanted your girl to win. Help gain favor." It seemed like his American accent started slipping and a bit of the Polish peeked through.

"Our girl, huh?" Sal said with a chuckle as the third-round bell sounded. The amusement on his face didn't lighten the hatred in his eyes, making him look more like a smiling shark just before it ripped off a person's leg.

"How much does she owe?" I asked, standing as the girl she was fighting threw her first punch, being immediately blocked, then "Blue" landed a viscous knee to the ribs.

"Five thousand," Marek growled, watching as Blue's opponent stumbled back, gasping and holding her ribs.

"Consider it paid."

"What?" Marek asked, rocketing off his chair like he was going to fight me.

"We could be taking everything away from you and Piotr," Sal said, leaning back in his chair and sipping lightly on his whiskey once more. His eyes were locked on the blue-haired girl as she bounced from one foot to the other.

"You wouldn't—"

"Wouldn't what?" Sal asked, tearing his gaze away as the ref announced the blue-haired woman the winner. "Tear your tiny operation down because you don't know when to leave the big dogs alone? Have you met my father? You're lucky we even met you like this and didn't send your *tatuś* for a swim in the river with cinder block shoes."

Marek was left floundering on the platform as Sal slammed the last of his whiskey, brought his honey-colored eyes to meet mine, and stood, walking off and toward the private exit. I followed, because that's what we did. Sal and I gravitated toward one another; we always had.

"So now we've bought the girl from them, Adrian?" he asked once we were well away from any ears who would care to hear. I'm sure my face twisted into disgust. While that wasn't my intention, I could see why anyone who heard that exchange would have thought that.

"Freed her, was my intention, Sal," I grumbled, running my hand through my hair and tugging at the back nervously. He broke out in a grin, loving the tortured look on my face.

"Have Enzo look into her. We'll see if we can help her out, so she doesn't have to deal with the Polish again," he said, slapping a hand on my shoulder and giving me a playful shake.

"Will do," I said, already pulling out my phone to text his brother.

As I pressed "send" on the message, moving down the hall with Sal, I had a strange feeling of relief come over me. It wasn't an unusual feeling, but one I certainly kept to myself. Sal and Enzo both had to join the life, forced into it by their father. I was also forced in, to keep my sister from being sold off, but I took that responsibility on my shoulders, because if there was one thing my father taught me before he died, it was that it was *my* responsibility to keep my brother and sister safe.

As long as I was able, Benny and Carmen would never be part of this mob life. Sal didn't have that same relief. The only one of his siblings to not have been sucked in by their father was Leo, who was off in some foreign country, fighting for our country.

Sal hoped, and I did too, that Leo would do better than I did when I was discharged from the marines. We hoped Salvatore stayed well away from him.

I stopped at Sal's car, Travis climbing into the driver's seat. Sal reached over, dusting something off my shoulder, but he was clearly trying to stall leaving. There was only one reason he would put off getting to his next appointment, and that meant his father.

"Heading to see Salvatore?" I asked, knowing exactly what the tightness in his eyes meant.

"Always," he grumbled.

"I can come with you," I offered, though I knew I was supposed to stay at this damn warehouse a while longer to talk to some of the gang leaders in the area that did work for us. I would have much rather gone with Sal though, if for no other reason than to be a support to him.

"No, I don't want you to deal with it. It's just a small thing," Sal said, though I could see the strain on his face before he slipped into the back of the car and drove out of sight.

CHAPTER 2

ASH

FOUR YEARS LATER

"**Y**ou're going to look fine, Ash!" Carmen called from across the parking lot of the restaurant we had just left, Daph and Rory, her two best friends from child-hood, giggling as they scrambled into their car parked just a few spaces away from me.

"I don't wear dresses, Carmen!" I yelled as she ducked through the door, closing it and giving me a grin and a dismissive wave.

I faked a glower at the three of them as they drove away, only narrowly managing to hold it before I broke out into a grin of my own when Rory looked a little worried from the passenger seat while Daph drove them from the lot, leaving me at my car, which sat beside Ingrid's.

"You're going to wear a dress," Ingrid said, having watched the interaction with a bemused smirk on her face.

"I'm not," I insisted, finally fishing my keys from my pocket.

"Carmen is the bride. She wants you to wear a dress, you're wearing a dress."

"Then I'm not going to the wedding." Even as the words left my mouth, I knew they were hollow. There was no way I was missing the wedding of Carmen LaMartina and Leo Lupo in a few weeks. The Lupos and LaMartinas had essentially been a family since before the now-adult kids had been born. Now with the two youngest of each family getting married, it was about to be official. I wasn't a member of either family, but like Ingrid, who still stood watching me between our cars, I was part of their circle. One of the people they invited to come to family dinners and participate in their lives.

Ingrid was more than just the outsider they brought than I was, now. She and the middle Lupo boy had very recently become quite an item, not that all of us hadn't seen the way he pined for her from the moment she stepped foot in Lee's Summit three years earlier.

"Pfft!" Ingrid snorted, laughing loudly as the absurd words came from my mouth. "Sure," she managed between laughs. "Me either!"

"You're Enzo's date, of course you have to go," I grumbled, but I knew there was no way I'd be able to miss this wedding. Only an act of god would be able to keep me from going, and unfortunately, a dress was not that. "Besides, I'm a fighter, not a lover."

As soon as the words left my mouth, I immediately felt the itch that had been nagging at me for nearly two months. I used to be a fighter. I used to go into a ring and win, but the special matches that Salvatore used to set up, mostly to schmooze businessmen and prominent politicians, went away with his death, I was feeling a skin-crawling desire to get back in a ring with tape on my fingers and sweat on my skin. Not just at the gym where I taught.

"I'm sure there are a few people that would *love* to see that hot body of yours in a dress," Ingrid said, finally calming her chuckles before she looked me over suggestively. Ingrid wasn't referring to what I was wearing now, or anything I could potentially be wearing at all. She was referring to two men in particular who either loved me or loathed me, it was hard to determine which way they leaned on a given day.

Adrian LaMartina and Sal Lupo were partners in business, my bosses, and of course Carmen and Leo's oldest brothers respectively. They were two men who drove me crazy with their overbearing ways, their dominance, and sometimes outright ignorant stupidity, but at the same time inflamed me with a voracious need. Maybe it was because I loved to fight with them, maybe it was the fact that both oozed dangerous confidence. Sal was much more reserved, and therefore so much fun to goad, while Adrian was always ready for a fight. While they both had dark Italian features, Sal had a much more angular face, a sharp jaw, dark eyes, and a Roman nose, while Adrian's features were a bit softer, and his eyes a deep blue. Different and yet similar. Two sides of a coin.

"They see my body all the time in the gym," I said, trying to be flippant, but I realized my face was heating, my breath quickening with the image that had just popped into my head of me in a dress that had both men on their knees before me.

Ingrid must have noticed because her face broke out into a wide grin.

"I think you'd love for them to see a little more, wouldn't you?" she asked, quirking her eyebrow before slipping into her car and starting it up, leaving me standing there in the parking lot alone, trying to reel in my own untoward thoughts.

Almost as if he could read my mind, my phone rang as I drove back to my apartment complex. Adrian's name flashed on my screen, and I stopped at the light to answer it.

"Had to wait until the last ring to pick it up?" he asked.

"I was still debating letting it go to voicemail," I fired back, smiling as the little grunt of disapproval sounded through the speaker.

"Are you driving?" he asked, when the light changed to green, and I started moving once more. He must have heard the engine.

"Yes. On my way home from your sister's dress shopping lunch," I told him.

"Oh yeah," he murmured, his voice a little distant, as if he was recalling details he had been informed about at some point recently. "Was anyone with Carmen?"

Normally, Adrian's concern about his sister was endearing, but now that she and Leo were engaged and she was in school to be a pastry chef, very much out on her own and being a grown adult, it sometimes made the feminist in me rear its ugly head to hear questions like this.

"Does it matter? She's a grown woman, Adrian," I snapped, stepping on the accelerator, perhaps a little too much for this neighborhood.

"I know she's a grown woman, Ashley. There are just some things happening right now that…" His words trailed off, like he realized he had said too much to me or was about to say too much.

It wasn't uncommon for that to happen in my presence. I worked at the gym that he and Sal owned. I had worked there since they merely ran it for Sal's father,

Salvatore, before he died. I knew the sorts of business they worked with and ran; I knew far more than I probably should have, but we didn't openly discuss it. Confirming things I did and didn't know to them would mean I would either have to be brought into the fold or be a loose end they needed to cut. Clearly, neither of them wanted me gone, so we just maintained this little limbo, one foot in and one foot out.

Sometimes I wished I could have been fully in, because it was times like this, when it concerned people I cared about, like Carmen, that I wanted to know what was going on. I knew far more about her kidnapping last summer than they would have liked, but part of that was because Leo had come into the gym nearly every day to work out his aggression while they tried to plan to get her back.

But there was more, and it seemed like Carmen was still a target. I just wasn't privy to why.

"What is happening, Adrian?"

"I'm going to be with you to close the shop today," he said, instead of answering me, just ramping up my frustration.

"Joey is fine. I'm used to him being there."

"And when I get there, I'm sending Joey home."

I pulled up into my parking spot a bit more abruptly than I would have liked, my tires screeching against the pavement in front of my building angrily.

"Why?" I asked through gritted teeth.

"It doesn't matter why. I'm the boss," he said, before hanging up.

How that man heated my blood in both anger and desire in a matter of minutes I had no idea, but I was fuming as I scrambled out of my car and headed toward my building.

The mail person was just closing up the last box as I got closer. I didn't usually get much mail, but the box below mine did, so much mail that an orange envelope was sticking out of the bottom, like a beacon, catching my attention.

"Did I get anything?" I asked, pulling out my keys and gesturing to my box.

"Everyone did today," he said, with an odd expression. His smile was kind, but his eyes were filled with sympathy … or perhaps pity? Now I was infinitely more curious.

I opened my own box to reveal a similar orange envelope sitting there, as well as a few others; bills most likely, but none of them filled me with dread the way the orange one did.

"Thank you," I said, closing my box as he walked over toward the next building, and I slipped up the stairs to my apartment, closing the door with a loud snap as soon as I was in there. There was a weird pressure I could feel forming in my chest.

Obviously, I felt something weird was happening in the lives of the people closest to me. My job and general life revolved around the Lupos and LaMartinas. Their businesses and the people who worked and ran them were central to my life now that I had moved here from St. Louis, but the anxiety that I was feeling in this moment wasn't because of them. No, something about this note I received felt like problems from my past. It felt like the weight of my father's sins coming back once more to rear its ugly head.

But that was ridiculous. *Everyone* got the orange envelope. It wasn't just me.

I moved through my small apartment from the door, setting the new mail on my small, scuffed kitchen table next to the only other thing on it, which was the wedding invitation from Carmen and Leo. That card was beautiful. Maria and Liliana had handwritten each one in their delicate handwriting against the soft cream paper with real flowers pressed into the pulp. Now, next to it, sat this hideous orange thing.

I knew I should read it, but I had just come back from a trip with the girls. I had just been included and part of something. I had joked and laughed with these ladies who had become a family to me over these last four years more than anyone else had been for most of life, and something about this note and maybe even these envelopes sitting there told me all of this could very easily come crashing down.

It was with hesitant hands that I reached down and took up the envelope, tearing it open and letting my eyes rest on the words there.

Ashley Torres - Tenant Building C, Apartment 204

Ownership of the complex has changed.

Krakow Invested has purchased the property and you are one of the tenants who is being asked to leave.

We know you have been a loyal tenant, but it is up to the discretion of the owners who we are to retain. Your lease will be up at the end of the month. You have until then to vacate the premises.

If you have any questions or concerns, please feel free to reach out to:

M. Lewandowski,
Property Management.

I felt sick.

Four years ago, I managed to get away from the sins of my father once and for all. I would have liked to say it was on my own, but I knew it was helped along by Adrian and Sal. It was after a fight I had at one of the underground matches they had organized that I was cut loose from the Lewandowski leash. Ever since my father's death, I had been trapped under their boots. My father was a flawed man, and his gambling habits got him into more trouble than they should have. I was only twenty-two when I found him dead in his apartment from what the cops had deemed a suicide. I knew better.

It wasn't long after that when I was contacted by Marek Lewandowski. My father was killed because of his debts, debts that I now inherited. My options for how I could pay were limited. I was already on the path to being a professional FMMA fighter. I had sponsorships that I was negotiating; my life had been on the precipice of completely changing for the better, and now I was faced with somehow coming up with the money within a week. That wasn't possible given that it was over twenty thousand dollars. Option two was to sell my body in one way or another.

My skills in the ring, thankfully, were enough to sway them. I was allowed to keep my sponsorships and start my career, but I had to fight for them when they wanted me to, whether it hurt my career or not.

And it did.

Fights for Lewandowski somehow seemed to line up with sponsored ones regularly, to the point I lost all my funding. Legal fights were no longer an option for me, no, now I was at the mercy of Lewandowski and working only at bars and restaurants where I could pick up shifts, because they became so frequent, I couldn't reliably give a job any sort of availability.

Slowly, breaking my mind and my body, I was whittling away at the debt, but at what sacrifice?

The fights started being rigged. Sometimes in my favor, sometimes not. I had a hard time throwing fights. The women I was up against were not as skilled as I was, often not as clever, and yet I had to appeal to Marek's desires, feigning losses at the cost of my pride. If I didn't adhere to his demands, whatever money he lost would be added to my debt.

It had been an odd request for me to travel with him across the state for a fight. Most of the fights I had were in St. Louis, where he had a foothold, but something about that fight four years ago, the one that ultimately established my freedom, was important to him. I didn't like traveling with him and his men, but it was a necessary evil. I couldn't refuse a fight, not when I was so close to being out of his debt.

And then, suddenly, I was free and offered a job by Adrian LaMartina to work in the gym he ran here in Lee's Summit. I was to train people, make money doing that, and have time to fight legitimately if I wanted to. The only odd request on occasion was from Salvatore Sr., who asked me to fight in private events, but I honestly didn't mind those or the extra money it gave me. At least I didn't have to throw fights.

My life here in Lee's Summit was like a dream come true, at least in comparison to the nightmare I had escaped.

But this letter on the table made me realize it had been just that, a dream. I may have had a few years of freedom, but it wasn't supposed to last. Not really.

The end of the month was two weeks away. In two weeks was the Lupo-LaMartina wedding. How the hell was I supposed to move somewhere else on such short notice?

And I knew what was coming if I called the number listed and asked for help. Marek would find a way to get me back under his thumb, saying I didn't finish paying off my debt or some other made-up crap about my father that would pull me in.

I tore my eyes away from table, dropping my bag that I had been clinging to onto the floor and turning to take in everything that I called home over the last four years. My apartment wasn't matching or upscale, but it was all mine. The black sofa I had bought at an estate sale, and the blue swirly rug I had purchased on clearance from a rug and carpet store in Kansas City proper. The lamps that I had remade the shades for with salvaged scarves, and the curtains that were made from thrifted sheets.

I *made* this place a home, and now I was going to have to pack it all up and move ... somewhere.

My shift at the gym was going to start soon. I had a class I was teaching and then I would take over desk duties until close. I supposed I would have to figure out how to make a little more money on the side over the next few weeks to pay a deposit on someplace new, especially since I assumed I wouldn't be getting my initial deposit back from the complex management. Being told they weren't renewing your lease almost guaranteed that in these more run-down areas.

People who lived here couldn't usually afford lawyers to fight for rental deposits. I certainly couldn't.

I pulled open my laptop, an old decrepit thing, but it still worked, just slowly. I honestly wasn't sure what I could afford around here, not anymore. I had been grandfathered in with the price when I renewed my lease each year. They only once raised the price, and that was by $40 so they could pay for lighting the parking lot.

As the price of comparable apartments in the area popped up, my eyes widened. I knew Ingrid had been renting for her and Nora up until recently, but I had no idea everything was so expensive. It was nearly double what I was paying now, and that was for something that was essentially a studio apartment.

Panic was setting in, a deep-seated feeling that I hadn't experienced since I moved here. How was I supposed to come up with not only a deposit that size, but that sort of monthly rent?

The gym didn't pay me poorly, I was paid well to run the desk, teach classes, and provide personal training, but it didn't pay me enough money to afford to live anywhere close by. Not anymore.

I shoved the computer away again, moving to my bedroom to change into clothes for the gym, while my mind raced trying to figure out how I could make this work. Would I be able to make enough fast enough by picking up bartending or serving shifts somewhere?

Getting back into the legitimate fighting circuit would take too long to see any actual money.

I frowned as slipped on my tennis shoes and headed back out my front door, realizing I only really had two paths forward. Neither path made me especially happy.

CHAPTER 3

ADRIAN

There were very few times anymore that it was just me and Ash in the gym, alone. More often than not there were guards here, because I wasn't able to stay, but that wasn't the case today. I had sent them away. I wanted to be the one to make sure Ash was safe, because I missed being here as often as I used to be now that Sal and I predominately stayed in Kansas City proper.

I missed her.

There must have been a switch that flipped within me at some point in the last few months. Maybe it was seeing my sister, Carmen, falling in love with Leo, or even Enzo and the strange way he transformed with his devotion to Ingrid, but I was feeling so much less desire to hold my feelings for Ash back anymore.

It could have also been the need for something that lit me up instead of the dread that seemed to be bearing down on us all as of late. The aftermath of Sal's father dying at our hands after he tried to sell off Carmen to the Irish had caused a difficult enough hurdle, since Manzo Morelli, the big boss, wanted us to prove Sal's worthiness of taking over as Caporegime. But of course, that couldn't be the only obstacle we faced. Not eight months after everything had gone down with Carmen, did a new problem arise.

Ingrid, the sweet single mother who had been working at Sal's mother, Liliana's, coffee shop for the last several years, was found to be some sort of genius hacker working for the O'Sheas who Enzo had been battling for months. It turned out she had been willfully ignorant as to who she was helping, and switched sides immediately, solidifying her feelings for Enzo in the process, but that little problem revealed a much bigger one.

The O'Sheas were after Carmen and weren't going to stop until they got her.

I may have been the overprotective older brother, but I felt like the fact that Carmen had a target on her head was a good enough reason to always find her walking around without a guard an insult and a serious problem.

Ash apparently disagreed; though Ash didn't know everything that was going on.

I sat in the office, the door open, and watched as she went through the motions of closing everything up. Her class had ended a few hours ago. Mitch, the young man who ran the desk for a few hours in the afternoon while classes and training happened, was sent home, and now the gym was closed. She was finishing up counting the register down. Soon she would be coming back here to put the till in the safe before she headed off to her life that was separate from here.

I had hoped, years ago when I offered her the job at the gym, that maybe someday she would open up a little more to us, especially after she had been included in many family events over the years, but she was a lone wolf. What she did outside of the gym was kept close to her vest. And thus far, only Carmen and occasionally Ingrid had been given permission to be part of that outside life.

I watched the way her hair, now a faded purple, rippled over her shoulders as she moved. The long straight strands looked silky, despite the amount of bleach and dye she applied to them. The pale hair against her tanned skin was a beautiful contrast, as was the shock of her gray eyes. She had mesmerized me from the moment I laid eyes on her four years ago, and now wasn't any different. We may have been a little older, but that didn't mean I wanted her any less. I was certain actually knowing her only made me want her even more.

Knowing her made me immediately realize something was wrong with her when she finally crossed the main room from the counter, heading back to where I sat in the office. I may not have known what her life was like outside of here, but I knew her well enough to be able to detect there was something very wrong happening. Her dark brows were drawn together, one cheek sucked in where she was chewing on it.

There was worry there. Ash wasn't one to worry.

"Why are you still here?" she asked when her eyes finally met mine and she was pulled from whatever thoughts were plaguing her mind.

"I'm waiting for you. The other guards are gone for the night," I said, leaning back in my chair and watching with amusement as her face scrunched up. When she was displeased her cute little nose would wrinkle while her full lips pouted.

"I can take care of myself," she insisted, turning toward the safe and flipping her long ponytail over her shoulder.

"I know. Doesn't hurt to have a little backup though," I said, standing and moving to lean on the front of the desk as she put in the safe combination and set the till in its designated spot beside the smaller safe that sat within.

"You can't always be there to back me up," she muttered, clearly not meaning for me to hear, but I did.

"What's going on with you?"

Admittedly, that wasn't the most subtle or caring way to go about asking that, but I wasn't someone who was particularly good with subtleties. The venom in the look I received from her as she slammed the safe door closed told me I would have been better served to have not said anything at all. But it was too late now, and she was charging toward me, those gray eyes filled with anger.

"Why is it, Adrian LaMartina, that you think you have any right to know what's going on in my life outside of this gym?" she snarled, jabbing her finger into my chest with each word. I grabbed her hand, stopping her assault and managing to pull her a little closer in the process.

"You're my employee. I should know about what's happening in your life."

"Why? So you can see if I'm fit to do my job? Are you going to fire me too?" she yelled, ferocity from her eyes burning into mine.

"Fire you?" I snapped back, my anger getting the better of me. "Any other boss would have done just that for this kind of behavior."

"Then do it," she said, her voice low and menacing, hand balled into a tight fist above where I held her wrist.

While the fighting, angry part of me wanted nothing more than to yell right back, to fire her, if only for a day to make her learn her lesson, the look on her face when she first came into the office echoed back into my memory. It pulled just enough of my rational mind to the forefront to keep me from saying things that would only push her further away.

"Why can't you just accept that there are people that care about you?" I snapped back, instead of the litany of other far more hurtful things I could have said. My voice may have been harsh, but at least the words weren't.

The tugging she had been doing to get her hand free stopped. The look in her eyes changed to something foreign that I had never seen there before. Vulnerability?

She opened her mouth like she was about to say something, but then snapped it shut a moment later, shaking her head and moving to turn away. I could have let her. I could have let her wrist fall from my fingers and watched her walk out the door. Our lives would return to normal, this just another spat in the long history of seemingly insignificant arguments we had had since she came to work here, but instead I tightened the grip on her hand, pulling her farther between my legs.

The feel of her body being engulfed in mine was amazing. For so long, I wanted her to be this close to me. I wanted to hold her, to have my hand firmly pressed against the small of her back as it was now. She stiffened, turning her head from me, the sight of tears welling in her eyes tugging at my heart in a way that I had only felt a time or two before.

I pulled my hand reluctantly from her back to grasp her chin, turning her face back to mine.

"I care about you, Ash. I don't know what's going on, but I'm here if you want me to be," I whispered, watching the way those small pools of tears that had sprung in her eyes filled further still. The anger that had burned in those gray orbs was now replaced with pain and fear.

This woman was one of the most strong and powerful women I had ever known, and that was quite a feat, considering the women who raised me and the person my sister had become. To have Ash look into my eyes and show me what lay in hers in this moment was profound.

I couldn't help myself. Years of pent-up desire, trials and tribulations, laughter and fun, made this proximity, the feel of her skin against mine, unbearable and my actions uncontrollable. I wanted to heal the hurt there. I wanted to be the comfort that helped ease this pain. I wanted her to confide whatever caused it to be there, so I could fix it. But I wasn't sure how. I could only show her.

I leaned forward, my lips brushing against hers. I paused there for a moment, waiting for her reaction. She seemed to have stiffened, but she didn't shove me and step away. She simply stayed there, just like that. The feel of her lips on mine with her body heat radiating off her skin, infusing into me, nearly took my breath away. I forced myself to keep still, to let this moment linger for a little longer.

She wasn't pulling away, but she wasn't kissing me back either.

My heart beat wildly. The years of desire for her as well as the need to comfort her, to know what was wrong so I could be the one to help her, was warring with the fact that this was probably not at all what she needed and wanted right now.

I started to pull away, the touch of her lips against mine slowly dissolving, but it was she who pressed forward just a little more, solidifying our lips together.

Her body shifted to touch more of mine, her chest leaning against my torso, and I risked it, pressing my lips a little more firmly to hers. I was rewarded with a quiet moan as her body leaned even more heavily into mine.

Whatever pent-up desire had been within me had apparently been locked within her as well. The gentle press of our lips turned into a frenzied kiss. My hand plunged into the hair at the back of her neck, while the other grasped her waist, fighting the urge to squeeze or wander. Her fingers raked across my scalp.

A shiver ran down my spine, a tightness settling into place within my chest with each touch of our tongues, with each moan, and with each pass of our hands.

But all at once, it ended abruptly when my phone rang where I had left it on the desk. Our mouths parted with an audible smack, eyes looking into one another with pupils blown from desire. Our labored breathing mingled in the small space between us. A blush fluttered across her tan cheeks, and she pulled away slightly, looking away from me.

"You should probably answer that," she said quietly, fully removing herself from my reach now and turning toward the door.

"It can wait," I insisted, even though I hadn't looked at it. Quite frankly I didn't care in the slightest. If someone was dying, they wouldn't be any less dead when I got there, even if I left immediately.

She turned back, a cheeky smirk on her lips.

"Oh really, Adrian? What if it's Sal?" she asked, not with the solemn expression from earlier or the embarrassment from a moment before, but that playful and flirtatious teasing look was firmly back in place.

Of course, she was right. If it was Sal, that was one phone call I couldn't ignore. And I gave her a little smirk of my own before I turned away to snatch the phone from where it sat behind me.

"This is Adrian," I answered, still not having looked at who was calling.

"I hear you got more than one enemy moving in on your territory." I stiffened at the rough sound of that voice. It was so similar to Sal's dead father, it could have been him. But I knew he was dead. I watched the life leave Salvatore Lupo Sr.

This was Romolo, Sal's uncle, the Caporegime in Chicago. He had been an ally for us on more than one occasion since all this mess with Carmen and the Irish started, but those tides could turn quickly. In this business, you couldn't count anyone as being your true friend. Not really.

"Romolo, you know something I don't?" I asked, watching Ash as she grabbed her bag from under the counter and slipped her jacket over her shoulders.

"I know that my nephew is doing good so far with impressing Morelli, but you're about to get hit with another hurdle. I heard from Bosko that his little Polish cousin might be making moves over there."

"Again? That fucking idiot!" I hissed, watching Ash more closely now that the Polish were brought up. It wasn't long ago that she escaped the Polish scum, and just like the Irish, they kept rearing their ugly head.

"Lewandowski thinks you two are weak. Salvatore's death, the crap with the O'Sheas. You might want to keep your eyes peeled or get that other nephew of mine looking around to see what they're up to."

He meant Enzo. Enzo's, and now Ingrid's, focus had been on trying to find out what exactly it was that the Irish wanted Carmen for so badly. She still couldn't remember anything more than what she had told us, and that meant O'Shea definitely had an advantage over us. Whatever it was that my father, Bernardo

LaMartina, hid away must have been bad, because for him to use his own child…

Well, my father was very different than Salvatore. He loved us. Yes, we were trained like the Lupos to use weapons and fight, but my papa saw that as more of a necessary evil, a way to help keep us safe, especially given the world he was involved in. For his baby girl to be used to protect whatever it was he was hiding, meant it was serious, deadly.

I shuddered to think of what it could be.

"Noted," I said, standing and turning off the lights to the office when I saw Ash was waiting with an irritated look by the front door.

"Tell Sal he should answer when I call. I don't like wasting my time."

"You are always appreciated, Romolo. I'll find out what he's up to," I said, before hanging up the phone and setting the alarm.

"Sal?" Ash asked as we hurried out the door.

"His uncle," I said without thinking. We didn't share details with her. Based on her adjacent affiliation with organized crime in the past, she definitely knew that we were involved, but I had no idea how much she knew, other than what Leo shared last summer. Sal and I had agreed to keep her as in the dark as possible, unless one of us started a legitimate relationship with her.

Not that there had been much conversation about that. It was understood we both were drawn to her.

"Uncle, huh?" she asked, clicking her tongue against the side of her cheek as if she was thinking.

Shit.

"You Italians and all your family. You sure do like to breed, don't you?"

I choked a little, between my sigh of relief and the laugh that wanted to burst from my chest. I turned to her, one eyebrow cocked, and smirked a little before I said, "I think it's more that we like to fuck. The *breeding* part happens incidentally."

Her cheeks were set aflame, but those fiery eyes didn't stray from mine.

"Thank goodness for modern medicine, or else I'm sure we'd have hundreds of little Adrians running around here, wouldn't we?" The snark in her voice was there, and the pointed smirk along with it, but there was an edge to her tone and a sharpness in her eyes that told me she wasn't at all pleased with the idea that I had fucked other women, many other women in her estimation. That jealousy hiding there emboldened me a little. The passion we felt in my office was not just her other emotions taking a backseat for a moment; she was jealous.

I wanted more.

"Thank you, modern medicine," I said with a grin, watching with glee as she rolled her eyes and stomped toward her car.

"Goodnight, Adrian!" she yelled.

"Goodnight, Ashley! Don't think about that kiss too much!" I yelled after and watched with pleasure as her shoulders tightened before she slipped in her car and slammed the door behind her.

CHAPTER 4

ASH

*G*oddamn Italians.

I was tossing and turning in my bed. The combination of the uncertainty of my living situation, coupled with that damn kiss, had me coiled up tight when I should have been sleeping.

For all the times I gave Carmen LaMartina shit for staying up too late for our sessions early in the morning, I was going to be the one who came in like a zombie tomorrow. Saturdays, there was no pastry school, and even if there was, her semester was over as of a week ago, just in time for her to do all the last-minute things involved with getting married.

But she wasn't skimping out on her training, no. If anything, since she was done with school, I saw far more of her at the gym. It made me wonder what happened during the week when she was in Kansas City. Was there another gym she went to there?

And then I thought of her brother again. The taste of his lips, the tickle of his beard on my face, the feel of those long fingers as they wrapped around my waist and threaded through my hair.

I was practically panting.

I sat up, realizing there was absolutely nothing I could do to get my mind from replaying what happened, at least not until I either exhausted myself or quenched the thirst he had started in me.

I may have lusted after him and Sal for years, but never before could I not stop thinking about one of them. And of course, thinking of the second side of that Italian coin, Sal, had a whole other wave of need and an odd mixture of guilt rolled in. The guilt I would either need to explore later, or most likely, it would just get shoved to the back of my mind, like most of the unpleasant things in my life.

My drunk, gambling father? I rarely thought about it, because when I did, a wave of emotions I didn't want to handle came through.

My childhood? Just as bad.

And now I had made myself angry.

Out of bed now, I glanced around my disheveled room. It wasn't fancy or perfect, but it was *mine.* While so few things in my life before had been mine, I hated that when I finally had a semblance of freedom and independence, there Marek Lewandowski was to rip it all away. Again.

I went to my tiny bathroom. The counters were littered with my various hair products and my minimal makeup selection. If I was going to be lost in my head, I might as well be productive with this awake time. I started cleaning the counter, organizing the chaos I had left, when I caught a glimpse of the singular photo of my mom I had.

Admittedly, the bathroom was not the place for such a thing, but it had become a tradition for her to be here, on the bathroom mirror. When I was younger, it reminded me of when she was alive, singing to me as she did my hair each morning before school. The tradition had just carried on as I got older, though I rarely glanced at it anymore.

She was a slight little thing, with pale eyes and light hair, the very opposite of what my father had been with his dark Puerto Rican features. I always liked that I had gotten her eyes. Somehow those genes came through despite the dark depths of his. She was not a fighter, not someone ready to face the harsh underworld that my father had led us into.

I was very different, and it showed. Becoming a fighter like my father was not something she would have chosen for me, but she was gone long before that even became a reality.

My fingers gripped the edge of the counter. Memories and taunting possibilities of what my life could have been like flashed through my head, only ramping up my anxiety.

Nope. No more bathroom.

Time to start trying to solve one of my problems. I went out to my living-dining-kitchen room, slumping on the couch and pulling my previously discarded laptop over to me. I didn't have many contacts that were current in the world of underground fighting anymore. Those came and went rather quickly unless it was an organizer, and most of those I knew were predominantly from St. Louis.

St. Louis fights wouldn't really help me in this particular predicament. I needed fights nearby and fast, that I could get into and still maintain my regular life. That meant close by.

But as I tried to hunt down old contacts, an email popped up with the newest schedule for the gym.

Normally it was Adrian who sent those, but this time Sal's name was listed. I glanced at the clock. 3:00 a.m. Not usually a time that I'd think Sal would be up working on legitimate business stuff, but also not entirely surprising.

And my tired brain began wandering again, wondering what exactly Sal and Adrian's lives were like. Two best friends and business partners, tied together in their life of crime and their families. To have a friend who you've known your whole life was a foreign concept to me, let alone someone you still share almost all aspects of your life with. Hell, their mothers even lived together.

The kiss with Adrian flashed into my mind again, and it made me hot all over, as well as the new image that popped up. Imagining Sal at my back, his strong arms wrapping around and gripping onto my waist as Adrian's tongue danced with mine. They shared everything else, why not share me in my fantasy? It was just that, a fantasy, after all.

Nothing was ever going to come of it. That kiss with Adrian was a mistake and wasn't going to be repeated. He was my boss. *They* were my bosses. It didn't matter how much flirting and fighting we did, I was never going to cross that line, even if my soaking wet core was tempting me to do the very opposite.

I got up, pacing my apartment for a few minutes before I let out a frustrated grunt. I wasn't going to get anything done, not sleep or otherwise, as long as Sal and Adrian kept popping back up in my mind, tempting me.

Back into my bedroom I went to lay in the comfort of my old bed, the sheets soft with wear, and the memory of Adrian's taste and scent lingering at the forefront of my mind. My hand reached down, determined to relieve myself, at least just a little, so I could quell the desire that seemed to have a mind of its own, and perhaps get a few hours of sleep before my alarm went off at 5:00 a.m.

I pulled up at the gym, wishing I had time to grab a coffee from Liliana's shop on the other side of the parking lot, but seeing Carmen, Leo, and Paolo meant there was no such luck for me. I wasn't *late,* but perhaps not as early as I usually was, especially for these early morning training sessions with Carmen. I could already see the snarky look on her face as I turned off the car.

"Late night, Ash?" Carmen asked, one dark eyebrow rising on her forehead, a smirk on her lips.

"I had a hard time falling asleep. That happens sometimes when I close," I said grumpily, slamming my car door and trudging to the door of the gym.

Leo could have opened it on his own, technically so could Paolo, but I wasn't going to point that out to any of them. This was usual Lupo and LaMartina behavior. They really liked to take opportunities to goad people. That's probably why I liked them so much.

"You okay?" Carmen asked, her voice now switched from teasing to concerned. I shrugged, still too groggy to even think about what excuse I could make for my racing thoughts that didn't involve her brother and Sal or my current monetary issue.

We all piled in, Paolo last, and I darted over to the alarm to turn it off while the others went to stash their bags.

"You warm up, I just have to get the till and start the computer," I told her, shoving my bag and jacket under the counter and watching as she moved over to where we stashed the tape for her fingers to get her stretches in. Leo was right behind her, the two of them talking quietly as she went through the motions I had taught her. I could see the blush creep in her cheeks as she talked to him. Funny that even though those two had known each other forever, and had seen one another in some of their darkest and worst moments, they still flirted like it was brand new.

If I ever fell in love, I imagined that's what I'd want too.

I went to the office, opening the safe, and pulling the till, glancing at the smaller safe within that I only ever saw Sal and Adrian get into. It was one of those things about working for them, even if the gym was a legitimate business with plenty of normal, non-Mafia members, that always left me questioning. What code could I use to break in and find the secrets I had been wondering about?

I needed someone like Enzo or Ingrid, hell, even Leo, but none of them would choose me and lose the kinship and trust that Sal and Adrian had with them, especially not to sate my curiosity.

I went back out, placing the cash in the drawer and starting the computer, when Leo's phone rang.

"It's Sal," Leo said when he picked it up from the bench he had set it on, swiping to answer it. "Yeah," he said as a greeting. The muffled sound of Sal on the other end of the phone piqued my interest, especially with whatever had been going on with the families, but not enough to move over there until I finished with the computer.

"Yeah, she's here," Leo said, glancing over at me, which had Carmen turning her gaze to me as well.

Great. They were talking about me. I wrinkled my nose in their direction, getting a grin out of Carmen and an eye roll from Leo.

"I'll tell her. See you at the house," Leo said, ending the call before he made his way over to the counter.

"Sal said he sent a schedule, but he forgot to add Benny. He noticed you approved it right after he sent it." He paused for a moment, his eyebrow quirked, I assumed about the hour I approved it. A little late for me to up reading emails, but I already told them I had a hard time sleeping. "He needs you to remove your approval so he can add to it."

"Okay," I murmured, pulling up the scheduling software on the computer and pulling my approval in moments.

Leo continued to watch me for a moment, like he was trying to figure something out, but I kept my features schooled. I didn't need any of these people catching on to my problems. They meant well, but liked to put their noses in other people's business. While I appreciated them, I was only an employee, a peripheral person in their lives. I wasn't going to have them go out of their way for me when they had other, probably much more pressing, problems to address.

Leo went back to Carmen, giving her a sweet kiss when she stood back up out of her stretch, before he moved over to the treadmills, and I finally walked over to start taping my own fingers.

"There's something going on with you," Carmen said, taking the tape from me once I had finished.

"Nothing out of the usual. Maybe it's the fact that a certain *friend* keeps threatening that I'll have to wear a dress to their wedding," I said with a playful smirk.

"You would look so good though!" she insisted.

"Can't move in a dress," I said, demonstrating by widening my stance and hitting the bag between us. "See?"

"You shouldn't be throwing punches or kicks at my wedding, Ash," Carmen said, rather disgruntled.

"With your family? There's always that possibility," I deadpanned, making Carmen burst out in laughter.

"That's fair," she said after a moment, her laughter dying down to chuckles.

"Alright. Let's see how sloppy you got over the course of the week."

CHAPTER 5

ASH

My fingers shook as I taped them. It had been a long time since I was back in the ring. Not so long that I had forgotten what to do, and I had been training people at the gym for the last several years and it had only really been about a year since the last time Salvatore had been to a private event, but it had been long enough that the nerves of going into an illegal match were getting to my head a little. Illegal matches had been what I did for Lewandowski. I had gotten away from that, escaped that, and here I was again, but this time of my own choice.

It hadn't taken long to find a contact. I knew enough people from the old days who still had their fingers in the fighting scene. I could have lined up fights for days if I lived in St. Louis. The trouble had been finding someone in town who could hook me up without alerting Sal and Adrian.

Oddly enough, it had been Joey who helped me. The idiot of a man-child was almost always at the gym and overheard me making calls to old contacts after closing one night. I thought he was in the bathroom or outside smoking while he waited for me to finish counting down the till, but apparently, he had been eavesdropping just around the corner by the treadmills the previous night.

"You're wanting to fight?" he asked.

"Not that it's your business, Joey, but I need a little extra cash," I snapped, my face deepening its snarl as he grinned at my reaction.

"There's a fight in Blue Springs tomorrow. I can give you the number, see if you can get in on a match." The offer was so unexpected.

I knew Sal and Adrian ran these sorts of events. It was a good way to make a little money, have a setting for negotiations, and potentially recruit new people. That was a very common thing in the line of work they did, but I didn't want to be involved with anything they could touch. They would ban me from doing it just as soon as I stepped foot in the ring.

"I don't want the bosses to know," I told Joey honestly, hoping he'd keep his mouth shut.

"Blue Springs is a gray zone. It's not theirs."

That was surprising.

"Whose is it?"

"No big names or organization behind it. Just some old fighters that wanted to make a little money. My uncle is one. Opted to try that on his own before he offered his services to Sal."

Oh, Joey, I loved him. That was definitely more information than he should have shared, because if I hadn't known already, he would have just revealed to me that Sal was the boss in these parts. Not just of us at this gym, but the crime lord of this area. And not only that, but that Blue Springs wasn't their territory.

I took the number and thanked Joey, but not too profusely. Didn't want him to catch wind of how much he had overshared.

And call his uncle, Cal, I did. Not even twenty-four hours later was I sitting in the locker room area of this massive warehouse, taping my knuckles with a number painted on my stomach and back.

I closed my eyes and breathed through my nose, taking in the scents of sweat, blood, and fear that were permeating the air. I knew these scents. I had grown up surrounded by them. I had made it my everything for so very long. They were woven into the very fabric of my being. Something about being here felt so very right.

"Hey, new bitch!" came a voice, making my eyes snap open again. Coming toward me was a beast of a woman. She had to have been at least five inches taller than me and clearly outweighed me by a lot, based on the broad muscles. Her face was fixed in an angry pinch, and her finger was pointed in my direction.

"I don't know who you think you are to step into this fight. This was Rhema's fight, and you took it!"

"I don't know who Rhema is. I called Cal, Cal said there was an opening," I said, turning my attention back to my finger taping.

"There was no opening. She was booted for you!"

"Talk to Cal," I said, before tearing the end off the tape with my teeth and standing. It put my eyes at her throat, and being that she had gotten so, so very close to me, I was only a few inches from her.

That proximity helped when I saw her muscles flex to move, ducking low before her arm even made it to grasp my throat. There were many advantages to being smaller; one was being quick.

"This is bullshit!" she called once she had recovered from the little stumble I had caused by dodging her attack.

"Not my problem."

"It will be if we meet in the ring," she said, her voice full of promises of pain. Though I knew exactly how I would take her down. It would barely take a minute with the weakness in her lower half and how slow her reaction time was.

I was trained by a fighter, fought professionally for a short time, and had done nothing but teach people the very things to look for to defeat their opponents for several years. She had no idea who she was messing with. None of these people did.

The first handful of matches left and came back, and my adrenaline started pumping full force in my chest as I counted down to my own match. One more to go.

Two men had left the locker room, but only one came back. He was being dragged by two men who I recognized as being bouncers at the back doors when I got there hours ago. I knew right away that he was concussed. His face looked like a bloody mess; Picasso himself couldn't have done a better job. That meant the winner of that fight was either getting some serious praise, a beating of his own, or fleeing in case this poor guy died back here.

No one said a word as his friends started to patch him up and clear his airway of blood and spit. He was still breathing, that was obvious from the violent gasps that were coming from his open mouth. He would be in a lot of pain, probably need to see a doctor, but he'd live.

"It was that new piece of shit," said one of the fighters who had come over to help as soon as he was laid out on a bench.

"Probably work for the same scum as this newbie," the woman from earlier spat in my direction.

I knew there would be people who worked as I had in the past, fighters who were working off a debt, but I wasn't expecting such fervent hatred for them. In the past, the only thing other fighters had against us was if we threw fights. The only thing worse than losing a fight was winning, but not knowing if it was your skill that got you that prize.

The door opened, and a man stepped into the room, his expression giving the impression he had just been dealing with some problems out front that he was not too pleased about.

"Next fighters!"

I realized that meant me. I stood, glancing around to see who else was approaching the doorway, when I spotted the movement. The woman was about my same size, perhaps a bit taller than me, but otherwise similarly shaped. Her hair was buzzed to her scalp and her eyes were smudged with black makeup.

We made eye contact as we got to the door. Her expression, though clearly trying to remain stoic, gave away the little bit of anxiety that was running through her.

Me too, girl.

The open warehouse turned arena was teaming with people. All walks of life were in this building; from men in threadbare clothes, probably spending their last few dollars on drinks and their bets for the evening, hoping this would be the night they won enough to get by for another week or month, to men in suits, sitting leisurely on raised areas and being catered to while they chatted and proposed business deals, their bets less about making actual profit and more for show.

The crude ring had blood smears that hadn't fully been wiped away, still staining the floor. Cigarette smoke hung in the hair like a heavy fog, and the sounds of talking amongst the crowd were deafening.

Odd to think this felt so much like home, despite the negative history I had with fights like these.

We were announced, and the bell rang. My eyes zeroed in on my opponent. Didi, they had called her. That probably wasn't her real name. Real names weren't often used in these situations. I was announced as "Blue." Whatever anxiety Didi had in the locker room was whisked away with the sound of that bell. Like a cool wave washed over her, the tension left, and it was replaced with a cold fierceness in her eyes.

I wanted to see how she moved. I wanted her to strike first, but I wasn't sure that was going to be how this fight happened. We danced for a minute or two, moving around one another, with neither of us taking a chance on lashing out.

Yeah, I was going to have to be the one who made this fight happen.

The first "boo" rang out from the crowd, and I knew this couldn't continue any longer. My heart lurched a little as I dipped down, kicking my leg out to get her in the knee. She wasn't expecting that, only barely managing to partially block my attack, so her knee buckled. She tried to fling out a fist, but my arms were already up, blocking my face from her swing, before managing to punch her squarely in the side which she had left unprotected.

The crowd screamed, but I barely noticed them. What I did notice was the way she stumbled away, trying to protect herself as her diaphragm spasmed with the blow. Her eyes never left mine as she fought for air. As a teacher and a trainer, I would have stopped here, let my student recuperate, and tell them how their technique should have been better. Here there was no stopping.

I moved swiftly over to where she was, seeing that with her efforts to breathe normally, her hands dropped. It left her face wide open. I took my opportunity, landing a blow to her jaw that caused her head to whip to the side. Another and she was on a knee, one more and she was on the ground.

"Enough!" the ref screamed, grabbing my arm and pulling me up as I was about to get on the ground and keep beating her. "Winner!"

The cheer of the crowd flooded me. A euphoria I hadn't felt in at least a year filled me up. I would have a little more money in my pocket for sure after this night, and the complete and utter rush of the fight back in my veins.

I could get used to this.

CHAPTER 6

SAL

I sat in the chair next to Enzo with Adrian behind us, watching the footage for a third time. There, in black and white, was Marek Lewandowski, checking into hotels, eating at restaurants, and generally just *being* in our territory. Not that he was banned from visiting our little slice of Missouri, just that he wasn't invited here, at least not by us, and he certainly wasn't vacationing. That little slimy bastard only meant trouble.

He and his father were really nothing more than a mild irritation, but we had enough on our hands without one more issue.

"Let's get someone on him, at least until he leaves. I want to know who he's meeting with, if not why he's here altogether," Adrian said, turning to talk to Travis.

"On it," he said, slipping from the room.

"What else do you have?" I asked Enzo as I pushed my chair back, moving to the cabinet on the far right side of the wall to grab the whiskey.

This room had been my father's office. The Kansas City house had unfortunately been where Adrian and

I had to come back to after we dispatched the old bastard from this living plane. I still rarely used this room, hating the memories that oozed from the walls and furniture like a caustic substance, filling me with nothing more than fear and hatred. But this room was the most secure in the house; soundproofed with secure connections.

With Enzo and Ingrid's recent issues, it made more sense to have briefings here. Hell, I had already considered moving everyone to the city, at least until the ground settled a little under our feet. The moms would hate it, Ingrid would give Enzo so much shit for it, but with Leo and Carmen already in town, it really made so much more sense.

"I haven't turned up too much on Coleen Smythwyck. April Smith, though, has been very busy organizing underground fighting across the Midwest. Big events."

"Oh really?" Adrian asked, leaning closer to look at the image Enzo had pulled of her on the screen. I was less interested, though it made sense why Adrian would be. She was apparently his late father's mistress, a fact none of us knew anything about until Maria dropped that lovely bit of knowledge on us a month previously.

I moved back over with my whiskey in hand to stand beside Adrian and look at her. She was the opposite of everything Maria was. Light hair, pale skin, thin delicate frame. Maria was strong and dark with a mane of hair that her children had all inherited. It was hard for me to imagine Bernardo cheating on Maria. While my mother loved my father dearly, his side of their relationship was far less devoted. Bernardo, however, from the memories I had, was deeply in love and doted on Maria whenever he could. Then again, the men in our line of work were very good at lying. It shouldn't have been as much of a shock, but somehow the memory of who Bernardo was cast him in such a different light than Salvatore, that it left us all reeling.

What other secrets did Bernardo have?

That was the biggest question lately, especially given it was a secret Bernardo took to his grave that Colin O'Shea was bound and determined to get Carmen to reveal.

While I understood why the others were not as keen on interrogating Carmen, I was itching to know what it could possibly be that she had the key to. The only thing she had said so far was that she remembered her father taking her to a strange place. Mind you, she was only eight, but there was a lot there she couldn't recall alone.

I had suggested hypnosis. Leo, my youngest brother, and Carmen's fiance, had been completely against it. Adrian, while my second in command and my best friend, had suggested maybe *after* the wedding.

"I'm working this lead. Ingrid said she'd take over on some of the O'Shea tracking, so I can try to find something out about what Bernardo was hiding all those years ago," Enzo said, finally pulling his eyes from the screen to look up at us.

I hadn't looked at Adrian's face. I didn't need to. I could tell, simply from the way his shoulders had tensed and the white knuckles of his hand gripped to the back of Enzo's chair what he was feeling. Adrian was emotional. He was volatile sometimes, but he had me to keep him grounded, and he was the pillar that kept me from feeling like all of this would crush me under its weight.

"We'll figure it out, Adrian," I said when it seemed like Enzo didn't know what to say.

"But will it be too late?" Adrian whispered.

"Enzo, I want everyone organizing to come to the city a little earlier than planned," I said, diverting the attention from Adrian, who had snagged the whiskey from my hand and took a long swallow as he moved around me to the cabinet, most likely to refill the glass.

"It's only a few days—"

"No. I want everyone close to us and here. We need to keep the family safe, especially before the wedding."

Leo and Carmen were getting married at a hotel here in the city. It was in Kansas City, proper, so the plan had always been to have everyone come stay at the city houses. If we weren't going to get many more answers before the wedding, I wanted everyone here.

Close.

Safe.

"The ladies aren't going to like that," Enzo grumbled, slapping his laptop closed.

"Well, they'll get over it. I'm tired of fighting them all about protection anyway." Enzo chuckled, standing and moving toward the door.

"Fair enough," he said, running a hand through his hair at the threshold. "How close are you to the Morelli meeting?"

"June," I said. As the word left my mouth the gravity of how soon that meeting was hung in the air between the three of us. I glanced at Adrian who had refilled the whiskey glass and had stepped one pace closer to me, before he stopped, taking another mouthful, before coming back to where I stood and handing it over to me.

"Crunch time," Enzo said with a nod, before slipping from the office. The only sound in the house was his footsteps walking through and out the door. Then it was nothing.

Adrian and I stood side by side, still facing the door for a few moments longer. There was a lot resting on my shoulders. I was very nearly the Caporegime of this territory. It was mine, in everything but name from the

Big Boss, but really, the reality was, it was never *just* mine. I couldn't have done any of this without Adrian.

I took the last swallow in the glass and followed where Enzo had just vacated, slipping from the room quickly, Adrian right behind me. He also hated that room.

That room was where he traded his life as a good citizen for one under my father's rule. He didn't do it by choice. He did it to save his sister. But secretly, I had always been glad he was in this with me. I wasn't sure I'd be able to do any of this without him.

We moved to the den; a room that had been the place we had hung out as children on the rare occasions when we stayed in the Kansas City house. It didn't happen often back then, but as such, the large basement room which held more cushions and couches than it did any other furniture, felt more comforting than the lavishly decorated upper rooms.

Nine months ago, when it became clear we had to move here to take hold over the territory, I hadn't had time, let alone the will to change this house. As such, it was still very much my father, Salvatore's, house and aesthetic, not mine.

I swiftly shrugged off my jacket, while Adrian moved to the bar cabinet. In minutes, we were sitting side by side, passing a bottle of whiskey between us as the local news played on the television for no less than half an hour. It was a comfortable silence. We had always been the type of friends who could simply be in each other's presence, even without barely interacting. It was how we managed to live and work together.

"I kissed Ash," Adrian said very suddenly as I brought the bottle to my lips. It stayed there, barely touching my mouth as I processed what he had just said.

My heart raced, both with jealousy and intrigue over the mental image that recalled.

"Just kissed?" I asked. That wasn't so farfetched a question. Adrian wasn't one to go too long without company joining him in bed, though he hadn't brought anyone here since we moved into this house together following my father's death. I went longer stretches, not because I didn't want sex, but more that I was far too busy to be seeking it out.

"She was upset about something. I…" He trailed off like he wasn't sure how to articulate what he wanted to say. The silence hung there for a moment, and instead of pushing the particular point, I could tell he didn't know how to explain, I just moved on to what I was far more interested in hearing about.

"Did she like it?" I asked, not looking at him, but I could feel his discomfort.

"She kissed me back, so I'd say yes."

A strange thrill ran through me, which seemed odd. Of course, jealousy made sense, but the rush of tingles that went through my body was as if Adrian was describing *me* kissing Ash.

It wasn't the strangest thing, both of us wanting the same girl. It happened quite often in the past. It seemed like our tastes were very similar, even if our personalities seemed to be two sides of the same coin. In fact, there had been a time or two we had considered sharing a woman. Once in high school, but we never approached her about it, and the other not long after he had been home from his time in the Marines. The woman in question ended up deciding that being in a relationship with two men, even if it was always separate, wasn't for her, but it was a possibility that had excited me more than any other sexual prospect I had ever anticipated before.

For two men who were raised very traditionally, it was strange to think we didn't mind the idea of having a shared relationship. We shared everything else; I supposed.

But with Ash it was different. I may have had plenty of women at my disposal if I so chose, but when Adrian and I saw her in that ring four years ago, it felt different. She was different than any other woman either of us had ever pursued. And because of that, it seemed Adrian and I both had some problems with approaching her as anything other than her bosses.

Until now.

"Upset about what?" I decided to ask, even though he had clearly been struggling with that aspect of the explanation. It was easier to bring that up again than delve into my strange feelings and thoughts about both.

"She managed to avoid telling me. And then Romolo called."

Ah yes, the reason we had Enzo look into Lewandowski and if he had been in our territory in the first place.

I finally turned my head to look at Adrian, his gaze fixed on the television but clearly not seeing anything on it. One hand was balled into a fist against his leg, body rigid as he sat beside me. Anxious.

But what was he worried about? I knew full well he also had feelings for Ash. He knew about mine. Hell, everyone knew we both wanted her, our siblings teased us about it relentlessly, especially since Leo and Carmen got together.

Was there something more there he wasn't telling me?

"What does it mean?" I decided to ask, watching as his thick brows furrowed and his jaw clenched.

"I don't know, Sal. I wanted to make sure—"

"Look at me, Adrian," I said, not capable of hearing whatever this was without viewing his full face.

He sighed, then turned to me, looking at me with a pained expression. I had seen this look there before, but I was one of a very few people who had. He didn't show this side of himself often.

"I know you want her too, but your friendship is more important to me. If you don't want this to happen, then I won't let it happen again," Adrian said. The subtext there was that he very much wanted it to happen again but was leaving it to me.

I took a long moment of seeing that discomfort there, that concern, before I let one of my eyebrows raise just a little bit.

"Maybe she would consider being shared."

I hadn't brought the prospect up of doing that with Ash before this moment, because something about our instantaneous attraction to her felt too powerful. Our friendship was already a strange force all on its own, our families twined together, and then to add this unwitting siren to the mix was asking for trouble. It was trouble we didn't need right now, but maybe it was unavoidable. Maybe we were always heading down that path.

Adrian's face seemed to melt a little at my suggestion, relief washing over his features. There was the tiny part, in the back of my brain that acknowledged that Adrian could refuse, wanting her all of himself, but the reality of our close lifelong friendship was that those concerns, while valid and human, were not the choices either of us made. Adrian and I were a team.

"You think she'll go for that?" he asked, a grin spreading over his face.

Settling back on the couch and taking a heavy swig from the whiskey bottle I shrugged.

"I guess we'll have to find out."

CHAPTER 7

ASH

A week passed. By day I was working and training at the gym, sometimes joining Carmen and the other girls for wedding preparations. By night I was fighting my way to financial security, I had made almost enough for the deposit on a different apartment, but not enough to cover the rent each month.

I knew I could go to Sal and Adrian, but not only was my pride keeping me from asking for a raise, but that kiss between me and Adrian lingered in my memory. Somehow, it felt like I was betraying Sal by kissing Adrian, which was absurd. That was the first sort of romantic encounter between me and either of them after all these years. Sal and I weren't anything, just like Adrian and I weren't anything.

I had to keep reminding myself of that though, especially when I was in the tiny dressing room at this little dress shop looking at myself in the mirror after I had slipped into one of the dresses Carmen and Rory had picked out for me to wear at the wedding. It was deep blue, like the shade of Adrian's eyes, with black swirling designs. The dress accentuated my figure beautifully, hugging all the right places, hinting at others in a subtly seductive way.

What Ingrid had said a week ago seemed to echo in my mind as I looked at myself in the mirror.

"I'm sure there are a few people who would love to see that hot body of yours in a dress."

My face was certainly hot at the thought of their reactions to seeing me in this, especially when I turned to the side and realized some of the black details were peep-through, all along the torso and down the sides.

"Come out, Ash! I want to see!" Carmen called from the other side of the curtain.

"I don't think—"

But I didn't have time to protest, Carmen barged right in, stopping and looking at me. The slack-jawed expression transformed into a wide grin that looked nearly identical to the devious grin I often got from her oldest brother.

"*That* is the dress," Carmen said with such finality, I could only fight back with a fervent shake of my head.

"Let me see!" Rory said, rocketing off the little bench outside the dressing room to stand behind Carmen.

"No, no. I can't wear this," I said, trying to close the curtain on Carmen before Rory could get a look.

"You can and you will. That dress looks like it was made for you. Painted on your skin," Carmen said, shoving the curtains open against my efforts so Rory could get an eyefull too.

"Even more reason to not wear this to your wedding. *You* should be the center of attention," I protested.

"Every single man is going to be drooling over you," Rory said, her eyebrows wiggling.

"Not … helping," I said with gritted teeth, turning away from them to look back at the mirror.

"But, Ash, *look* at you," Carmen said, stepping a little closer behind me.

"What are you afraid of?" Rory asked, causing me to look up at their faces again through the mirror.

The attention of two men who I want but can't have.

But I couldn't say that out loud.

"I can't afford this right now," I said instead. It was true, but not the actual reason.

Carmen snaked her arms around my waist, resting her chin on my shoulder and sighing.

"I get it," she said, her face forlorn. "I won't make you buy anything new. This was silly anyway. You'll look fabulous in whatever you pick to wear. I'll just be happy you're there," she said, squeezing me a little before she released me and turned back to leave the dressing room.

I let out a breath I had been holding, feeling slightly relieved that she was seemingly leaving this topic alone now. I knew she had far more important things with the wedding to worry about, my dress, or lack thereof, was low on the totem pole of priorities these days.

But Rory froze for a moment in the doorway, brows furrowing as she stared at my back.

"What the fuck is that?" she asked. The twins were not known for their subtleness, both rather harsh and to the point, at least in our company. Carmen immediately whipped around and looked at the spot on my back where Rory was pointing.

I knew what they were seeing. Top heavy bitch was my opponent the night before and got exactly one hit on me. I wasn't so bothered because the placement made it easy to cover up in normal clothes, not so easy in a backless dress.

"Ash…"

"Lucky shot from one of my students," I said turning to face them, but the mirror that was now behind me took their focus as their eyes zeroed in on my bruise once again.

"Who the hell are you training that can land a blow that hard? Are you sure you didn't crack a rib?" Carmen asked, stepping back in and coming around me to take a closer look.

"It's fine," I lied, knowing I most certainly did have a cracked rib, and unfortunately would have to protect that side when I was fighting tonight.

"Will you let Benny look at it? He'd have suggestions on how to get it healing faster," Carmen said, her fingertips lightly brushing against the inflamed, discolored flesh.

"Benny would laugh if I came to him for something so minor," I said with a forced chuckle.

And that wasn't the first or last time I would be lying to the people around me. Though I was rather tired of the omission of what they all had going on, since it was now starting to affect my life. It was clear I had a guard trailing me after I closed the gym later that evening. Guards at the gym I was used to, but being guarded at home? That was far different.

It wasn't Joey. Since he closed with me, I knew the car he drove and this was not the forest green beater he somehow kept driving, despite the horrendous sounds it made. This car I recognized as one of Sal's men, but it wasn't anyone I saw with regularity, and they weren't very discreet.

Whoever it was following me, driving far too close and parking in my apartment lot within view but not getting out of their car at all, was someone different than my day-to-day encounters. I wasn't going to let a little pest like that stop me from getting to the fight tonight though. I needed to be out of my apartment in a week, the wedding was only days away, so I needed a new apartment immediately.

I changed hastily, grabbing my bag and throwing my hair into a ponytail that was quickly hidden with the hood of my jacket, and sighed loudly in my small bathroom as I thought of how well I seemed to avoid the two men since I kissed Adrian, yet I still had to fight to get away from their influence. I may not have seen either physically, but they were always there in other ways, like the man still parked in my lot.

It was going to be hard to get past him to get to the fight. This night was different. Change of location, higher stakes. More money for wins. This night could make or break things for me because it could give me a cushion where I could slow down on the fights. Fighting and working at the gym every day was starting to wear on me. I could feel the exhaustion seeping in, and the desperation I felt didn't help.

I slipped my bag over my shoulder, snatching my keys from the table, before opening the door only to be met with the chest of a man standing right outside it. My breath caught in my throat, the familiar musky cologne that I hadn't smelled in years filling my nostrils.

"I heard a little blue bird was living here."

I felt sick.

Marek Lewandowski was standing in the hallway of my apartment building, the disgusting, but reminiscent smirk on his lips.

"What are you doing here?" I asked, though I knew quite well that his family was now the owners of the property. In fact, he was probably the reason my lease wasn't being renewed, to get me back under his thumb.

"I come to check on you. I saw you living here, then fighting tonight," he said, his Polish accent a little thick, meaning he had already had a drink or two, loosening his lips.

Shit.

The fact that he knew I was fighting meant he was somehow involved.

My head whirled with the strange coincidences that were being laid out here: his company taking over ownership of *my* apartment complex, my lease not being renewed, and the way I so quickly got into this underground fighting ring that was not associated with any organized crime syndication. It was all too perfect.

Not to mention whatever the heck was going on with the Lupos and LaMartinas. There was never a moment I wanted to know what exactly was happening in the Italian mob more than right now.

"I'll give you a ride," Marek said, his hand clamping firmly at the back of my neck. In my slightly stunned state, I didn't notice his arm move around my side, but now I was trapped in his clutches, literally.

He led me out to the back, where there was essentially a service road, the dumpsters, and the woods. Instead of the empty alley, there was a handful of cars. Marek and his entourage of men. Four years ago, he had far fewer people in his employ. I wondered what could have changed.

As soon as I got shoved into the black sedan, I knew what the change was.

"This was the stop you had to make before?" the man in the passenger seat asked, turning around to give a glare at Marek. The glare looked more like some sort of terrible grimace, what with the scarring on the man's face. And then I saw the other features, the blue eyes, the dirty blond hair, the Chicago accent with just a hint of a lilt, all suggesting that this man was Freddy O'Shea.

I had seen him around Lee's Summit last summer, right before Carmen was taken. That information was something I wasn't technically supposed to know about, but like most things surrounding my employers, I knew far more than they would like to tell themselves, just not everything I wished I knew. At the time, Freddy and his brother Jeremy, who had been a frequent loiterer at the gym had been around, creeping. After Carmen had been taken, I never saw Jeremy again, and the name "O'Shea" was the topic of many whispered and heated discussions in the family.

Leo had told me who took her and told me updates while she was gone, but I never got the details of how they got her back, only that Salvatore was dead and Sal set to take over whatever he had overseen before.

"This lovely girl is Ashley. She used to work for me as a fighter, didn't you?" Marek asked, reaching his hand over to grasp my leg and squeeze. Marek never forced actual sexual acts on me, but he certainly held the possibility over my head, especially when I didn't play along at throwing fights like he wanted. That hand on my thigh was a show of possession, but Marek held nothing over me anymore. My father's debt was paid.

I resisted the urge to fling his hand off me, because like it or not, this situation was dangerous, and I needed to be cautious. Freddy's eyes looked me over a smirk adorning his mangled face. Yes, he was just as much a disgusting predator as Marek.

"Fine," was all he said before turning back to face the front and signaling to the driver to move.

I knew one of Sal's guards was sitting out front in the parking lot, waiting to be by my side if I left my apartment. But they didn't park out front, they came around back, as if they knew someone was there watching and waiting.

The drive wasn't long, just fifteen minutes outside of Lee's Summit once we got on the highway. The streetlights passed by in a blur as I tried to keep myself calm. I told myself I was never going to be in a Lewandowski's clutches again, but here I was. The very thing I had been trying to avoid with the situation in my apartment was coming to fruition.

The caravan of cars pulled up to the warehouse and I grasped the door handle before our car had even come to a full stop. The handle was useless, of course, child locked so I was trapped in here until Marek released me. I had no way of getting home after this fight unless I dipped into some of the precious money I had saved, no way of getting away from Marek now. I was desperate prey trapped by a predator, but I had to remain focused if I was going to find a way out of this, otherwise I would just fall deeper into his grasp.

"I need to get ready," I said, gesturing to Marek's door to indicate he should let me out.

"I'll come with you. We must catch up," he said with a grin as he opened his door set to climb out first.

"Don't forget why you're here, Polack," came Freddy's voice from the front seat.

It didn't comfort me to know that, with that simple sentence from Freddy, Marek was not the one in charge. Marek was the devil I knew, the one I could predict. Freddy was clearly dangerous, but unknown to me. I resisted the urge to look back toward the gnarled face, scrambling from the car as quickly as I could and trying to put distance between me and Marek.

Somehow it seemed just as chilling as the idea that Marek would be coming with me in the back. This was a skewed relationship on its own. The Lewandowskis were doing something for the Irish, but perhaps it

was less of a partnership than Marek would have liked to admit.

Marek said nothing, but I could see the way he stiffened at the derogatory name he had been called. I could feel the eyes of Freddy and his driver on me even as I sped toward the back entrance of the warehouse.

"So Ashley," Marek began after a few silent moments as we walked. Marek was only a few paces behind me. "You seem to have a problem with the apartment, don't you?"

Advancing from the low-level petty money schemes Marek and his father had been pulling when I worked for them, to owning properties outside of their city of origin seemed like a stretch, but it had been four years. I supposed I shouldn't have been too surprised that they could have managed to gain enough money and resources since I had completed my work for them, but then again, they weren't the smartest men.

"You seem to have a new daddy," I said in response, just as we approached the door. The bouncer at the back was a man who sometimes fought too. He and another man switched out being the ones who watched the back entrances. Only fighters and important people could come through this way, and unfortunately, I suspected that Marek fell in the latter category.

"Ashley Torres," I said, fishing through my bag for my ID, in case he needed it.

"Lewandowski," Marek said, tilting his chin up as if daring the man to ask for identification.

"Go on," he said, waving us in as he opened the door. I pushed through first, glancing at the signs on the walls to indicate where the locker room was. Not that it would provide any protection from Marek, but maybe with the other fighters around he'd be less likely to try to mess with me.

I didn't make it though, he caught up to me just as I got to the door, grabbing my elbow and spinning me around before slamming me into the concrete wall.

"We all do what we have to for survival, don't we Ashley?" he asked, his fingers a bruising force on my skin as he leaned closer.

"I don't owe you anymore, Marek. What do you want?" I asked, trying hard to keep myself from screaming at him, so my words came out clipped.

"Don't you? I never got that last five thousand. What paid off your debt was that Salvatore Lupo wouldn't come after my men, but Salvatore is dead, his organization weak and in shambles, and you…" His voice trailed off as he leaned closer, his nose grazing my neck as he breathed in my scent through his nose with a disgusting needy sound. "You will be my little fighter again, just as soon as the O'Sheas deal with the pests who pay your bills."

An electric jolt ran through me. My first impulse was to smash his nose in, which I narrowly avoided by pinning my fist behind my back. I didn't like him talking about Sal and Adrian that way. But it wasn't just my unreciprocated feelings for those two men that were causing my mind to reel, it was the subtle little hint of additional information that Marek revealed.

"Weak and in shambles," was what he had described. That's not exactly what I had felt over the last nine months or so, but I wouldn't have been shocked if they were just very good at hiding it from everyone. Something had definitely changed when Salvatore died. There was both a freedom and an additional weight that seemed to be pressing down on everyone in those families. Especially Sal and Adrian.

I had assumed it was just because of what happened with Carmen, but it was clear I hadn't even scratched the surface of what had been going on.

"Until then," I started, pulling my fist from behind my back and pressing it to his shoulder, pushing him far enough from my body that I could slip away from the wall. "I work for me."

I barely had enough time to dart through the door before he took a step, but once I did, I was in the locker room, surrounded by other fighters. There wasn't anyone I was particularly close to here, but as a rule, we had each other's backs, and the locker room was off-limits to aggressive outsiders.

It wasn't until I saw a familiar face that it finally dawned on me that this wasn't going to be a situation where I kept my fighting a secret any longer. The door opened as I was tying back my hair and there stood Elio with Vallo, otherwise known as "The Tank." I helped him train twice a week with Elio. He was Sal's go-to for these types of fights. Not that he didn't have other fighters in his employ, but Vallo relished in the fight. He lived for the bloodshed.

If Vallo was here that meant Sal or Adrian were very likely in the crowd.

I was screwed. There was no amount of covering up my hair or my face that wouldn't clue either of them in that it was going to be me up there in the ring, fighting.

I glanced down at the lineup. I was fighting Hurricane.

Great.

The brute of a woman had been itching for the opportunity to flatten me since our first encounter a few weeks ago, and even more so since I won our first fight against each other just days before. I knew I could win, simply because I was faster than her, it was just a matter of how many hits would I take in the meantime? I had a wedding to attend in less than a week, as well as packing to do, and she had already cracked a rib that I was still sporting a nasty bruise from. I couldn't be out of commission or beaten up, obviously.

Shit!

Between her and whichever of the duo were sitting out there, I was well and truly fucked.

Vallo was first, though he usually made some excuse or got into a fight in the locker room that put him lower on the line-up. His rationale for this, when he told me about it at the gym one day, was that he was saving the best for later in the evening. At the time I had laughed at him, but the longer he was in this locker room with me, the more likelihood he or Elio would notice me before my fight. The last thing I needed was an angry Lupo or LaMartina barging in and demanding to know why I was fighting here. Or worse, demanding I leave and not fight.

Another familiar face came through the door. My head whipped up, expecting to see a bouncer calling for the first fighters, but instead, I was met with the face of April Smith. Four years ago, she had been one of the main people who arranged underground fights like these across the Midwest. Most of her time was spent between Chicago and St. Louis during my time fighting, but I knew she had sometimes crossed the state of Missouri and organized fights in the Kansas City area when my father was still alive.

There had been some kind of scandal, though I didn't remember the details since my life had been absorbed in taking care of my drunk father while attending high school. The controversy had apparently made her halt working with this side of the state. But here she was, a ghost of a former life, like Marek had been, standing in the room and scoping us all out.

I quickly came to realize why she was in the locker room in the first place as the door slammed closed behind her and she cleared her throat. Her blue eyes darted around the room; blonde hair pulled back into the tight bun I remembered. She looked like she had aged since I had last seen her, though it had admittedly been a few years. A lot could happen.

"Fighters!" she called, finally getting everyone to quiet down and give her the attention she was seeking. "Tonight isn't going to be quite like it has been with Cal these last few months. This will be a tournament style. There are a few high-valued people attending tonight and Cal has so graciously given over his little operation here to facilitate some *entertainment*." She grinned, her eyes dancing with something other than joy. It was malevolence. It was bloodthirsty.

"Fighters who win move on to the next round. The bracket starts you with your current match. If you win, you'll get your next opponent."

"What about the women?" came one of the men sitting closest to her. I didn't recall his name, but he was friends with Hurricane and her friend Rhema. Another wide smile came over her face, this one perhaps even more frightening than the one before.

"What about them? You're all fighters. Equal rights and all that," she said, a slight laugh coming from her tight lips, before she turned abruptly, sauntering out the door which closed with a jarring slam, given how quiet the room had gotten with her proclamation.

This was going to be interesting.

CHAPTER 8

SAL

I hated everything about this. The scent, the sound, the dim lighting, the greedy looks on the people's faces. I hated it all even more, because this wasn't my event. I had no control here. I was just a spectator, like everyone else.

The invitation had come the night before, and with April Smith's name attached to it. I couldn't say no. So while Adrian, Leo, and Benny were tracking down a lead about a property that Bernardo may have owned under a different name, I was here. I could have not shown up. I could have snubbed them, but I knew I would get more information if I came and made an appearance. I just wasn't happy I was doing it alone.

The moment Adrian and I had opened the invitation, I knew Adrian wouldn't be able to handle being here. His temper needed help sometimes, and being in the presence of his father's supposed mistress would not have been a calm situation. An insult to Maria LaMartina may as well have been a death sentence. It would have been for any mistress of my father's in my presence too. That was why my father had taken such great lengths to keep his various lovers separate from us.

I didn't often attend the fights we put on, let alone come to one that didn't fall under our rules. We had been letting Cal put on these fights, mostly because of his connection to Joey, but ultimately it would prove to bring in more revenue and control of more areas near our territory if we ended up folding Cal and his operation in with ours at some point. But this was not Cal's operation tonight. April had apparently bribed him to allow her to take it over as she saw fit.

April hadn't been operating here on this side of the state since before I was truly in the life. I was only fourteen years old the last time she did anything this way, I had no way of knowing what was different, and my father surely hadn't given me that knowledge before he died.

I didn't come alone, I wasn't so stupid as to do that, not that Adrian would have let me if I had tried. Five of my men were here with me, Travis at the helm. He stood near me, eyes assessing the crowd from where we stood with other "prestigious" guests. There were city politicians, smaller gang leaders, high-end drug dealers, and me.

But my unsettled feeling only became worse as I saw a few familiar-looking men enter. I couldn't quite put my finger on why they were familiar, until Travis made a signal to one of the other guards. Four fingers meant four men, and one pinky up after that meant Irish. My eyes focused in on the door as a man, still sporting a cane, was revealed to be none other than Freddy O'Shea himself.

I clenched my fist, forcing my gaze to go back to the crowd. He was going to be in this VIP box with me, and I couldn't let his mere presence get the best of me. Perhaps this was going to be quite fruitful with information if I played my cards right. Despite how much I relied on Adrian, there was never a moment I was grateful he wasn't here more than this one. I wasn't sure how well Adrian would have been able to hold back from killing Freddy if they sat a few feet from one another.

"Well, well," Freddy said as he reached the few steps up to the box. "I shouldn't be surprised you were invited here."

I turned my eyes to look at him. That once handsome face was now scarred beyond repair. If only Leo and Carmen had finished the job all those months ago.

"No, you shouldn't be," I managed to say, my voice even and cold.

"But where is your lovely pet dog? What was his name? Adrian?" The sneer that spread across his lips looked more monstrous than amused. I managed to hold back the urge to rage at him for daring to call Adrian that, instead, stretching my neck and glancing toward the doors that led to the back rooms.

"My second is dealing with more pressing matters than a silly fight," I said. But as the words left my mouth, another jaw-dropping sight was laid out before my eyes. Marek Lewandowski came out of those doors like some sort of slimy weasel. His greasy hair shined in the lights from the ring as he moved through the crowd, heading directly toward us.

"He'll be sad he missed this show, I'm sure," Freddy said, holding up the hand that wasn't grasping the cane to wave toward Marek.

Oh, Adrian most certainly would be sad at missing the possibility of taking both Freddy and Marek down a peg, but that would have helped nothing.

"Salvatore! What a good surprise!" Marek said with unwarranted joy. He looked a bit too pleased with himself for my liking, but I supposed having O'Shea as an ally would embolden him a little, especially against me.

"Marek," I acknowledged with a stiff nod. "I'm also surprised. Didn't think you'd step foot around here again after the last fight we attended together."

I thought mentioning our previous understanding would help put him in his place and remind him of how much lower he was than the other men here, but he only smiled wider.

"It has been so long since we've watched our girl fight, hasn't it?"

Our girl?

I tried not to visibly recoil with disgust. Who on earth was he talking about? The only person he could have been talking about was Ash, but that couldn't be right. He couldn't mean Ash. She didn't need to fight in these things anymore. She was free of all that now. The only reason she would ever go back to this, instead of legitimate fighting would be for money, but she knew she only needed to ask us. Didn't she?

I didn't respond to Lewandowski, because I couldn't. I had no idea what to say to a comment like that, not when I wasn't sure what was really happening here. Why was I invited to this? Why were they here?

April Smith, or Coleen, was associated with the O'Sheas, that much I knew, so Freddy being here wasn't so much a surprise as a confirmation. His association with the Lewandowskis however, was new, and I suddenly felt very caged in.

Almost as if my thoughts called her, April stepped out onto the ring, microphone in hand. Much like the picture Adrian and I had seen of her recently, it was almost shocking how very different from Maria this woman was. I would never have thought Bernardo to have such varying taste, especially when it was rather obvious who was more beautiful out of the two women, but then again, he died when I was fourteen. There was clearly much about him we hadn't known.

"Good evening, everyone," she said, her voice raspier than one would have expected from her appearance. "Tonight is going to be a little different than usual. I know many of you have already placed your bets, but now your winnings will bring you even greater amounts as long as you picked the right fighters."

A murmur went through the crowd as April grinned, holding up her hands to quiet them back down.

"This will be a tournament. Winners from the fights you bet on will move on to the next round. If you pick a winner, you get paid. Sounds nice, right?"

Cheers and mournful sounds echoed through the room. My stomach clenched. Ash better not have been fighting in this thing. Not with The Tank being one of the fighters. I pulled the little card that had the fighters listed on it from my pocket, glancing through until I saw the name I didn't want to see.

Blue.

"And now, without further ado, let the fights commence!"

The Tank was announced by the ref, as well as whoever the poor man was that he would be fighting, and I watched as Vallo and Elio marched out of the doors and to the ring. This had to be a joke. This had to be some sick nightmare I was having.

My phone buzzed with an incoming text message, and I fought the urge to run back into those locker rooms and see with my own eyes what I feared was the truth.

[Adrian: We just got to the location. Nothing so far. How is it going there?]

I almost laughed out loud at the absurdity. How was it going? I supposed it hadn't broken out into a firefight, but there was little about this situation that was going well.

[Me: Freddy and his new best friend Marek are here.]

[Adrian: Should have known...]

[Me: I think Ash is lined up to fight.]

I held my breath as I waited for Adrian's response. I could almost imagine him trying to hold back the rage but failing miserably. At least Benny and Leo were there to calm him. Or at least keep him restrained.

[Benny: Leo is staying to check this out. I called for some men to meet him here. Adrian and I are heading back to the gym, just in case.]

That would take an hour at least, but who knew how long this thing was going to last. Not surprised that Benny texted me back instead of Adrian. I didn't love the idea of Leo being out there alone, but I was very much stuck in this situation, forced to see this through instead of being out there with them.

Vallo finished the fight quickly, his opponent very nearly weeping when they pulled him from the mats. I didn't know who the next fighter was going to be, I was holding myself together with a thin thread of control as Freddy and Marek kept chattering beside me.

"Your man is quite formidable. Can't imagine how the ladies will handle him," Freddy, ever the misogynist, said.

"We'll find out soon enough. Fight two is Hurricane and Blue," Marek said, his voice filled with more excitement than I had ever heard from him.

"I can tell you are protective of your women. I suppose that should have been obvious with the show you and your men have been putting on for very nearly a year now," Freddy said as the ref stepped back into the center about to announce the next fighters.

"Not just our women," I said, sparing only a searing glance Freddy's way, before I turned back holding my breath as I watched the doors open again for the next set of fighters.

At first, I felt relieved, since the woman who stepped out first was a tall broad woman, who looked like she would have been better suited in deadlift competitions than a mixed martial arts tournament. But then my fears were confirmed. Behind her came Ash. Her hands were taped, a number four painted on her toned bronze stomach, and her hair, which she had apparently recently redyed was a shocking blue, braided tightly to her head.

She didn't look at the crowd of of us in the box where the VIPs sat, she simply walked to the ring, her head held high, despite the varying reactions from the audience. She was so much smaller than Hurricane, I couldn't help the way my fingers folded tightly into fists, nails cutting into my palm as I kept myself from barging over and ending this fight before it even began.

Ash was a trained fighter. She was skilled and taught people how to do this very thing. Her training was one of the reasons Carmen was alive in the first place. Ash was smart and resourceful. She wouldn't enter a fight she couldn't win, or at least not one she wouldn't walk away from. Right?

The bell rang and Ash was light on her feet. Moving from side to side while the mountain of a woman seemed to simply stretch and watch her. They clearly knew each other's moves, since it was a long few seconds before either of them even made a move to strike. Ash was patient, Hurricane, evidently was not. One heavy swing in Ash's direction had Ash dodging and landing a kick right at the knee of her opponent.

Jeers and screams were echoing through the warehouse, while I watched, enraptured in the action, the way Ash moved around the mat, landing hit after hit, while Hurricane barely got a moment to swing, let alone a punch.

"I'm surprised she's in such good form after not fighting," Marek said beside me. I didn't want to miss a moment of what was happening in that overly lit square of potential death, otherwise, I would have made sure Marek knew better than to speak about her that way.

"You see what I can do, Salvatore?" came Freddy's voice, suddenly much closer to me than it had been. "I have much more influence than you. It may take us time, but we can make anything we want happen. You like this girl, have her under your protection, but haven't named her yours. She's not untouchable until you make that official, and therefore I can pull all the strings I want."

Ash kicked Hurricane in the stomach, causing her to double over, providing Ash with the opportunity she needed to land a solid blow to Hurricane's ear. That should have been it, the great beast of a woman should have been sprawled on the floor, reeling, but instead, just as Ash landed the hit, Hurricane punched hard at Ash's unprotected side.

Somehow, over the commotion around me, I could hear the distinct sound of Ash's gasp. A thin, pained sound rushed through her lips and struck me in the chest.

"I can make sure you and everyone you have around you feel all sorts of pain until I get what I want," Freddy whispered.

"You'll never get Carmen, and I'll be sure to cut all your strings," I gritted out, as I watched Hurricane, though clearly not balanced from her ruptured eardrum, grab hold of Ash's arm as she fought for air, pulling with all her strength so the whole crowd could hear the sharp crack of her shoulder either dislocating or breaking, it was hard to tell.

Anyone else would have screamed, but instead, Ash merely hit the mat, the ref already prepared to end the fight.

"You think this is all I have to offer you, you are very mistaken," Freddy said as I tapped Travis, telling him to prepare to leave.

"I am not mistaken on anything, O'Shea. But so far, I think you forget we've bested you in every attempt you've made. What makes you think we won't again?" I asked, turning to look at him now that Ash was slinking off the ring and heading back to the locker rooms.

Freddy's smile fell as he took in my expression, which I could only assume was frightening, given how his eyes went wide and he physically took a step back from me.

"Taunt and test me all you want. We are not your lap dogs. Unlike your new best friend here," I said jerking my head in Marek's general direction, "we bite back."

CHAPTER 9

ASH

*F**uck!*

My arm was limp at my side, my previously cracked ribs were maybe actually broken now, and I was certain I saw more than one man who was a guard for the Lupos and LaMartinas in the crowd.

I was cooked.

Extra crispy.

Well done.

I could have still beat her, but I knew I wasn't going to make it through the other rounds with my shoulder this way. Much better to just get out before serious damage took place. And I needed to get home somehow, before whichever one of my men was out there watching came back here to yell at me.

I let out a laugh at that. Neither Adrian nor Sal was *mine.* It was insane I would have even thought that. With one hand I grabbed at my things, roughly stuffing everything I could into my bag, because there was no way my jacket was getting back on until I got my shoulder working.

"Hey, Blue, are you okay?"

I glanced up at Didi. There was genuine concern there, but I didn't have time.

"Just need to get going," I said, putting my bag over my unhurt shoulder and giving her a stiff nod as I moved to the locker doors and stepped out into the hallway. Almost as soon as the door shut behind me, the doors out to the main warehouse opened, and Sal was standing there.

Where Adrian was more of the wild Italian hotty, with curly hair, a beard, and very seldomly put together, Sal was a cool, collected Italian in a suit, with slicked back hair and dark eyes that would root you to the spot. He always seemed to be calm and have it together, but I had seen him let loose some anger at the gym before, and it was a sight to behold. I couldn't take my eyes off him.

But now was not that time.

Now was the time for me to run.

"Ashley!" he called as soon as I turned away from him, darting in the opposite direction to get back outside.

I could hear his footfalls as he chased after me, but I didn't care. He was going to catch me, but I had to try to get away. I didn't want to face whatever this confrontation was, because I had been avoiding a lot more than telling him about this. All the weight of the problems that had come down on me, on top of the feelings I had for him and his best friend was just too much. I didn't want to deal with it. I didn't want to discuss it. I didn't want him to think he could take care of me.

I took care of me. No one else.

The door slammed behind me; the bouncer startled as I sped past him, heading through the mass of cars and trying to figure out exactly how I was going to get home, while not alerting Sal. That didn't matter though.

Sal was basically right behind me, the door opening again before I got more than five paces away.

"Ash! Stop!"

"Just let me go home, Sal!" I yelled back at him without looking behind me.

He didn't stop coming, because why would he?

I zigzagged between cars, my limp arm painfully hitting them as I went, but I couldn't stop. I needed to get home, to try to put my shoulder back into place. I had done it before, and then maybe I could figure out how to face Sal. But it didn't matter, I got as far as the last row of cars before he finally reached out and grabbed my uninjured arm, spinning me around to face him.

"What the fuck are you doing here?" he practically snarled, those brown eyes like black inky pits of anger. I had never seen him this mad before. The twisted, damaged part of me liked it, my stomach clenching with desire as I looked into those enraged black depths.

"None of your business!" I yelled back.

"Oh, it's my business, Ashley. Everything is my business," he said coldly, before he turned, dragging me behind him.

"Where are you taking me?"

"To Benny," was all he said, marching me to his car where Travis waited. I couldn't really argue with that. Benny LaMartina was a doctor, specializing in physical therapy. Other than an orthopedic doctor, that was probably my best bet with this shoulder. But my stubbornness wouldn't allow me to admit that to Sal, practically making him scoop me up and set me in the backseat of the car.

"The gym, Travis," he said before he promptly put the partition up between us and the front seat and grabbed my chin to bring my face up to his. "Why are you fighting again?"

"Maybe I like it," I snapped.

"That's not why you're at these fights, and you know it. You want a legitimate fight, you'd get in. I know you would. So tell me the truth."

It was like he saw through any lie I might have told. Those dark eyes could peer into my very soul if I let them.

"I needed money."

The way those eyes narrowed, and his fingers tightened only slightly on my chin.

"What happened?"

The fact that he asked that question instead of asking why, told me more about him than I liked to admit. He knew I was comfortable with the amount of money I got from working for them at the gym. He understood I didn't care for lavish or expensive things. He and Adrian watched me, looked after me, even though none of us had ever acted on any of these low-burning feelings we had had for years.

I hadn't wanted to tell him or Adrian, because I didn't want to admit anything to myself. Not that I needed help. Not that I wanted two men at the same time. Not that I craved being part of their inner circle, now more than ever before because Ingrid had most recently stepped out of this periphery we had both been in, and I was left an island alone.

I was always alone.

"Lewandowski bought my building. I'm being evicted."

Sal's nostrils flared as he took in a deep breath. He looked into my eyes for a long moment, thoughts I was not privy to dancing within his.

Without a word, he rolled the partition back down.

"How much longer?" he asked Travis.

"Five minutes," Travis said.

"Good."

We pulled up to the gym. The parking lot of the strip mall was mostly empty. Well into the night and a Wednesday, meant even Breakers, the bar, wasn't all that busy at this point. Outside the door stood Adrian and Benny, though the lights inside the gym were on. Travis pulled the car right in front of them and Sal quickly got out.

"You can go, Travis. Head to Ma's. Carmen is staying there tonight."

"Are you sure? I can come back and get you when you're—"

"Adrian will drive us," he said before Travis could offer more.

"Yes, Sir," Travis said, before Sal climbed out, bending down to help me out as well, which was harder than I felt it should have been. I'd been in worse shape than this before, it had just been a while.

As soon as I was out of the car Adrian was in front of me too. His eyes took in everything about my appearance with a fierce rage building in his eyes.

"What the fuck is this?" he asked, practically spitting.

"I'll tell you while Benny takes care of her," Sal said, nudging Adrian out of the way with his shoulder so I could go toward Benny.

"Come on, Ash. Let's see how bad you fucked yourself up," Benny said, a small smile peeking at the corner of his mouth.

We all went inside, Benny bringing me to the newly remodeled room that was now for exams. Previously it had been an unused second office. I dropped the bag from my good shoulder and managed to get myself onto the exam table. Benny zoned in on my shoulder first, of course, because that was the most obvious injury. Adrian and Sal stood side by side on the right side of the room.

"Dislocated. Not the worst I've seen," Benny said as he lifted my arm slightly, watching my minute facial changes. "Let's have the guys come hold onto you while I put this back in."

I shook my head, but it was no use, a moment later Sal was at my side and Adrian right in front of me, holding onto my hips.

"On the count of three," Benny said.

"Just fucking do it!" I snapped, making Benny smile wide.

"Three!"

A sharp jerk and upward push and my shoulder was back where it was supposed to be, accompanied by searing pain. Then came relief.

"Barely a grunt from her," Benny noted with an impressed tone.

"No crying in boxing. Well, martial arts. My dad used to say it when I'd stitch him up after fights," I said, then almost immediately regretted it. It wasn't that I didn't want to talk about my dad, it was more that it brought up bad memories of what came after he died. Adrian and Sal said nothing, but I noticed the look they exchanged.

"We heard that a lot too growing up. Maybe not about boxing though," Benny said, turning his focus to the bruising he could see on my ribs now.

"This is old?" It was a question, because of the coloring, I assumed.

"Reinjured. She hit me there again tonight," I said, trying and failing not to flinch when he brushed his fingers over it.

"Hmm…"

"Clean break, though it's going to hurt for a while. Lucky it didn't puncture a lung."

"No backless dresses for me," I sighed sarcastically.

"That's what you're worried about?" Adrian asked, and Sal just shook his head, a tiny hint of a smile on his lips.

"Joking, dumbass," I said, while Benny went to the cabinet to grab some gauze rolls to wrap my ribs.

"Actually, it might not bruise too bad for a backless dress. You got hit more toward the front this time. The old bruise should fade," Benny said, a little wicked-ness hiding behind his eyes. Either he knew about the dress Carmen had me try on, or he was trying to get Sal and Adrian to react, which was clearly working on some level.

"Just going to wrap you up. You should probably do it every day for a couple days at least. Plenty of time so you can sport a backless dress for Carmen's wedding. I'm sure these two won't mind the view," Benny said, chuckling as both shifted uncomfortably.

"I'm still waiting to hear what happened," Adrian said, glaring at me. Sal pulled him away from me, and back to their little corner of the room. In a quiet voice, Sal gave him the rundown of what I had said in the car, and then quieter still, there were coded things he began relaying, probably about something that happened at the tournament that didn't involve me.

"You're going to drive them crazy you know," Benny said for only me to hear as he wrapped my ribs. Having the pressure there felt good, but also painful at the same time.

"They're driving me crazy already," I admitted, gaining a chuckle from him.

Benny's life had taken a strange turn too. He was a practicing physical therapist in Kansas City proper and had come back to work here of all places. I didn't particularly understand it, other than wanting to be back home after what had happened with Carmen, but he didn't have any sort of resentment surrounding the change of life. He had settled in here and didn't seem to mind being back in the town he had grown up in.

"She's as good as can be done. No more fighting for a while and I'd say you'll be back to normal in a week or so. Take it easy when you're training," he told me sternly.

"Heading to the moms or are you going to the apartment?" Adrian asked.

"Moms. I know Travis is there with Peter, but I'd feel better if one of us is there until Leo comes back," Benny said, getting nods from both men. "Don't be too hard on her," he said pointedly at both of them, before quickly leaving the room, the ding of the front door chiming the only sound a moment later.

CHAPTER 10

ASH

The silence felt heavy as I sat on that exam table. Sal and Adrian still stood together on the far side of the room, looking at me. I was starting to feel like I was going to crawl out of my skin if someone didn't say something. Or I could just go. My apartment wasn't too far. Much easier to walk home from the gym than it would have been from the warehouse. I slipped off the table, moving to the spot near the door to the room to grab my discarded bag.

"Thanks for the ride and getting Benny," I said as I put it over my good shoulder once more.

"You aren't going anywhere, Ash," Adrian said with a scowl as he stalked over to me and practically ripped the bag back off my shoulder.

"What the fuck, Adrian?" I hissed.

"You didn't think you could tell either of us about your apartment? Didn't even think to confide in Carmen or Ingrid?"

"And what? Have them blab to you two?" I snapped.

"Why didn't you want us to know?" Sal asked, still rooted in the same spot, but almost pulsing with unreleased tension.

"Why should you know? You're my bosses! Nothing about my life outside of this gym has anything to do with you!"

The moment the words left my mouth I regretted them. That wasn't true at all, and I knew it, even if that's what I had told myself. It was like I had slapped them both in the face. Sal strode over to us, each step deliberate as if he were approaching a wild animal or perhaps holding back his own anger, something Adrian was clearly struggling with as he breathed heavily before me.

"It could," Sal said, placing a hand on Adrian's shoulder, something I had seen him do many times when Adrian was on the verge of exploding. It seemed to ground them both.

"What do you mean?" I asked, trying to keep my voice steady.

"We want your life to be our concern, if you'll let us," Sal said.

There were two very opposing feelings that came over me at the same time. One was the immediate desire to revolt, to push this away and close down, be the solitary person I had essentially been all my life. The other was the overwhelming urge to let these men in as I had wanted from nearly the moment I had met them.

It hadn't been the same night as the last fight I did for Lewandowski, it was a few days later when I got a call. Adrian was the one who was on the other end of the line, letting me know he had a job offer for me after seeing me fight, and it would be waiting for as long as I needed. Not long after that, the details of the trainer job were sent to me. Marek unexpectedly told me my

debt was paid the very same day the job description landed in my hands.

Something within me told me that I needed to take this job. So what that it was across the state? What did I have in St, Louis that I was really leaving behind? I didn't have real friends; anyone I spent more than a few minutes with was because I was in a locker room with them or punching them in the ring. No one would miss me there, and I definitely needed to get as far away as possible from the Lewandowskis.

I drove the four and a half hours to Lee's Summit the next day, pulling up at the quaint gym in a little strip mall and instantaneously falling in love with it. It wasn't fancy, but it wasn't run down like the places I was used to in St. Louis, and I felt an odd sort of comfort. I was never *comfortable*.

I met both of them that day. Sal had sat behind the desk, crisp suit and slicked back hair, while Adrian stood in standard gym attire beside him, his beard and wild curls making them look so opposing, yet they were clearly a team. They were dangerous, I could sense that from the moment I saw them, but beyond that, they were offering me a life free of the influence of my father's shortcomings. Over the years they had shown me so many facets of who they were and what their principles were. They put their people first, always, and they had chosen me to be one of those people.

Now I just had to finally make that choice, and I wasn't sure I could do it. Not to mention I couldn't be sure what they were offering? Was I going to be folded into the organization? Did they want to use me for something? Or was this more personal?

"What does that even mean?" I asked, my voice barely a whisper.

Suddenly Adrian let out a chuckle, glancing back at Sal.

"She's not going to go for it," Adrian said, his tone almost bitter.

"For now?" Sal said, ignoring Adrian's comment, but giving him a squeeze on the shoulder he was still holding onto. "You let us take on some burdens for you," Sal said to me. I let out a shaky breath. That still wasn't very clear, but at least that was something I could handle letting them do.

"I guess I could do that," I murmured, looking at them skeptically.

"Tonight, you're staying with us," Adrian said, gaining a nod from Sal.

"I don't think that's—"

"Freddy O'Shea and Marek Lewandowski are in town. That Polish scum not only knows where you live but owns the building. There is no way in hell you are staying there tonight," Adrian said, his voice harsh, but as he said it, his hand came up, as if unconsciously, cupping my cheek softly.

"Please, let us help," Sal murmured, his other hand reaching for a moment like he wanted to touch mine. The hesitation and then flash of sadness in his eyes made me think perhaps he wasn't sure if he could touch me like Adrian had.

"Okay," I said, before swallowing loudly and stepping away to gather my bag that Adrian had thrown.

The drive from the gym to their Kansas City house was quiet and tense. But I was so tired that I found myself dozing before we got there. It wasn't that far of a drive, but it seemed like a blink before I was being lifted from the car. I was expecting Adrian, but as I let my heavy lids open just a bit, I realized it was Sal who was holding me.

"I-I can walk," I tried to say, squirming a little, even though the strength of his arms and the delicious spice of his cologne was so comforting.

"Just go to sleep," he whispered.

The next time I woke up, I initially became aware of the strange scent. Odd scents on my person were fairly normal. Working with people at the gym all day tended to leave me smelling like others, especially their body sweat, but this wasn't body odor, it was *fresh*. Clean laundry, but not my generic store brand detergent, like my sheets often smelled like. The next thing I was acutely aware of was the horrible pain in my shoulder and ribs.

I groaned, rolling over from my stomach to my back, and opened my eyes to see, not my small bedroom, but a very garishly decorated bedroom I had never seen before. I sat up abruptly, which I immediately regretted because of my ribs, hissing slightly for a moment, before resuming taking in my surroundings.

Everything about last night came back into focus, Marek, the fight, Sal and Adrian. And then the reality of where I was settled within me, a deep-seated dis-comfort taking up residence where confusion once was.

Opulent.

This room was more expensive than the money my dad owed the Lewandowskis. More expensive than any car I had owned. More expensive than my whole life from birth to now, probably. And they brought me here. They let me sleep in this bed with sheets that smelled like heaven. They put my sweaty, grimy body on this bed with no qualms.

I slipped from the sheets, still dressed in the clothes I had fought in, a little of the paint from the number painted on my torso smearing against the pale blue fabric. A little relief filled me that Sal had clearly just put me in here, only taking off my shoes but leaving me clothed. And now that I noticed my feet were bare, my eyes darted around in the semi-darkness, trying to see where those shoes could have been placed.

As soon as I spotted them, I quickly moved to grab them, having been set beside my bag by a chair in the corner. Both items of mine in my grasp, I hastily headed for the door, where a knock resounded just as I was about to turn the knob.

"Ash? It's Carmen. Are you awake?"

Why did Carmen's voice make me feel so much better and worse at the same time? It both felt like a relief she was the first person I saw instead of either of the men, and like I was caught doing something wrong.

I opened the door, adjusting the bag on my good shoulder as I gave her a halfhearted smile.

"I'm up! Just about to head out," I said, quickly trying to move past her.

"Oh my god! Are you okay? Adrian really down-played what happened," she said stopping me and gently inspecting the bruising on my shoulder.

"I'm fine. I'll be better when I get home and shower before I head to the gym," I said, still trying to wiggle away from her.

"The boys said you can't go back there until other arrangements have been made. Whatever that means."

I paused in my attempts, letting those words settle on my shoulders for a moment. I couldn't go back.

"Because?"

"Not safe," she said, sighing heavily and looking at me with sympathetic eyes. "I know this sucks, but eventually things will go back to normal. Though they've been saying that to me for months." Her grumble was cute, and normally I would have poked fun at her for being the little sister amongst all these men, but at the moment I saw no humor in anything. "Let's get you some coffee and food."

Feed people. That was what Maria and Liliana did, so it made sense Carmen would find that the first comfort she would want to perform. But my stomach decided at that moment to remind me it had been far longer than normal since I had food, so perhaps it wasn't necessarily the comfort and more of an observed necessity.

We walked down the hallway. It was just as lavish as the bedroom. Rich wood paneled the lower half of the walls, while the top was beautifully painted textured plaster, adorned with paintings and other art. I didn't see any photos of the family, but that didn't necessarily mean much. This must have been Salvatore's house, which Sal inherited after his father died.

Which meant we were in Kansas City, not Lee's Summit. And I was still without a car to leave if I wanted.

Trapped.

Although not the very worst situation to be stuck in, but still not ideal.

And I already knew that. My mind pulled back the pieces of the disorienting night before, reminding me I had already known they brought me here; I had just fallen asleep before we arrived.

"I'll give you a tour later. It's kind of a maze until you get used to it," she said, grabbing my hand. There was a hint of her own anxiety. I wasn't sure if it was about giving me a tour, the wedding, or something else, but I decided to let us anchor each other. Carmen was not an enemy, not that any of them were, but she had my best interests at heart.

Carmen led me to a set of stairs at the end of the hall, it was narrower than I expected, but no less beautiful than the rest of the house. I could hear the sound of activity as we got farther down the stairs. Talking and the sounds of pots and pans accompanied the scent of food and coffee. My stomach lurched again, the scent triggering hunger pains like I hadn't felt since I was a teenager at home with my dad. I hadn't eaten anything since sometime before I went to the gym for work yesterday, having rushed directly from there to get home, before I was whisked away by Marek for the fight.

We finally hit the bottom of the stairs which opened directly to the kitchen and a sight I had never truly experienced before. Maria and Liliana were whipping up breakfast, and talking loudly about what they needed to do for the wedding. Leo and Sal were bent over a phone at a kitchen table, while Adrian was leaning against the island counter, happily chatting with Nora who sat on Enzo's lap. Benny stood next to his mother, Maria, laughing as she swatted his hand away from the food he was trying to steal bites of. The only person missing in this equation was Ingrid, who, given the hour, was probably at the coffee shop Liliana owned.

"Oh good! She is awake!" Liliana said, bustling around the island counter with her arms outstretched. Liliana and Maria were huggers, I had discovered when I first came to one of the Christmas parties.

"I'm pretty disgusting," I warned, holding out my good arm to show her the smeared paint and my bandaged ribs.

"Carmen! You didn't find her clothes?" Maria admonished as Liliana, unfazed by my dirtiness, pulled me in for a hug anyway.

"She needs to eat, then shower, Ma," Carmen grumbled behind me as Liliana pulled away from the warm embrace, cupping my cheeks and giving me a soft smile.

"Let's get you a plate," she practically whispered, pulling me to the closest stool and taking my bag off my shoulder in one fluid motion.

A delicious hot plate of eggs, fried onions and tomatoes, sausage, and toast was placed in front of me a moment later.

"Coffee with almond milk," Carmen said, setting a mug by the plate before I could even start in on the food. She knew how I liked my coffee from years of working at the coffee shop. I supposed Ingrid and perhaps Liliana would have also known, but something about all these kind gestures made me feel strange.

"Had quite a fight last night, huh?" Leo asked as he left Sal where he sat to grab the plates and pass them around to the others. Benny did as well, getting Nora's child-sized dish, and Enzo's for him since he was stuck with her on his lap.

"Something like that," I said, glancing over at Adrian who had taken up the spot Leo had vacated next to Sal, their two sets of eyes now focused on me.

"Didn't know you were still fighting, dear," Liliana said. It wasn't a question but clearly was a prompt. A few times at the private events Salvatore had put on, Liliana had come with him, more often than not, it wasn't her, but some other random woman he brought with him. If I could have gone back in time I would have gone to Liliana and told her about the infidelity I witnessed, but as it was, I suspected she already knew all about what Salvatore did when she wasn't around, and he was dead now, so it really wouldn't change anything.

"That's up to her, Ma," Sal said, casting her a harsh look, before turning his attention back to me, and then Adrian.

Conversations resumed, thankfully I was mostly left out of it. I ate my food, which my stomach gladly thanked me for, and felt somewhat human after that, though I was far more acutely aware of how disgusting I was than even the short time earlier when I got out of the lavish bed.

"Alright, Carmen. Do you have some things Ashley can wear until we can get her some clothes from her apartment?" Maria asked when she grabbed my empty plate and seemed to take in my uncomfortable expression.

"I can just head home," I said, standing from the stool and looking around for where Liliana had set my bag.

"But Mommy said you were going to stay until the wedding. Like us!" Nora said, happily wiggling in Enzo's lap.

"Until the wedding?" I asked. I'm not sure what my face looked like, but everyone seemed to look back at me with strange sympathetic expressions.

"Maybe the tour and a shower, first," Carmen said, quickly moving from the seat she had been sitting in next to Adrian and Leo and coming to my side.

CHAPTER 11

SAL

The room was quiet as Carmen and Ash left, and then I was met with the scornful look of both of the moms.

"You didn't tell her the plan?" my mom asked, her hands on her hips as she moved swiftly over to the kitchen table where I was sitting next to Adrian.

"She fell asleep. We were going to tell her, but everyone decided to come over first thing this morning instead of waiting until we had enough time to talk to her. Now she's overwhelmed and bombarded. Much harder to convince a stubborn person who has been blindsided, than someone who has all the facts," I said, standing with my own empty dish to head to the sink.

"The wedding plans need to happen whether or not some Irish man is in town. We only have five days, *Salvatore*, don't try to make *me* feel guilty," my mom yelled. I cringed at the use of my full name, a name only really associated with my father. Salvatore was my father; I was Sal.

"We will tell her, if Carmen doesn't do it for us," I said, but the stern looks from both her and Maria were making me feel like I was twelve and had just broken a window. "I have some work to get done," I said, glancing at Leo and Enzo pointedly.

Adrian and I needed to go over what Leo found out last night as well as discuss the next steps, because until we knew exactly what the Irish were hunting for, this was never going to be over with them, not unless we took them out. But killing off the O'Shea clan would only bring more problems down on us, since Gregor Stepanov, the Russian boss in the Midwest, wanted Colin O'Shea's head for his own trophy.

I moved quickly before the moms could try to start another argument or conversation and slipped from the kitchen and into the dining room. Before I could move to the hall and subsequently up to the office, I was stopped by the little bit of conversation I could hear coming from the main hall by the stairs.

"…but you know what they do?" Carmen asked.

"I've known, just not at what scope. Leo maybe told me a bit more than he should have when you were taken. I'm getting more of an idea of it now though," Ash said, and I could practically hear the way her face would shift into that sassy, tough expression. Carmen laughed, confirming that for me.

"The Irish have been trying to get ahold of me because they think I can help them find something my dad locked away before he died. That's why the extra security has been on me. You, from what I gather, have some Polish dude after you that is linking up with these Irish assholes. Adrian and Sal and the rest of us don't want anything to happen to you," Carmen told her. It was a little less eloquent than I would have liked it told, but Carmen wasn't really one to sugarcoat if she could help it. Adrian came behind me from the kitchen and

I held up a hand to stop him. He looked at me quizzically, but then Ash spoke again.

"Your wedding is, what? In five days? I can't even get to work from here," Ash said, making me roll my eyes. That was enough.

"And you won't need to. Classes have been canceled, the others can run the gym without you," I said, finally moving around the archway from the dining room to the hall and into view of both women. Carmen sighed and crossed her arms and Ash scowled.

"What the hell? I'm just kidnapped now?" Ash demanded.

"Carmen, get the clothes for her, please," Adrian said, also stepping into the hall, and though it was asked nicely, there was an edge to his voice that apparently Carmen listened to, because she stomped up the stairs and out of sight.

"Come to the office," I said, heading up the stairs after a moment of listening to Carmen's footsteps fade away.

The three of us went up the stairs, Ash entering the room behind me and Adrian closing the door behind him a moment later. I wasn't going to sit behind my father's desk, and the only reason I came into this room at all in the first place was because it was soundproofed better than most of the other rooms.

"Okay, Ash. What do you want to know?" I asked, leaning on the back of the desk as she stood in the middle of the room between me and Adrian. She sputtered a laugh, throwing up her hands and shaking her head as she looked around the room.

"Everything?" she said, like it was a question.

"I am Salvatore Lupo Jr., the son of Salvatore Lupo Sr., the former Caporegime of this midwestern territory of the Italian Mafia," I said pausing so she could take in that information. Her brows rose a little, but the expression she gave was more resignation, like she had already known that, maybe not concretely, but had deduced as much.

"My father was killed by myself, my brothers, and Adrian for trying to sell Carmen off to the Irish. I did not take over his position immediately, because the boss wanted me to prove myself. I have been trying to do that, while the Irish continue to try and take Carmen from us in various ways because of something Bernardo LaMartina did before he died. You are part of our family, even if only in the little bit you will allow."

She looked surprised, glancing back to Adrian, who nodded.

"Your old boss, Marek Lewandowski traded your debt to us to keep us from killing his men for stealing from us. That's why you were freed. That is why we want to protect you, now that we know he's been weaseling his way back by trying to have you evicted," Adrian said.

"But other than him, I'm not a target. I only have a few days left to move," she murmured.

"That wouldn't be the biggest worry, if he wasn't clearly allying himself with the Irish now. None of what happened last night would have come to pass if the man I had keeping you safe hadn't been alone. You leaving the apartment, not to mention being taken by Marek would have been noticed, but we have been stretched thin with trying to keep everyone we hold dear protected," Adrian said, having stepped a little closer to her, probably without even realizing it.

"Having you here in the house will help keep everyone else safe too, at least while some things are in motion," I said.

"What about my things?"

"What do you want to do with them? After it's safe and Lewandowski is taken care of, you can find another apartment if you want. We have places to store things," I said, though I knew both Adrian and I really didn't want her to find another place to live. Maybe she would agree to be something more with both of us … but that wasn't what we were discussing right now. That would have to be something we talked about another time.

"I don't like this," she said, rather pointedly.

"We know," Adrian said, a smile coming to his lips.

"This is only for now?" she asked, though the under-current to her words were that she was *telling* us it was temporary.

"Only until we can be sure you aren't threatened," I said carefully, making sure there was understanding in her expression that just because the wedding was five days away, that didn't mean she was living on her own after that.

"Fine," she said, her voice a little harsh. "But I'm packing my own stuff. I don't need your *men* going through everything I own without me there.

"Fair enough."

CHAPTER 12

ASH

It was a strange thing, not going to work. My routine lately had been wake up, eat, gym, eat, fight, sleep. Now there was nothing but time ahead of me and it felt more surreal than anything else. The SUV I was being driven in pulled up to the apartment complex, the second one that had Carmen in it parked right beside us a moment later, and then Benny in his jeep.

Adrian had argued that it wouldn't be enough space for everything, and they should get a service truck from their car storage, but I assured them I really didn't have much, just a lot more than my small sedan could carry. Three large vehicles and my sedan would probably end up being too much.

"I'm sorry, Carmen. You don't have to help. I'm sure you have a million other things you need to do today than this," I said when I got out and stood next to her between the cars.

"I need a break anyway. Mama is driving me crazy with the centerpieces and seating arrangements, so I'm just going to let her do it without me," Carmen said with a strained smile, clearly not pleased to hand over the reins to someone else, but not capable of dealing with the wedding planning whirlwind that had become Maria. "This will be good. Maybe I'll find out a little more about you," she said, wiggling her eyebrows.

It wasn't so much that I had kept things from her on purpose, I just hadn't felt the need to share everything. I hadn't had real friends that I shared my whole life with until I moved here. Now it was Lupos and LaMartinas everywhere, every day.

"So how much is crammed in there? I nearly broke my back helping Carmen and Leo move all her junk to their apartment. And Ingrid and Nora had an ungodly amount in their tiny apartment," Benny said, getting an elbow to the ribs from Carmen in response.

"It's really not that much," I assured them, finally leading the way up to the second floor and my apartment, unlocking the door.

I wasn't sure why I was shocked by what I saw when I opened it, but I was. My home, my one safe place that I got to call my own, was now in shambles. The table had been knocked over and broken, my couch was on its back, the cushions having been thrown across the room and frames were knocked from the walls. Drawers were emptied and left lying on the floor.

The only thing I could imagine had happened, especially because the door had been locked, was Marek had come in to trash the place. This wasn't someone looking for something in particular, and there weren't any valuables to steal, this was a message.

"Shit," Benny said, sighing as he ran his hand through his hair. Odd that in this moment I could see exactly how similar the LaMartina siblings were, with their worried and angry expressions, they looked so much like Adrian.

"I'm so sorry, Ash," Carmen said, stepping closer and taking my hand as we looked over the mess.

"Let's just get started," I said stiffly, moving farther into the apartment and taking in the rest of the destruction.

We broke into groups. The two guards and Benny were busying themselves with the furniture, while Carmen and I decided to take care of my bedroom and bathroom. Thankfully it didn't seem like Marek had done much in there. My mattress had been thrown off the frame and my clothes were strewn about the room, but I was going to be packing it all away anyway.

Petty and childish was the best way I could describe this, not that I expected anything different from the man-child. He was little better than a toddler when I had been working for him, making me adjust to his whims at a moment's notice. This tantrum he threw in my apartment was nothing in comparison to what it could have been if I had been here.

I would never admit to Adrian or Sal the gratefulness I felt, knowing they kept me from whatever Marek had planned for me when he came back here last night.

"So what's the deal with this Polish guy anyway?" Carmen asked once we had decided how we were going to get everything packed. It didn't need to be perfect, because I just going to be unpacking all of the clothes again when we got back to the house.

I glanced at her, looking over the friend I had made over these last few years. I was older than her, sure, but she had been an unwavering rock of a person for me, even if I didn't share much of myself in return.

"My dad owed him money before he died. I had to work for him to pay off the debt," I told her. The only thing Carmen or the others knew was that my parents were dead. It was partially why, I suspected, they made such a point to invite me to events and holidays. I was alone.

"And now he's followed you here from St. Louis all these years later?" she asked, raising an eyebrow at me through the mirror over my small dresser.

"I'm thinking my being here was more a convenience than a reason, since he's got the Irish backing him now," I said, recalling our conversation earlier that morning.

"These men do thrive taking opportunities when they present themselves," she grumbled.

We were silent for a few minutes, the gravity of the conversation making the air feel heavier as we shoved my life into bags and boxes, the sound of the men grunting as they moved the furniture the only real sound.

"Are you excited for the wedding, at least?" I asked, hoping to lighten the mood a bit, even if it was my life that was being upended, not hers.

"I'd be more excited if you wore a dress," she said, grinning at me again through the mirror. I rolled my eyes, shaking my head and gesturing to the pile of clothes that had formerly been hanging in my closet.

"If you want to take a look, you'll find there are no available dresses to wear to your wedding, but there is a very nice pantsuit that I was thinking I'd wear."

"Ugh! You're no fun! That dress we tried on was *perfect*! I *need* to see the looks on Sal's and Adrian's faces when they see you wearing that!" she said, the mock desperation in her voice making me crack my own smile.

"I can't afford it, Carmen," I said, though the idea of it was rather tempting. Especially with how much they both seemed so vested in my safety. Sal's rage last night only seemed to inflame my desire for him more. So angry that I hadn't come to them with my problems, that I had gotten myself mixed up in their world on my own. And they always spoke of them as a unit. Both men. Sal and Adrian.

Suddenly, the image of me in that dress and the two of them unable to contain themselves flooded my mind. They would be so consumed; they wouldn't mind sharing me with each other. I was thankful my blush wasn't noticeable, as I looked back down at the shirts I was putting back on hangers. If I had been Ingrid, I would have been flaming red with the path my thoughts had gone down.

"I wonder who you'd choose," Carmen said, turning around to face me and watching my reaction.

"What?"

"Which one? Adrian or Sal?" she asked now.

That was pure Carmen, blatantly asking the question on her mind instead of beating around the bush. Her expression was genuine curiosity, but I had no idea how to answer. How could I say to her that I wanted both? How could I tell her I didn't *want* to choose?

"I—"

"We got most of the big stuff in my jeep. I'm just going to run and take it to the warehouse and then I'll come back," Benny said, having popped into the room and interrupted me. For a moment I was glad he came and cut me off before I could spill any of the thoughts in my head. Adrian was their brother after all.

"Great," I said, my voice a little more pinched than it normally would be.

"You okay?" he asked, glancing at my shoulder and ribs, clearly assuming I was having a hard time from my injuries, not what his sister had just asked me.

"She's just having a hard time because I asked her if she would choose Sal or our brother," Carmen said, grinning at the transformation of Benny's expression from concerned to a little embarrassed.

"Oh," he said, straightening back up and heading straight back out the door.

"You know you want to know the answer too, Benito!" Carmen called after him.

"I'm sure you'll tell me later!" he said back before the apartment door slammed. Carmen laughed, and I couldn't help the little chuckle that left me. It was our favorite pastime, to embarrass her brothers and the Lupos, even if this time it was also at my expense.

"So?" she asked when her laughter died back down. I sighed, standing to start putting the bag over the bundle of hanging t-shirts.

"What if I don't want to choose?" I asked, purposefully not looking at her.

"You going to make them fight over you?" she asked. "That might be fun at first, Ash, but they are like family. We've all known each other our whole lives. I don't want you to ruin what they have."

What they have.

No, I didn't want that either, which was why I was trying so very hard to not have any sort of romantic relationship with either of them, but then Adrian had to go and kiss me and Sal had to be chivalrous. But what seemed strange was that even though I was certain Sal and Adrian had the kind of friendship where they would tell each other if such a thing happened, the fact that Adrian had kissed me didn't seem to diminish Sal's desire.

"Me either," I said.

"You'll have to let them down easy," Carmen said, clearly coming to the conclusion that I wouldn't be choosing either of them. That was safe. That was probably how it should be, because what I really wanted was to have them both.

Not possible.

S al and I were driving to my mom's house, which I supposed was more like Enzo and Ingrid's now, since she had moved in next door with Liliana now that Carmen and Leo had their own apartment in Kansas City.

Not long after Carmen and Ash got picked up from our house to pack up Ash's apartment, did we get a call from Enzo saying he needed us to see something. It seemed urgent, his voice had been almost panicked when Sal answered, and we immediately rushed to meet him.

Pulling up to the house was far too familiar. These two houses that sat side by side were *really* our home, not that mansion of a place that was decorated for showing off the wealth and power of the Mafia that Sal and I now lived in.

We walked in without knocking, though only because we knew Ingrid was at work and Nora was at school. If Ingrid had been home, we would have been polite. Ingrid wasn't quite used to how open and comfortable with each other we all were, though she was making a valiant effort. Her agreeing to move in with Enzo had been something we weren't sure would happen for some time, but she surprised all of us.

"I was going through some of the intel we managed to copy from when Ingrid pulled it for us. Deep in some video footage they had saved, probably for blackmail purposes, I found this," Enzo said, his breathing a little erratic.

We quickly moved through the living room to the dining room where he had made an office with multiple computer screens and now two workstations, since Ingrid was just as adept, if not more than Enzo in all of this computer stuff. On the screen that he pointed to was the still image of a video.

A man was strapped to a chair, his face bloody but it was unmistakable who it was.

My father, Bernardo LaMartina.

"Did you watch it?" I asked after swallowing the lump that formed in my throat.

"Not yet," he said.

Sal braced his hand on my shoulder, the touch immediately making me feel so much more grounded, as it always had.

"Play it," I said to Enzo. I almost wished I could take Sal's hand, because if the slight tremor in my voice wasn't enough proof, I felt like I needed something a little more than the usual to keep me on my feet for whatever this was going to reveal.

Enzo nodded, moving the cursor to hit the play button. There was no sound, but my father was sitting stoically, his hands tied to the arms of the chair, but his head held high. Another man came into the frame, his back to us, but I could tell from his overall shape and coloring who he was.

Colin O'Shea.

Whatever O'Shea was asking my dad, he merely shook his head no. To a few questions, he didn't even do that, he simply spit blood in O'Shea's direction, never adverting his eyes.

"You are stupid if you think I'll tell you anything," I saw my father say, reading his lips.

And then O'Shea turned, his profile a mask of fury as he beckoned someone from outside the frame.

"Luckily I don't need all of you for this," it seemed like O'Shea said, just before a very young Freddy came into the frame. In his hand was a saw. He looked frightened as his father beckoned him closer, whispering something in his ear once he was right beside him.

I watched, in horror as Freddy went to my father, grabbing his hand and proceeding to slowly saw it off his body. My hand involuntarily reached out, grasping at Sal's jacket and holding on for dear life as I watched both hands get removed, my father's face twisted in agony, body thrashing against the restraints, as blood started pooling on the floor at his feet.

When it was done, Freddy immediately threw up behind the chair while his father clapped him on the back, a sinister grin spread over his face when he turned to grab a cooler that one of his men held out to him. The hands were packed in the freezer, Freddy stumbled out of frame, and Colin O'Shea leaned over saying something in my father's ear as he slumped forward in the chair, still shaking, but no longer screaming.

Colin left, and for a long time, the video was just watching my father slowly die of blood loss. His breathing was irregular, and then it was still.

"I'm going to stop it," Enzo said, moving the cursor again.

"Don't!" I said, my eyes still glued to the screen.

Just as I suspected, another person came into frame, this time it was none other than April Smith. She kicked his corpse as another man entered with a bag in his hand. He was a smaller man, almost comically so standing next to April, but he just simply got to work, laying out instruments from his bag on a table he had rolled close from somewhere in the room.

"Who is that?" Sal asked.

"I'll find out," Enzo said, noting the time stamp of the video on a piece of paper with the word "who?" written above it so he could get the face off it later.

To my horror, the man came over to the back of my father, pulling his head so his face was toward the ceiling. His mouth was agape, eyes closed. I knew the image would haunt me forever and I fought the urge to let my knees buckle beneath me. Then, using those instruments he had just pulled out, the man proceeded to cut my father's eyes from his face.

"That's enough," Sal said, and Enzo promptly stopped the video. "Adrian, look at me."

I turned my head to look at Sal, it felt heavy to do so, hard to move, hard to breathe. I had seen a great many terrible things during my time in the Marines, and more since I was working in the Mafia, but something about watching my father get brutally tortured and killed, then have his body desecrated afterward, had hit me differently than anything that I had seen before.

"Adrian, look at me," Sal repeated, but his voice seemed far away or muffled.

"I-I can't—" I couldn't get the words out. I couldn't say how disgusted and horrified and upset I was at just witnessing what I saw.

"I know. I've got you," Sal said, his eyes never wavering from mine, his hands holding on to me as I clutched onto him for dear life. When had he stepped in front of me? When did he press his forehead to mine?

"I've got you," Sal said, but his fury was coming to the surface. It was not only on my behalf, but also for the sick things we had to witness. The things we had to do.

We sat there, holding each other for a moment and the world started to stop spinning, the blood stopped whooshing in my ears, and I could breathe once more.

"There you are," Sal said, his hands softening on my shoulders and moving up to cup either side of my face. They felt cool against my overheated skin.

"We need to find whatever the fuck this is Bernardo hid before they do. Whatever this is has to be big," Enzo said from behind us. At some point, we must have slid to the floor, because that's where Sal and I were now, and I didn't remember that happening.

"Has Carmen remembered any more?" Sal asked me. I shook my head. Even though I had checked in fairly regularly, she was busy with the wedding and honestly seemed like she was going to cry any time I tried bringing it up.

"Hypnotism will work. I have the name of one we might try," came my mom's voice from the kitchen. She must have come through the back door, a noise so common to our ears in this place we didn't even register it.

Sal and I scrambled from the floor just in time for my mom to step into the dining room.

"What are you doing here, Ma? You're supposed to be in Kansas City!" I said, my heart beating wildly again, hoping she didn't catch any of what we had just watched.

"We forgot a few things. Peter brought us here to grab them," she said indignantly.

"You think hypnotism will work?" Enzo said with skepticism laced in his voice. Sal and I hadn't mentioned that suggestion to everyone just yet, and Enzo, ever the skeptic, looked at my mother incredulously.

"It worked for me and your mom," my mom said back, her tone a little sharp. That was news to all of us.

"Why did you two do that?" Sal asked, clearly as surprised as I was.

"As a wife, there are many traumas your brain tries to help you forget to keep on living in that situation. When I had cancer, Liliana did research on *other* things that might help."

"Oh yeah, you both did that sound healing thing," Enzo said, and she nodded.

"Some people theorize that holding onto traumas and not working through them leads to illness. I agreed to try it for her and all of you. She agreed to do it, so I wasn't alone."

Such a strange admission from my mother but somewhat illuminating. She seemed to be stronger as a person after having gone through her cancer, even if her physical body was much weaker than before.

"Do you think it will work for Carmen?" Sal asked.

"If Bernardo took her somewhere, she should be able to remember it with that," my mom said with a nod.

Carmen wasn't going to like it, but it was worth trying.

ASH

I was putting my clothes away in the room that had been designated mine when I heard the door from the garage into the kitchen open. I left my bedroom door open, listening out of habit. I liked privacy, but I was not exactly used to the sounds of other people in the house. The sounds of my neighbors at the apartment had seemed far easier to ignore, given that they weren't going to walk into my kitchen any moment.

Living in a house with others was something I hadn't ever experienced, and I was trying to make myself get used to the noises here, so I could maybe relax a little more. Emphasis on the "maybe."

Two sets of feet hit the kitchen stairs and came down the hall a moment later. I noticed immediately who the footfalls belonged to, and I should have known before I glanced at the doorway and saw them, that Adrian and Sal were back. I had no idea where they went while Benny, Carmen, and I had been packing up my apartment, but they had been gone for hours since we got here.

They both glanced at me through my open door, and I looked right back, expecting some kind of greeting, but was met with their backs a moment later as they pushed up the next flight of stairs, presumably to head into the office.

Adrian looked distraught, an expression I only saw once or twice during the time Carmen was gone last summer and that was it. Something horrible had to have happened, there was no other explanation.

I found myself abandoning the clothes I had been putting away, wandering up the stairs, and stopping just outside the office door, which hadn't been closed.

"I'm going to kill him," Adrian said, his voice breaking a little, like he was going to cry or scream.

"Stepanov," Sal said sadly, and then there was a crash, like someone had just flung something across the room. "They'll all come up here wondering what's going on if you keep doing that," Sal continued, so I imagined that Adrian must have been the one to make noise. Adrian, the emotional, volatile one of the pair.

"I'm sick of all these games we have to play, Sal. I just want a minute where something is blatant and real," Adrian said quietly, his voice just as desperate as it had been before, but stifled, like his face was pressed to something.

"We'll get through this, but there will always be these games, Adrian. As long as we're in this life, we have to play very carefully," Sal said and I could hear the footsteps in the room move before there was the sound of glass upon glass.

I shouldn't have been there. I shouldn't have listened. I should have stayed in my room or let my presence be known just as soon as I came up these steps, but instead, I was rooted in place, unable to leave, as my heart was breaking for whatever it was Adrian had just gone through but wanting to desperately escape before they found me there. I was about to take a step back, to force myself to walk away, when Adrian spoke again, his voice a little hoarse.

"And what about Ash?"

"You want to talk about this now?" Sal asked.

"Thinking about her is better than what we just saw," Adrian said.

"True."

Now I was far too intrigued to leave.

"You think she'll stay after the wedding?" Adrian asked.

"I doubt we'll fix all of this before the wedding. I don't think we'll be able to keep her safe until we find out whatever your father was hiding," Sal said, sighing.

"You think she'll want to once it's all said and done?"

"I guess we'll have to see. She didn't say no to letting us take care of her. Maybe she'll say yes to the other proposal."

What other proposal? What on earth were they talking about?

Now being there was treading into dangerous waters. I finally forced myself to take that step back, and of course, the wooden floors creaked beneath my foot, making me freeze, but only momentarily, before quickly and quietly sprinting back down the stairs and flying into my room.

I went back to my stacks of clothes, trying to calm my breathing, which was labored from my fear of being caught and the thrill of hearing them talk about me. I could tell one of them stepped into the upper hall, before going back in the office and promptly closing the door.

While I may have gotten away with eavesdropping, it left me with plenty more questions than it had answered. My conversation with Carmen earlier popped back into my mind, and I realized I was hoping far more than I had been before I overheard that conversation that the strange fantasy I had in my head of not needing to choose between the two of them would come true.

CHAPTER 14

SAL

Family dinner. We hadn't had one in a little while, what with all the wedding planning and how busy the rest of us had been. But instead of having it at my mom's house like we usually did, it was happening in the Kansas City house. I hated it.

Not that I didn't like being with everyone, but the idea that we were all meeting here instead of at *home* really seemed to hit me hard as I walked past the dining room and saw Ingrid and Ash getting the places set.

It had been two days since Adrian, Enzo, and I had watched the horrific footage of Bernardo being killed. Two days that I agonized over the idea of mentioning hypnosis again to Carmen and Leo, to get more clarity through her memories. The other option, which we were trying to figure out, was if we could get to April.

April was not a guarantee, just like trying to get Carmen's childhood memories to tell us the location we needed to look in was not an assurance. The wedding was in three days, and it was now or never, if we were going to ask. Carmen was already in the kitchen with the moms, putting the finishing touches on the dessert she had been making for us, but Leo wasn't back from making a visit to one of the gangs in the area.

I hated having Leo do those things, but he was the enforcer and was known as such now. Just his appearance somewhere seemed to motivate the underlings to stay in line.

Ash looked up to see me watching her, a little smile hinted at the corner of her mouth. The only bright spot had been having her here. Just a few days in the same house, seeing her not just when I made a trip to the gym, had me yearning even more for her. The tension between me and Ash, and Adrian and Ash was almost palpable, enough that Enzo couldn't keep his mouth shut.

"Why don't you just claim her already?" Enzo said as he popped in from the butler's pantry, watching the exchange while eating a piece of fresh ciabatta he had stolen. I hoped Mom had given him a good smack for it.

"Enzo," I warned as Ash stiffened.

"You and Adrian are making moon eyes at her all the time and neither of you are doing anything about it. Hell, she's not doing anything about her obvious feelings for both of you."

"Shut it, Enzo," Ingrid said, walking over to him and stuffing the rest of the bread in his mouth. He grinned with his mouth full, leaning in to try to kiss her. She laughed, pushing him back out of the room and following behind, leaving us alone, or as alone as we could be with my family two rooms away.

My eyes went back to Ash, her smile now firmly in place as she finished putting out the silverware.

"Everything get moved okay?" I asked, leaning against the doorframe. We hadn't talked about her move, only briefly passing each other in the house, much to my dismay.

"Yep, my whole life was easily stuffed into two SUVs and two trips in Benny's jeep. Kind of weird to think about," she said, raising her eyebrows.

"I heard there was some trouble there?"

Benny had called me when he was taking the first trip to the storage unit and told me the place was in shambles when they arrived. I felt justified but also relieved that Ash had agreed to stay at our house. Who knew what would have happened if she had been there when Marek trashed the apartment?

"Yes, I suppose I should thank you," she said, giving me a playfully sour face. She wasn't going to tell us what they had found there, but she knew Benny and Carmen would have told us.

"That face is all the thanks I need," I teased. She looked down at the table, clearly contemplating what she could get away with throwing at me when Leo came through the front door.

My youngest brother looked blank-faced as he entered, closing the door behind him a bit too care-fully, before walking to the stairs. That expression only seemed to show up when he had to do something that, while part of his job description, was not what he liked to do.

"Everything go okay?" I asked, even though I already knew the answer to that without asking. He looked at me, tipping his head toward the stairs, before taking them two at a time.

I glanced at Ash and then followed, watching as he went into the bedroom he and Carmen shared while they were staying here, and immediately into their bathroom. Hands in the sink, the water he started ran red with blood.

"What happened?" It was just supposed to be routine, a reminder.

"O'Shea approached them and offered the second a deal. I had to take care of him and remind the rest who is here in Kansas City," Leo said with a hollow voice.

"What deal?"

"Loosen their watch for us, give us smaller cuts, share information for an in on O'Shea's trafficking when they provide women." He sounded so monotone as he said it, but I understood. He had to compartmentalize this, or he wouldn't be able to function. He had seen much more and done much more than Adrian had in his time in service. More than he had ever told me. The human trafficking was especially hard on him.

"You think they'll listen?" I asked.

"They saw a side of me most don't live to see. I think I scared them enough to behave for now, but this O'Shea shit needs to fucking end," he said, the blank look giving way to the rage that regularly reared its ugly head, especially when reminded of what happened to Carmen. He wrapped his hand in the towel on the counter and punched the granite three times before he threw it across the room, breathing hard.

"The towel?" I questioned, smiling just a little. He chuckled a little, his breath calming some.

"I can't have split knuckles in the wedding photos," he said, shrugging.

"Ah, that makes sense. No need to anger your little Italian woman," I said with all seriousness.

"No, indeed," he said with a nod.

"Speaking of Carmen," I said, realizing there probably wouldn't be another good opportunity for us to chat about this alone for the rest of the night. "Maria mentioned something to me, Adrian, and Enzo a few days ago. About hypnosis."

Leo had turned around to pick the towel back up, but his head whipped around at my words to stare at me with a look of disbelief.

"You're mentioning this to me again? Now?" he asked. For some reason that reaction wasn't what I expected. Skepticism like Enzo? Sure. But immediate anger was not.

"The sooner we do it the better. They aren't going to stop trying to get her, to kill us, Leo," I said. The words coming out of my mouth were not meant to be cruel or harsh, but even though that may have been the case, I still felt like my father, imploring those in his employ to sacrifice for his ultimate goals.

"We get married in three days and you want me to let you hypnotize her? Do you know how dangerous that is?"

Clearly, I didn't. Up until Maria said something I had just thought it was a load of crap, made up mumbo jumbo, to be honest, but something that might be worth trying. We were running out of options and losing this race to get the information O'Shea was willing to do anything to get ahold of.

"We need answers," I said, though it killed me to do so, and I was certain it was written all over my face. Leo very calmly folded the towel once more, setting it just right on the counter, before walking up to me. He was the youngest of us three brothers, yet he was also the tallest. He looked down at me, our noses nearly touching, eyes menacing.

"And I want Carmen to have the best day ever, the most magical wedding. I don't want it dampened and ruined with Mafia shit. Our wedding will be about *us*, and we'll deal with the other bullshit afterward," he said, each word punctuated and distinct, to be certain I understood.

He was right, of course. We had waited this long, why push to do this before the wedding?

Because Salvatore wouldn't have allowed us to wait.

I wasn't my father. I wouldn't do this to them.

"We can work with that," I assured him, reaching my hand up to his shoulder as I did, and pressing our foreheads together.

Leo calmed, putting his own hand on my shoulder and we just sat there for a moment, as if he knew the thoughts that had just run through my head.

After a few moments, we parted, heading back downstairs, where Carmen was setting out the beautiful cake she had just finished on the buffet, while Liliana and Maria brought out all the various dinner items. With Nora's dairy allergy and the fact that there were now three more mouths to feed at family dinner, the moms had opted to do two main dishes. One was usually soup or a pasta that didn't have cheese and one that was loaded with cheese. Really, all that meant was we ate way too much.

The table at this house was a standard rectangle, instead of the round table at my mom's. As such, our seating was a little different. As I walked up to the table, I noticed Nora was placing little cards in front of each plate.

"What's this?" I asked, picking up the card and trying to decipher her handwriting. She could write; it just wasn't always the easiest to make out all the letters.

"Name tags silly. Your spot has been assigned," she said with a giggle, pointing to the seat at the center of the table closest to the wall. I set the name I had picked up initially down and moved around to view the others.

"I want to sit next to Carmen. Did you put me next to her?" Leo asked, after scooping her up in his arms.

"You and Carmen are here," Nora said, pointing to the opposite spot from my chair.

"Ah, so she can sit by Maria too. Very smart," Leo said with a smile.

"Enzo and Mommy are there," she murmured, pointing to the spots after Leo's.

I looked down and saw my name, then Ash, and then Adrian. My mom was next to me, and Benny was at the head of the table. A little shift in the placements we usually sat in, but not too far off.

"Is everyone here?" Maria asked as she brought the bread in and set it in the center of the table between both main dishes.

"Benny's down in the den," Carmen said as she brought out two bottles of wine and set them on either end of the table. For easy access, of course.

"Get him, would you, Little Song?" Maria asked, and I watched with amusement as Carmen stomped through the dining room and into the hall, going to the door at the basement stairs.

"Benito! Dinner now!" Carmen yelled. All of us grinned, the moms scowled, and Carmen smiled proudly as she walked back to the dining room and found the name tag that Nora had made her.

"Was that necessary, Carmen?" Maria admonished, sitting in her seat beside Carmen as Leo took his.

"It was, actually. We're all up here helping, some of us working, and he's down there lying around and watching tv," Carmen said, her eyebrows raised as she poured herself a glass of wine.

"Where's Adrian?" I asked, noticing he hadn't made an appearance yet. He had spent a lot of time alone lately, except for when he made appearances at our various business establishments and checked in on incoming shipments with Leo the day before.

"I'll get him," I said, standing again and moving around the table to head upstairs. He was coming out of his room, which happened to be the one across from mine, when I made it down the hall.

"I figured Carmen would be screaming my name for the whole neighborhood to hear next," he said, giving me a sheepish smirk.

"I thought I'd avoid that if possible. My eardrums couldn't take another," I said, walking back toward the stairs with him. "You okay? Need anything from me?" I decided to ask just before we hit the stairs.

"I—" His brows furrowed, hand smoothing out his beard a little. "I'll be okay," he said with a little nod of his head. "Just needed a little time."

That I understood. I grabbed his neck, pulling his forehead to mine, and looked in his eyes. Those blue eyes looked into mine like he was seeing into my soul, but he was really the only person I allowed there. A moment of relief filled his features at just this gesture, something I knew would help, even if only for a moment.

"I'm here, Adrian. Always here," I said, waiting for his nod before I released him, and we went back down to dinner.

CHAPTER 15

ASH

My days there were wearing on my control. The only thing keeping me from giving into my desires for Sal and Adrian were the rest of the family being there and the fact that they had been too busy to spend much time with me. But there had been a handful of moments that tested my resolve.

One day in the small home gym that was in the basement across from the den, I watched them work out through the mirrored wall while I was trying to get a run in on the singular treadmill. Adrian was spotting Sal standing over him, his gym shorts slung low on his hips, a sheen of sweat on their arms, and their tank tops stuck to their chest.

"You can take one more," Adrian said as Sal grunted, pushing the barbell off his chest. I wasn't sure how much weight was on there. Far more than I could do.

The words Adrian said, and the sounds Sal made, had my mind reeling with my nighttime fantasies, like they were coming to life before my eyes. The sudden jolt of need within my core had me almost tripping on the treadmill, forcing me to stop running to hold on to the side panels. When I looked back up in the mirror, both men were staring at me, eyes raking over my body.

Another day, I fell asleep on the couch in the den watching movies with everyone and woke up to my head in Adrian's lap and my feet in Sal's. Everyone else had left, presumably long before I woke up, so it was just the three of us. The temptation to touch was so much, especially when I shifted and one of them made a little groan. I knew I gave away my wakefulness with the little panted breaths that came from my lips. I had to sit up and nearly run from the room.

Now, I was going to be sitting between them at family dinner and somehow it made my heart race. I had been to family dinners before. Usually sitting beside one or the other, but not *between* them.

I felt like the discomfort was written all over my face when they came back down and sat on either side of me, their body heat radiating, their scents somehow overwhelming me when the smells from the food being dished out onto all our plates had been so prevalent before.

"Pass Ashley's plate down, would you, Sal?" asked Liliana. Sal grabbed my plate, leaning just a little closer to me to do so, and I swear he winked when he saw the expression on my face.

"Your classes will start again after the wedding, right, Ash?" Ingrid asked from across the table. She was dishing up Nora's plate, who was already hungrily munching on some bread.

"Um?" I looked over at Adrian.

"I hadn't told her yet," he said sheepishly.

"Oh good. Now that Nora's school is out for summer, I can actually start coming back. It was rough during pickup time," Ingrid continued. I felt suddenly excited.

Not that the little break from real life hadn't been nice in some aspects, but the idea of getting back to the gym, back to my job, back to fighting in some capacity, even if it was only to teach, made me immensely happy. Though not so happy that I seemed to be the last to know.

"Remind me of when you two will be back after the wedding?" Benny asked, looking at Carmen before he took a big bite of the ziti that had been mounded on his plate.

"Just a few days. We're going to the lake house," Carmen said. The glint of joy and mischief in her eyes was adorable, and Leo's smirk told me everything that wasn't being said.

Suddenly, I realized that the house was soon to be unoccupied. The wedding marked the end of this house full of people. While the rest of them had other places to go off to, I no longer had an apartment or any place to call my own. I would be alone in this house with the men that sat on either side of me.

Excited, nervous, and incredibly turned on were only a few of the emotions that flittered through my head.

"We'll make sure you two get a proper honeymoon after all this." Maria waved her hand in the air, referencing the unsaid strange times the family was going through. I suppose sitting at this table meant I was going through it too.

"It's okay, Mama," Carmen said, patting her hand and smiling genuinely.

One of our conversations during my unfortunate apartment packing day had been about how happy she was. And truly, it seemed like Carmen didn't really care about anything except the fact that she would be married to Leo. It was so funny how long she had been in love with him. Even I could tell from my few interactions and her clear frustration the longer he was away, and I had never met the man before he came home for the final time. Just the way she talked about him, it was obvious.

It made me wonder how blatant my affections for Sal and Adrian were to all of them. Enzo had said the three of us made "moon eyes" at each other all the time. I supposed at least my lust for both of them was clear enough.

Almost as if they had read my thoughts, two knees pressed against mine. I had only eaten about half of my food, and my glass of wine sat nearly untouched. Part of me wanted desperately to feign illness and get out of this situation, and the other part of me was resisting letting my hands wander.

Family dinner!

We had been eating together and spending time together for days. No one there had made me feel like an outsider, nor had they batted an eye when I stole away for time alone, yet somehow, sitting there with an itch I couldn't scratch made me want to crawl out of my skin, or maybe crawl into theirs.

"Are you okay?" Carmen asked, pulling me out of my thoughts. She was staring at me, concern written all over her features. Whatever face I was making, thankfully hadn't been showing my internal thoughts.

"Maybe if Sal and Adrian gave her a little breathing room, she'd be able to keep up with the conversation," Enzo said with a snort, getting an elbow from Ingrid.

"What? Yes! I'm fine," I said, realizing I had my glass of wine in my hand, and promptly took a nice big gulp.

"They like her, Enzo!" Nora said with a mouth full of pasta.

"We all know that," Benny said with a grin.

"Are you boys being handsy under there?" Liliana nearly shrieked, moving her chair back as if she was going to come around the table and separate us. The touches to my knees immediately disappeared, and even though they were making me a complete and utter mess of a person at this dinner table, I missed it when it was gone.

"No, Mama," Sal said, grumbling as he took a bite.

"Ashley, you'll tell us if they're being ungentlemanly, won't you?" Maria implored; eyes sympathetic, she looked me over. I wished I knew what expression I was making. I honestly was so consumed with the over-whelm, I wasn't sure. I probably looked pained.

"They are being perfect gentlemen, I promise," I said, though I wasn't sure how convincing it was, considering I didn't especially want them to be gentlemen.

"I don't want them scaring you off. You're family now," Liliana said. "And they certainly weren't raised to be heathens."

Benny and Leo burst out laughing, Carmen hid her smile behind her wine, and Enzo looked like a kid on Christmas.

"I, um … got up early to do some extra workouts. I think I'll head to bed, if you don't mind," I said, shifting my chair just a little.

"Oh dear, of course you can!" Maria said, the sweet woman just entirely too kind.

"Good job scaring her off," Enzo said to both of them as I managed to squeeze out of my chair without touching either of them and headed to the stairs.

"It's all of you stupid boys," Carmen said back, a clear bite in her tone. "Couldn't leave it alone, could you, Enzo?"

The knock at my door came about an hour later. I opened the door to find Carmen and Ingrid.

"Come with me!" Carmen said with a grin, reaching her hand out and snagging my wrist.

"I'm supposed to be in bed," I said, but let her drag me from my room anyway.

"Yeah, we all were very convinced at how tired you were while you hyperventilated sitting next to Sal and Adrian," Ingrid said, the sarcasm dripping.

Choosing to ignore that, I said, "Where are you taking me?"

"To my room," Carmen said, pulling me down the hall. It was only then that I noticed the grocery bag hanging over Ingrid's arm.

"What is everyone else doing?"

"Enzo's putting Nora to bed. Maria and Liliana went to their rooms, and the other four are cleaning up. Well, more like Benny and Adrian are, while Leo and Sal chat and cheer them on. Perfect," Carmen said, opening her door with a flourish.

I hadn't been in this room before. It was not exactly what I expected after being in the ornately decorated room I had been sleeping in these last few days. This room was much more utilitarian. Very minimalistic, masculine colors and barely any decor. I found I liked this much better than the flowery room I had been given.

"Looks like Enzo's room," Ingrid commented, setting the bag on a leather chair in the corner.

"Their dad was very insistent they all grow up to be 'manly men.' Didn't let them decorate their own rooms here. I'm not surprised they hated when he made them come," Carmen said, with a little wrinkle in her nose.

I had, of course, met the late Salvatore Lupo, but I rarely had any interactions with him. He didn't spend

much time in Lee's Summit, and from everything I knew about him, I was glad for it.

"Now, sit," Carmen said, guiding me to take a seat on the bed. "I have a surprise for you. Don't get mad at me."

I was immediately on alert, glancing at Ingrid as if she'd help me, but she only smiled in response while Carmen went to the closet, opening the door, and disappearing inside.

"Good surprise or bad surprise?" I asked Ingrid. She only shrugged.

Carmen came from the closet a moment later with a black garment bag.

"I know you were against wearing a dress, and I can take it back if you really don't want to wear it, but—" Carmen set the bag on the bed beside me, unzipping it, and pushing the bag apart to reveal the dress I had tried on with her last week. "It looks so perfect on you."

I reached out, my fingers tracing over the soft fabric. Very few times in my life had I ever received a gift. Certainly never one this expensive. Before my mom died, there were birthdays of course. I'd get one small item, usually a new pair of shoes or a secondhand toy, since our money was always tight. My father being the only one who worked, meant we were scraping by most of the time. After she died, the gifts I received were a wad of cash my father would hand me to go to the grocery store or when I got time to train with him in the gym.

"Carmen, I'm going to pay you back for this," I said, looking up at her face as it transformed from worried to overjoyed. I couldn't let this expensive dress be a gift. That was just inconceivable. It might take me a while to get the money saved, but she couldn't just *give* this to me.

"You'll wear it?" she asked.

"I mean it, Carmen. I'm paying you back."

She launched at me, hugging me tightly and squeezing maybe a little too hard with my sore ribs and shoulder, but I didn't mind, hugging her back.

"I got you something too, but it's far less exciting," Ingrid said, bringing the bag over.

"What is this? My birthday?" I asked, feeling far too overwhelmed by the attention they were giving me.

"Just take it," Ingrid said with a smile.

Inside the bag were a few boxes of blue hair dye. My most recent dye was fading again. Not that it looked bad, just that it certainly didn't look fresh and wouldn't complement the dress at all.

"Why are you being so nice to me?" I asked quietly. I knew these women cared about me, and I for them, but this felt like too much.

"You just had to uproot your whole life," Carmen said, reaching out and taking my hand.

"I just had to do something similar and the amount of love everyone gave me overwhelmed me too, but that didn't mean it wasn't exactly what I needed," Ingrid confided.

Ingrid and I were similar in many ways, not that either of us had opened up to each other about our past much, but I knew she was alone in this world, like me. Odd that we both found a pair of families that wanted us around when we had been shown for so long that we were destined to be alone.

I felt the tears well in my eyes, but was willing them not to fall. Crying over a dress and hair dye would be ridiculous.

"But now, as payment for this act of love, I need you to explain to me how Sal and Adrian aren't fighting over you," Ingrid said, pulling the chair over to the bed where Carmen and I sat.

"That's a good question," Carmen murmured, looking at me with confusion.

"I don't have an answer," I said, just as confused. It was almost like they were already a unit, Adrian and Sal, beyond just best friends and in sync. They already shared everything else in their lives, so why squabble about a woman they both wanted?

They could share.

"She won't go for it."

The echo of Adrian's words a few nights ago went through my mind. My fantasy renewed as I thought of both men. There was a different sort of tension between them, not related to me. They orbited each other, were tethered to each other in a way I had never seen between two men like them before. There were no concrete outward signs that they had any connection other than their friendship and partnership in their work, but I could somehow see, with the lack of jealousy between them, that maybe there was a chance I *could* have them both.

This little glimmer of possibility in my thoughts and fantasies blossomed a glimmer of hope. I desperately wanted to it shut down. Anytime I had hope, it was immediately squashed. I didn't want to be disappointed yet again.

CHAPTER 16

ADRIAN

Ash being there, in the house with us, while everyone else was there, was driving me absolutely insane, while also helping me keep my head above water. Watching my father's death had struck me much differently than anything else I had ever witnessed. I found myself in a fog, going through the motions for the most part, except when I left the house to check on something or found myself in Ash or Sal's presence.

The wedding preparations at the house didn't seem to be helping either. The moms were like some sort of force of nature, clear paths of destruction in each and every room they stepped into, only to then become tornados of rage when people dispersed without cleaning up.

Currently, I was trying to get a workout in before we went with Leo to pick up our suits from the tailor. I had narrowly avoided being roped into final touches to the centerpieces that were happening in the dining room. Thankfully Rory and Daph arrived at the house just as I was slinking through the main hall to go down to the basement.

I didn't particularly love Rory and Daph being at the house, but it really couldn't be helped since the whole family was staying there. But tonight was the last night we'd have so many residents.

Tomorrow, my little sister is getting married.

That thought echoed in my mind like some sort of strange mantra. No matter what my feelings about seeing that footage were, I needed to show up for the people in my life, now more than ever.

When my father died, I became the leader of our home. Of course, Ma was there, and we adhered to her rules, but for the first few years after he died, she was not all there. She had just lost the love of her life. She had just been thrust into being a single mother, still unfortunately attached to the very organization that had caused my father's death. I didn't want her to take on the burden of caring for us alone.

That was not who my father had shown me how to be.

So though my own feelings were very much in turmoil, my sister's life, her wedding, was not going to be brought down by me. Not if I could help it.

As I went down the basement stairs, I could hear a little talking already. Sal's voice.

"I don't think you should be lifting yet," he said as I rounded the corner and found myself in the doorway.

There they were, Ash and Sal, standing only a few feet apart. Sal did not look happy, while Ash clearly had a devious look in her eyes, stretching like she did before any workout.

"I'm not losing my strength, Sal. I feel good enough," she said, her tone a little clipped and insistent.

"I agree," I said, making them both turn to look at me. Ash with a confused expression and Sal with a slightly appeased, happy look.

"With who?" Ash asked, leaning over into a forward fold, her palms easily touching the ground with her legs straight.

"With Sal," I said, finally coming farther into the room. Her bruising was looking much better, only faintly visible and fairly unnoticeable if you weren't looking for it. She hadn't been lifting any weights, opting for the treadmill more often so she didn't re-injure herself, but that didn't seem to be the plan today. "Wait a few more days. Training too soon will set you back."

"I'm a trainer too, Sal. I know my body. I'm ready," she said, standing back up effortlessly from her bent position, glaring at me.

"Oh? Your body is ready for some rigorous activity?" I asked, my eyes unable to stop taking her in as she moved to do a different stretch. The way her muscles rolled with each movement, her small shorts and sports bra the only thing keeping her whole body from our view. I was entranced and immediately aroused.

"I think it is," she said, though the bite had left her voice, her eyes no longer fiery with anger, but now looking at me with a different kind of burn.

"You should let Sal spot you then. Just in case," I said, forcing myself to go to the ground and start doing crunches, because I felt like if I got too close to her right now, my hands would touch of their own accord, and I was trying so very hard to wait until she told us she was ready and willing.

"Fine," she said, trying to sound resigned, but I saw when she looked at him, saw when her breath seemed to accelerate at the idea of him being close to her.

There had been plenty of moments when we had been in close proximity over the course of these five days, the most recent when she had rushed up the stairs to hide from one of the moms' tirades about seating and food, only the find herself backed right into me and Sal. It was only a moment, but the feel of her pressing between us, her breath catching when she realized exactly where she had landed and the reaction being, not fear or disgust, but *need*.

That was something I very much wanted to repeat. Especially after her hands lingered against our chests for a moment when she pushed away from us.

She finished her stretches, moving a few steps away from Sal, and glanced over her shoulder at him. I went to the floor, intending to force myself to do something to keep myself from walking over to them, but had to stop my crunches when I watched him come behind her, his body hovering just a few inches from hers as she started to lift the dumbbells from their spot on the rack.

Trouble.

This was trouble, because I couldn't look away from them.

"Tighten your core," Sal said at one point, his voice low and husky.

"Hm?" Ash murmured, turning her head just slightly.

"This," Sal said, bringing his hands around, fingers pressing to her lower abdomen and splaying there.

I could see how her muscles contracted to his touch, the dumbbells wobbling a little in her grip, but not because of their weight.

"Don't," she said, her voice barely a whisper, but she stepped away from him, putting the dumbbells back on the rack and breathing harder than she should have been for only having finished one set.

Sal immediately dropped his hand and backed up when she said that, stopping only when I had to touch his leg, so he didn't step on me. I looked up at his face. It was perhaps the most distraught I had seen in quite some time. His face pained like her rejection hurt him. But she turned around, putting her hands on her hips and revealing the blown pupils and panted breaths of a woman who looked like she wanted to pounce on us.

"It's taking a lot of restraint here," she said with gritted teeth, seemingly to herself. "You want to touch me, Sal?" she asked, then her eyes snapped to me. "Adrian?" We said nothing. I'm sure the looks on our faces were enough. "It's not happening with your family upstairs."

Not with our family upstairs.

But it *would* happen.

"Is that all that's holding you back?" I asked, because I couldn't help myself. I needed to know this proximity was clawing at her control just as much as it was ours.

"Unlike you two, I am very good at controlling myself. Otherwise, I wouldn't have lasted so long on my own, but this—" She cut herself off, sucking in a breath through her teeth, eyes somehow simultaneously angry and full of desire. Without another word, she stormed off, back out of the gym and up the stairs where the sound of all the women's voices could be heard trying to get her in on the centerpiece final touches.

"Not with them upstairs, she said," Sal murmured when I looked back up at him. "Maybe she will go for it, Adrian."

"I wonder what the thing would be to make that control of hers slip," I wondered aloud.

Carmen and the others were staying at the hotel tonight, while the rest of us men would be staying at the house here, but after tonight, the house would be ours and Ash's. That knowledge seemed to settle inside of me, sprouting and growing tendrils of complete and utter yearning. I wasn't sure how I'd get through one more day. I couldn't contain myself anymore, and from the look on Sal's face, he was struggling with that too.

CHAPTER 17

SAL

Leo was pacing in the small room that was designated for the groom and groomsmen off the banquet hall as Enzo and I sat watching, amused, and Benny kept following him to bat his hands from running through his hair. He did that when he was nervous, and we all knew it.

"What are you worried about, Leo?" Enzo asked, chuckling again as Benny frustratedly looked like he was going to slap Leo the next time he reached for his head.

"This is too big," Leo said, causing Benny's frustrated face to turn enraged.

"You don't want to marry my sister now?" he demanded.

"Shit! No! I mean it's not safe for her, you idiot!" Leo yelled, pushing Benny from him a little more forcefully than I think he had intended. I got up quickly from where I sat, striding over just in time to put myself between them before Benny came at him with a fist.

"Sit down, Benito," I said quietly, but sternly. He listened, though clearly grudgingly, and went over to pour a glass of whiskey that had mostly sat untouched from the little table. I wanted for a moment, to let the room settle a bit before I turned my little brother to face me.

"It's all fine, Leo. You planned the security. Enzo has alerts all over the place," I started, tilting my head to where Enzo sat, his phone already out of his pocket while he scanned through all the camera feeds he had up.

"Ingrid's watching from her phone too," he chimed in with a grin.

"And Romolo even brought some of his men with him. Travis is having them keep watch," I continued.

"But what if it's not enough? What if they're planning something?"

Only one other time had I seen him lose it like this, and it was when Carmen had been taken.

"Today, Leonardo Lupo, you are going to get married to Carmen LaMartina," I said, pausing to let those words settle over him for a moment. His shoulders relaxed a little, the worried expression softening around his eyes. "You don't need to worry about anything else but that, my brother."

Benny walked over as I released Leo, offering a glass of whiskey to him as well. The two best friends clinked glasses, nodding before taking the two shots' worth back in one gulp.

Watching them made me wonder how Adrian was doing with Carmen, if she was also having any worries, but I didn't really need to ask since my phone buzzed with a message.

[Adrian: I hope Leo is still in there with you. Carmen is convinced he's going to leave.]

[Me: He's here. Just had to talk him down from freaking out about security. Worried for her. I don't think he's leaving.]

[Adrian: How much longer until the ceremony? I want to make sure Ash is okay.]

[Me:10 min]

At the mention of Ash, my own nervousness seemed to come front and center. We saw her earlier that morning before we left to come here and get ready. She wasn't part of the wedding party, but she was still going to help Carmen get dressed before the ceremony, so off to the hotel she went with a garment bag in hand. Of course, if something had gone wrong, Adrian and I would have heard about it, but I wanted to lay eyes on her to make sure she was alright.

I went to the door, prepared to peek out and see if I could catch a glimpse of her amongst the other guests funneling into the banquet hall, but the door opened a moment before I reached, opening and revealing our mother.

"Oh, Leo!" she said, tears already rimming her eyes as she moved across the room to him. She reached up, and he had to stoop down a little so she could cradle his face before she turned her attention to the rest of us. "Look at all you handsome boys."

I took the opportunity to peek out at the crowd of people outside, seeing just a moment of that blue hair along with a little flurry of blue and black fabric, before other people obscured my vision.

"Just a few minutes and you'll be walking down there to wait for her," Mom said to Leo, her body practically vibrating with joy and excitement.

"I wish it was now," he said truthfully, and the rest of us chuckled.

And those five minutes turned into no minutes very quickly, Enzo going first and escorting Mom to her seat beside Maria up front, me next, and then Benny, before Leo came down the aisle, standing beside the judge I had on hand that was going to do the honors. Of course, in previous generations, a full catholic wedding would have been called for, but my father had killed that within all of us.

I glanced out at the crowd for a moment before the music for the bridal party was going to start, the shock of blue hair sitting only a few seats behind the front row. She was already looking at me when I noticed her, those eyes taking me in with an intensity and anticipation I had only dreamed I'd see on her face. Her outfit was obscured by the other guests around her, but I could see the delicate swirls of black on blue that complemented her skin and bright hair.

I could have looked at her for hours, but my attention was stolen back to the event at hand when the music started. Nora came down the aisle first, her red curls bouncing as she flung flower peddles in the air with each step. Then Ingrid, her eyes immediately finding Enzo beside me and a blush taking over her face and neck. Behind her came both of the twins, Rory and Daph, who were acting as the maids of honor, since Carmen couldn't choose one.

Finally, with a flourish of changing music, the doors at the back of the hall opened again, this time to reveal Carmen and Adrian. Carmen looked beautiful, her gown all lace, flaring out just after her hips into a beautiful fountain of lace flowers. Her hair was mostly down, and her green eyes shone as she locked eyes with Leo. His face, once stoic, perhaps even solemn, transformed when he saw her, a wide smile spreading over his lips, and I saw the moment he held himself back from walking to her.

But it wasn't Carmen or Leo that made my heart beat a little harder in my chest. It was seeing Adrian. True that I had seen him for most of the morning, but it had been a few hours, and he had apparently cleaned up quite a lot. It had been years since I had seen him this done up. His beard was shaped more and combed out, his hair was still curly but had been trimmed, and the suit that matched all of ours fit him like a glove. I forced myself to look at Leo again, trying to school my face to something more normal, since I was certain it looked strange. When I glanced back at Ash, my fear was confirmed, since she looked at me, then at Adrian with a look of calculation, as if a puzzle was fitting together in her mind.

I forced myself to look back at Adrian as he kissed Carmen on the forehead and placed her hand in Leo's, before moving to take a seat beside our moms in the front row.

As the judge started the ceremony, I could feel eyes on me. I wasn't certain who was staring a hole into the side of my head, but I could feel it there. Some joke was made that I couldn't pay attention to, because my thoughts were far more preoccupied, but everyone laughed, and I used it as an opportunity to look around the room again. I was surprised to find it wasn't just Ash looking at me, but Adrian too.

I turned my focus back to the couple getting married. This wasn't the time to be caught up in my own head. I needed to be here for my brother.

"I believe the bride and groom have written their own vows. Leonardo," the judge said, gesturing toward my brother. He pulled a piece of paper from his pocket, only releasing Carmen's hands so he could hold it steady enough to read.

"Carmen, there have been many things that have changed in my life, but one thing that has been a near constant is how I feel about you. I'm not sure when it happened exactly. Maybe it was the time we stayed up all night making pies for Thanksgiving together, or the many times I drove you home from school, or maybe when you started singing that song all the time, which both killed me and made me adore you even more. I may not be sure when, but I have loved you for nearly as long as I can remember, Little Song," Leo said, pausing to smile and reach over, wiping a tear from her cheek. "If it weren't for the fear that your brothers would kill me, I would have probably tried to date you much sooner." That gained a chuckle from the crowd and animated head nods from Adrian and Benny. "I don't always like the idea of fate, but I can't deny that I feel like we are meant to be together. I promise you I will love you, fight with you, win with you, and take care of you with every day we have on this earth together."

The crowd laughed again when Carmen, unable to help herself, stepped forward and went on her tiptoes to give him a small kiss on the lips.

"I believe that's supposed to wait until the end," the judge said with a grin.

"Sorry, couldn't help it," Carmen said with a wide smile, not at all sorry.

"Carmen, your vows?"

She turned, reaching her hand out toward the twins, one of which handed her a slip of paper.

"Tough act to follow," Carmen said quietly. "Leo, you have been a dream it seems. Countless times in my life have I woken up to this very scenario having played out, only to be disappointed it wasn't real, but Rory pinched me a few times, so I'm fairly certain I'm awake." Rory swatted playfully at Carmen. "You have always been the kindest person, helping me, showing you cared, even if it made you less cool to the other boys. When you left for the military, I thought that was the end, that even when you came back for good, there would have been too much distance and time apart, but that wasn't the case. If absence makes the heart grow fonder, it seemed to work overtime for us. You're the person I have loved since before I even knew what love was. The person I have wanted every single day. I promise to keep wanting you, to keep loving you, through every hurdle, bump, and harrowing adventure we have to go on. You are who I choose," Carmen said, folding the paper back up and lacing her fingers in Leo's hand.

"Well, that was beautiful," the judge said, seeming to be just as emotional as the rest of us felt listening to them promise themselves to one another, something I felt certain they would do every day for the rest of their lives, because I had seen them, seen the way they had been toward one another and this was the kind that was lasting and true.

"Leonardo Lupo, do you take Carmen LaMartina to be your wife?"

"I do," Leo said without a waiver in his voice.

"And Carmen LaMartina, do you take Leonardo Lupo to be your husband?"

"I do," she practically sang.

"Then, I now pronounce you married! You may kiss!"

And as if that was the last string keeping them apart, they came together, Leo's arms wrapping around Carmen's waist as her hands found his face, and their lips locking in a kiss. I could tell it was hard for them to stop, but much longer, and it would have been strange for the rest of us to witness.

They grinned out at everyone, waving before they made their way down the aisle, and the rest of the wedding party followed behind them. My eyes went back to Ash and then Adrian, and again they were both looking at me as I descended the few stairs from the little stage and made my way out behind Rory and Daphne. I needed to pull it together, because there was no way I was making it through this whole evening if the two of them looking at me had my head spinning like this.

We moved out to the courtyard of the hotel for pictures. It was a whirlwind and took very little time, which had been Carmen's preference. She wanted pictures, but didn't need us all starving and frustrated before we made it in for the reception. But because it was so fast, there was very little time to talk at all, which seemed like the exact thing Adrian wanted to do as soon as we were within a few feet of one another. There hadn't been time though, and I managed to slip out and to the bar for a drink before he could catch me.

It didn't take long, perhaps a sip or two from my drink, before he was beside me, flagging the bartender and ordering his own whiskey.

"You okay?" Adrian asked quietly.

"Fine," I said, perhaps a little too quickly. I glanced at him, his eyebrow raised with skepticism, but in a moment, he shook his head, as if he were shaking out whatever other questions he wanted to ask me.

I felt a little ridiculous, especially considering I should have been making sure *he* was okay. He had just really seemed to rally out of the funk he had been in since seeing that video of Bernardo, and now he was offering to comfort me?

"I told Travis you'll meet with people after the food and toasts," Adrian said, bringing the whiskey to his lips.

"Good," I murmured.

What was wrong with me? Why was seeing Adrian cleaned up making me feel like I was losing my mind? Maybe it was how good he looked and the idea that Ash might just choose him and decide I'm just a third addition to an equation that only needs two? That was the most likely thing to be causing my blood pressure to skyrocket.

"Did you see Ash?" I asked, deciding to just move the conversation there, because it seemed better than to wallow.

"For a moment. I wonder where she is?" That was a good question, though I suspected she was probably hiding in a corner somewhere, not wanting to mingle too much. She knew people who were in attendance, of course. Our family, but also many of the other guests were people who came to the gym. A few people she had at least seen when she did private matches before my father died. But Ash was very much a loner and didn't like to mingle and socialize. That was why it had been so hard to get her to come to any family dinners in the past. She may have felt like an outsider, but she made herself one too.

I understood the urge. Being the leaders put me and Adrian in a strange position, often needing to separate ourselves from others. But having everyone at the house this past week had felt right, even if it wasn't in the house we preferred. Ash seemed to blend in seamlessly with everyone, finally getting comfortable enough around our family, as a whole, the last few days, while still stealing away time on her own to recuperate.

I hoped that being there with everyone helped her see we wanted her there, but I knew some wounds ran too deep. Whatever her life had been before coming to Lee's Summit hadn't been a happy one for a long time.

"The food should be starting soon," I said, pushing up from where I had been leaning on the bar and clapping Adrian on the shoulder.

"Well, let's go then!" he said enthusiastically. He was clearly trying to lighten my mood, something I had been trying to do for him over the last week. Too much gloom and despair in our lives, too much uncertainty. I was more than ready to shed some of that tonight, but I still had duties that needed to be done.

We walked back into the main room. The ceremony setup had been cleared while pictures were being taken so that tables could be set up around the perimeter, leaving a dance floor clear. On one side there was a long line of tables adorned and overflowing with food and standing just at the end, snatching a grape from a dish full of fruit, was the blue-haired woman in question.

Adrian and I both seemed to stop in our tracks as we saw her. The glimpse of the dress she was wearing did not do it justice. Yes, the deep blue of the dress complemented her hair and skin beautifully, but it was the black pattern over the top that really helped accentuate her body. It hugged her perfectly, showing off her lean figure. The sleeves came down all the way, and it covered the bruising that I knew was still on her shoulder from the dislocation, but though the collar was up at her neck, it was sheer fabric, going all the way down to past her navel in a point.

"I don't know if I can keep playing this game with her. Not tonight with that dress on," Adrian said, mirroring my own thoughts.

"I think we might need to just approach her about it tonight," I said as she looked up, catching sight of us, both of us unconsciously moving toward her as soon as she did so.

"How long is appropriate to wait?"

I laughed.

"Too long," I said and was met with a grunt of agreement.

Ash waited, even though it looked like she wanted to bolt, stealing another grape off the table.

"Boys," she said as a greeting after swallowing the grape. Her makeup had been done as well, sharp black cat eye eyeliner made her gray eyes look like they could cut right through you, her lips were a deep gray color, and her hair had been straightened, though I liked it when it was messy from the gym. Perhaps we'd make it messy again later.

"You look amazing," Adrian said, his voice gravely as he spoke. I understood the feeling. Seeing her like that, when we'd been in such close proximity for days, had me feeling like I should just go full caveman and tear the beautiful thing right off her. Up close was better than what we had seen at a distance. Not only was there sheer fabric on her chest, but other parts of the torso were showing through the black designs on the fabric.

"You both clean up well too," she said, a glint of desire in her eyes as she looked over both of us. Adrian clearly stood out, being far different in his attire and grooming than usual, but I was very much my normal, with the exception of a more formal suit. "I like that you're matching."

Well, that was interesting. I found myself wondering again what it was that seemed to clink inside her head during the ceremony. What had she been piecing together in her mind that we didn't know?

"Oh, Ash! You look absolutely fantastic!" called Rory as she pushed between me and Adrian and rushed in front of Ash. "I meant to ask you earlier how you got it. I know you were worried about how much it cost when we were shopping."

"I think Carmen got it for me," Ash said, glancing up at us with a bashful look on her face, before smiling at Rory. The smile was a little strained, but that could have been because of the obvious mention of her finances. We obviously knew she had been low on funds and that's why she had been fighting in the first place, but I didn't like how rude Rory was being. She was making Ash uncomfortable, something we really didn't need if we wanted her to open up to us later.

"Well, you look gorgeous! Let's get you a drink before all the men start harassing you for dances," Rory said, linking arms with Ash and whisking her away without a glance in our direction, as if we weren't even there.

"We'll be able to get her away from her at some point," I murmured to Adrian, downing the rest of my whiskey as we watched the two of them walk away.

CHAPTER 18

ADRIAN

The food was good, and despite the strange family members from out of state we rarely saw, the mood was perfect. My mother's Aunt Allegra, who we were surprised made it from New York to Missouri, stopped me more than once to demand that I go shave my beard. Thankfully, Ma took her back to the table where she was supposed to be seated before she could make more complaints to Carmen about her visible tattoos.

"It's probably for the best that Leo has long sleeves on, otherwise all the other old Italian ladies would be in an uproar about defacing your bodies again," I said to Carmen who was gripping the fork in her hand like it was the only thing keeping her from throwing it at our great aunt.

"I hope Mom knows this is exactly why I didn't want to invite all these old people," Carmen said through gritted teeth.

"I think she's finding out. Hopefully, anyone else who gets married won't have to deal with Allegra again,"

I said with a grin as I took the last bite of shrimp on my plate.

"Great! Thanks. I'm the guinea pig," she muttered angrily.

"You decided to go and get married first."

That was very much the wrong thing to say to a bride on her wedding day. Especially an Italian bride on her wedding day, who was my sister.

Carmen tilted her head, eyes wide and slightly crazed as she looked from me to Sal, to the table a few hundred feet away that housed Ash.

"Well, if you'd just get your foot out of your ass and make a move on the people you like, maybe you'd be getting married sometime too," Carmen said maliciously. Something about the way she said that was a warning, that if I poked anymore, she would say more than I wanted her to. More than *I* even knew.

"And on that note," I said, standing from the table. "I think I'll go grab a drink and check in with Travis." I glanced at Sal, nodding to him, before leaving the table behind.

"Coward!" Carmen called behind me, but it didn't matter. Duty called, and she had no reason to keep talking about my lack of love life. Hopefully, that would be changing soon.

The bar had cleared out since everyone had migrated to the ballroom, but standing at the bar, waiting for an audience with Sal with a drink in hand, was none other than Gregor Stepanov. The last time we spoke to him was about Enzo's predicament in Chicago with Ingrid, and he had undoubtedly helped us recover Carmen months ago, but with the understanding that Colin O'Shea was his to kill.

"Ah, Adrian. How do you fair on your sister's wedding?" Gregor said as the bartender slid me a fresh whiskey.

"Better when this is over," I said with a smirk in his direction, before taking a sip.

"These gatherings can be tiresome. More so for us who cannot just sit back. Enjoy. Work must always be done." Sometimes Gregor's accent was a bit more pronounced. This was one of those times.

"Sal should be around momentarily," I said, glancing back toward the ballroom where I saw Sal had been stopped by Paul, Rory and Daph's father.

We hadn't expected Paul to make an appearance. He usually had work or some other excuse to miss the numerous events we had invited him to along with his daughters over the years, but oddly, he made it to this one. Carmen didn't spend much time at their house, the twins often opting to come to our house instead since he worked long shifts as a detective. Funny that my sister, the daughter of a mobster, would become lifelong best friends with the daughters of a cop, but it never became an issue. That very well could have been because of the conversation that our father had with Paul not long before he died.

Ash was seated at the same table as Paul, a fact that I wished wasn't the case. She clearly already felt like an outsider, and there she was left alone with a group of people she didn't know instead of seated with the family. As soon as these meetings were done, I was going to make sure a chair was pulled in for her.

Sal managed to slip away from Paul, and I met him at the door, handing him what remained of my glass to down before we walked together toward the little lounge area we had sequestered off as the place we'd take formal meetings.

"What did Paul have to say?" I asked as we entered the little room. There were a few tables and chairs, as well as a leather couch.

"Drunk already. Kept going on and on about how much he appreciates his girls being included in our families," Sal said with irritation laced in his tone.

"Surprising that two families of mobsters did a better job taking care of those girls than a cop."

"Is it?" Sal asked, settling in the middle of the couch instead of one of the chairs. He unbuttoned his suit jacket, spreading his arms over the back of the couch. I got a flash of his father in that moment, a memory of the two of us in his office, being lectured on gestures of power.

"Taking up the most space when meeting with someone makes them think you are more important. Impressions are everything. If they think it, then it's true."

My stomach rolled a little, as it always did when I thought about Salvatore. I'm sure it was worse for Sal.

"Who's first?" Sal asked as soon as he had settled.

"Stepanov," I said just before a knock came at the door.

"Let him in."

I went to the door, opening it to see Travis there, with Gregor a few paces behind him, but the expression on Gregor's face was not too pleased, very different from when I left him at the bar.

"There's an unexpected audience request," Travis said with clenched teeth.

"Who?"

"Marek Lewandowski is here."

My eyes immediately flew to the hallway, and there at the bar was the weasel, chatting with Sal's uncle, Romolo.

"Put him last, and keep him out of the ballroom," I practically growled, hoping that Ash wouldn't go anywhere near the bar in the next hour or so.

"Yes, Sir," Travis said, turning to murmur instructions to one of the men, who then immediately headed to the bar. Gregor stepped forward then, and I gestured for him to enter the room with Sal.

"Sal," Gregor said, walking in and immediately sitting on the chair directly across from Sal, his apparent second stepping into the room after him, but staying beside the door. "Congratulations to your brother."

"Yes, we're all very happy for Leo and Carmen," Sal said, genuine affection clear in his voice. The ceremony had been emotional for all of us, I could tell.

Being the one to give Carmen away had been both an honor, but also gut-wrenching. My sister was one of the bravest and toughest people I knew, and we had very nearly lost her less than a year ago. If it hadn't been for Leo, who knows what would have happened?

But I could tell it had been hard for Sal as well. At one point, he had a strange expression on his face. I wouldn't ask him, but I wondered if he was trying not to cry. That was certainly something he couldn't do in front of all these people. He had to show he was strong, powerful, not swayed by sympathy and overwhelmed with emotion.

"I'm happy to see all worked out with them. Glad to have lent a hand in making sure they could be together," Gregor said.

"Yes, and we thank you. What can I do for you on my brother's wedding day?" Sal asked, tilting his head to the side. We didn't really owe Gregor, per se, since the only thing that was truly asked of us was that we *not* kill Colin O'Shea, but we still felt indebted to him. The plan for us had always been to make ourselves available for whatever move he was planning to make on the Irish pig.

"I merely come to remind you of our agreement. You don't put down the dogs that aren't yours," Gregor said, leaning his elbows forward on his knees and looking deeply into Sal's eyes.

"That is not the plan. The agreement still stands," Sal said.

"He continues to pursue your organization. I fear that you will come to a situation where you will put aside our agreement," Gregor warned.

"It shouldn't come to that, but if it does, we will call for your assistance," Sal assured, but the sharp, deep sound of a malicious laugh came from Gregor's chest.

"No," he said as soon as his laughter died down.

"No?"

"Colin O'Shea will die exactly as I want him to, when I want him to. I do not want him killed because you are too messy to avoid it. Finish this with him and leave him unharmed for me," Gregor said, standing from the chair. "You don't, and your new enemy will be me."

And with that, Gregor turned, jerking his head at his second, and exiting the room swiftly, without a look in my direction.

For a moment after the door closed, Sal and I merely looked at each other, both of us processing what had just happened. Threats were not something we didn't get, but we certainly hadn't been expecting it from Gregor, at least not right now.

"Should I—"

"Just bring the next one on," Sal snapped.

Sal being on edge, was fairly usual, and he kept it hidden well. But Sal snapping at me, was not. Of the two of us, he was far more collected. Instead of opening the door and potentially causing more harm by having him go off on whoever was next to talk to him, I walked over to him, gesturing for him to stand up.

"What? We need to get this shit over with," he said, downing the last of the whiskey.

"And we aren't doing that until you're back to yourself, so stand up," I demanded. He glared at me for a moment, the muscles in his jaw ticking as if he wanted to yell. But after a few seconds, he relented, standing in front of me, his shoulders tense, brown eyes filled with anger and frustration.

I stepped forward, bracing my hand on his shoulders and putting our foreheads together.

"Sal, you and I are going to get through this. We will not make more enemies. We will get Morelli's approval. We will finish this and party with the families, bring Ash to a room, and fuck her until morning because she wants us."

With each passing word I said, I could feel Sal's tension slowly dissolving. That is until I mentioned Ash and something within him went from a smoldering to an inferno. I was teetering on the edge of having to adjust myself at simply the suggestion I made, but then the heat in his eyes when I said those words made the suggestion of something earlier into a definitive.

Sal and I had never had sex with the same woman at the same time, but we had considered that possibility before and had no problem with it. There was only one man I would ever consider doing that with and it was him. So when he was clearly just as excited by this idea as I was, I was infinitely more turned on by the prospect.

I released him, stepping away and adjusting myself so the erection that was growing in my pants wasn't noticeable, glancing up to see him doing the same.

"You good?" I asked, watching him settle back on the couch, readjusting himself again.

"Yes," he said, though his voice was a little thicker than it had been.

I opened the door and this time it was Romolo. Unlike Gregor, he didn't have his second with him, not that he needed the protection from us.

"You two took long enough. Did Stepanov do something to you?" he asked as he unceremoniously pushed past me and through the door.

"Just warned about killing O'Shea again," Sal said as Romolo handed him a fresh whiskey.

"Yeah. That's to be expected. He's got some psychotic plan, I guess, for how he's going to get revenge," Romolo said with a headshake. "Just better to do it quick and get rid of the garbage, if you ask me."

"What is he getting revenge for, anyway?" I asked, because it had been such a mystery and a curiosity for so long.

"For his sister," was all Romolo said, as if that explained it. In some ways, it did. We knew what kind of people the O'Sheas were—dealing in human trafficking—but the specifics were what we suspected. The real insult had been between Stepanov and O'Shea. Whatever O'Shea did to Stepanov's sister had to have been horrendous for him to go to such lengths and potentially make enemies if he wasn't the one to rid the world of O'Shea.

"What can I do for you, Romolo?" Sal asked when it was clear we weren't getting any more information about that.

"Morelli sends a message."

My eyes slid over to Sal, who didn't seem to flinch at the sentence, but I knew his heart was probably beating out of his chest. I knew mine was.

"He's impressed with what you've done so far. Though I think that's an understatement. You have done a lot of work in a very short amount of time with many extenuating circumstances. But he thinks I'm biased," Romolo said, sipping on his own drink for a moment, before setting it on the table beside his chair. "He wants some proof of loyalty to him before he gives you the full title, *nipote.* What you choose to do to show him, that is up to you."

A show of loyalty? Wasn't that what we had been doing this whole time? Fighting off other rivals, growing our numbers, securing the supplies, and funneling the money back to him. What part of any of what we had done was not a show of loyalty? But of course, Morelli wanted something bigger.

"Any suggestions?" Sal asked.

"There are a few bigger targets Morelli would like removed. I will give them to Enzo before I leave, but even then, I'm not sure if those will be exactly what he means," Romolo said, shrugging.

"We'll just have to become creative," Sal said, glancing at me. My brain was churning, trying to think of what kind of thing Morelli would want, but there was already so much for us to juggle. Hard to add another problem to the mix when it felt like we were always playing catch-up and on defense.

"I'm sure you'll think of something," Romolo said with a smile as he stood up, taking his glass and clapping me on the shoulder before he let himself out.

"Do you want a minute?" I asked Sal once Romolo was gone.

"No," Sal said quietly, pulling the whiskey to his mouth once more.

I quickly opened the door, ushering in the next several people. Mostly lower-level people asking about resources, several wondering about bringing new

people into the fold. An hour had easily come and gone, and we finally got to the last one. Lewandowski.

He slipped into the room like the eel that he was, reeking of too much cologne and liquor. He was stumbling drunk from the open bar, and it showed when he tripped, falling into one of the chairs closest to the door, and decided to just stay there.

"What do you want, Lewandowski?" Sal grumbled.

"I have a proposition for you," he said, his words surprisingly clear despite his obvious inebriation.

"And what is that?"

"You need to know something that the Irish know, and I need to win."

"That isn't a proposition. What do you want?" Sal nearly snarled. Lewandowski laughed, clearly not picking up on Sal's overt hostility. I saw the frayed edges of Sal, barely keeping it together as the time ticked on. The rest of the wedding was waiting for us. We had already missed speeches and the first dance. Now we were going to miss the cake cutting if we didn't get out of here soon.

"I need my Blue. Let me have her back, and I tell you what I know about the Irish," Marek said, some of that drunkenness showing as his accent got thicker and his words more slurred.

Sal leaned forward, the expression on his face one of frustrated disbelief that quickly changed into complete and utter rage. In one very smooth and methodical motion, he stood, striding over to Marek, and grabbing him by the collar, lifting him clear off the chair so they were nose to nose.

"Let me be perfectly clear with you, Marek," Sal started, each word coming out clear and precise, but low and deadly. "There will never be a time where I help you. I do not care what information you think you have, or what you think you can offer me. There is no sane boss on this earth that would spend more than a moment with you and not know you are an incompetent idiot. When I told you to leave my city four years ago, I meant do not come back. This is your final warning. Leave!" As Sal screamed the last word, he threw Marek to the ground, his chest heaving with each breath as he watched the drunken fool scramble to get back up and bolt past me out the door.

I wanted to rage as well, but one of us needed to be clearheaded, and apparently today that was me.

"Let's get a cigarette from Travis and share it on the balcony before we head back inside," I suggested, gaining a nod from Sal before we headed out to the hall.

CHAPTER 19

ASH

Sal and Adrian had been gone for nearly two hours when they finally returned to the ballroom. Both looked like they needed a stiff drink and to lay down, but they came back over to the family table where I was sitting with Carmen. We had just danced with the other women in our "tribe" and sat down for a few minutes before the cake-cutting.

"Everything go okay?" Carmen asked, of which I was thankful, because I was going to ask the very same thing. Adrian leaned down and kissed her forehead.

"Fine now," he murmured.

"Ugg! You smoked, didn't you?" Carmen said with disgust, pushing him away a little, but clearly playfully.

"Only during a party, Carmen."

"If one of them is really stressed or super drunk, they usually share a cigarette together," she said as she turned to me with her nose still wrinkled.

Somehow, the image of Adrian and Sal sharing a cigarette was incredibly enticing.

"You're back just in time for the cake," Leo said as he scooted Adrian to the side so he could slip in next to Carmen.

"That is my favorite part. Wouldn't dare miss the cake," came Sal's voice behind me. Apparently, he had slipped into the seat just beside mine, though my attention had been turned to Carmen. A waft of his cologne and the abrasive, yet warm and familiar scent of cigarettes seemed to envelop me with his words. I shivered a little when his body heat hit my back.

"Bit of a sweet tooth, huh?" I asked, turning my head to look at him over my shoulder.

"Anytime there isn't something more delicious available," he murmured quietly so only I could hear. Goosebumps of anticipation radiated over my skin. I was glad I didn't really blush, otherwise the whole room would have seen my burning flesh. My eyes shifted to look at Adrian, who seemed to be the only person to notice, his pupils blown with want and watching the interaction between me and Sal.

"Ope! Rory's flagging us down," Carmen said to Leo. He quickly got up, holding out his hand to Carmen and leading her from the table to where they were rolling out the cake on the dance floor.

Adrian seamlessly slipped into the seat Carmen had just vacated beside me, angling himself so my skirt-clad knees fit between his legs.

"Seems like Sal said something you liked," Adrian said, his eyes glinting with mischief.

"I think she might be interested in what I like to eat instead of sweets," Sal said, his voice now dangerously close to my ear as his breath washed over my neck. The scent of whiskey joined the enticing, swirling scent of him.

"Mm, maybe you should tell her what you're *really* craving, Sal." Adrian's eyes flashed over my shoulder for a moment, his lips quirking into a smoldering smirk.

"The only thing sweeter than that cake they're about to cut would be what's between your legs," Sal said, his voice a rumble, vibrating within my chest and throughout my whole body. A tingle followed, spreading from the top of my head all the way down to my toes.

"Watch the cake cutting, Ash," Adrian said, though with the way he was looking at me, I didn't want to miss a single change in expression. Reluctantly, I did as I was told, turning my head to where Carmen and Leo were cutting the cake together, their smiles real and full of playfulness and love. I wasn't feeling that sweet playfulness, I was feeling full of dirty lust.

"I wonder what you like. Do you want to be licked from head to toe? Or quick and hard?" Adrian said, leaning closer now, his hand having traveled from his own knee to mine. It was too far away for him to touch anything inappropriate for public viewing, but close enough that my stomach clenched with anticipation.

"Are you the boss?" Sal murmured. "No, I think you like to be told what to do," Sal said, his hand snaking from behind my chair to caress my arm. The feel of his touch, even if it was through the fabric of my sleeve, was like a scorch of fire, heating my blood and dampening my panties.

"Do you need to wait for cake?" I asked, watching as Leo licked the icing off Carmen's fingers. He had his own glint in his eyes, promises of what was to come for her later. I didn't want to wait much longer.

Both hands on my body seemed to tense with my words and I could almost feel the silent exchange between them.

"If there's a better dessert I can feast on, I would much rather have that," Sal's voice rumbled.

My breath hitched in my chest, and the gravity of what I was about to do settled over me, but there was only a very tiny voice in my mind that was telling me this was a bad idea, that I was putting myself between two friends and coworkers. Two men who were deadly and dangerous. But I wanted it too much to say no.

I turned back to Adrian, my own hand slowly reaching forward to touch his thigh, and I found myself licking my lips.

"I'll be at the bar," I said, my voice sounding odd and sultry as it left my lips.

I stood up, walking around the table, fully unnoticed by the other guests who were watching the rest of the cake cutting, except for the two men I had left behind me. I could feel their eyes on me the whole way through the ballroom until I made it to the hall and turned to the bar.

I had just enough time to get a whiskey sour before Sal and Adrian appeared. Sal continued to the elevators, while Adrian paused, making sure I saw them, and nodding his head toward where Sal was. I watched him take those steps toward the elevator himself, the two men standing together, watching me, waiting for me. Drink in hand, I walked to the now open elevator, stepping in and feeling my fate be sealed as the doors closed.

The moment the elevator started moving, it seemed like a tether broke on Sal. He reached out his arms, grasping me by the hips and pulling me against his chest. I looked up into his eyes. They were black with need; his scent flowing back over me was like an aphrodisiac. His head tilted down, and our lips crashed together. I couldn't contain the moan that broke free from my chest at the taste of him. Much like when I kissed Adrian in his office weeks ago, I couldn't control myself. My free hand came up to rake through his hair, my chest pressing more into his as my nipples hardened.

I hoped the licking from head to toe was in the cards, because my body was screaming with want.

I felt Adrian come up behind me, his hands sitting just below Sal's as I felt his lips touch my neck. Another moan escaped as my brain registered that both men were touching me, both of them kissing me. The very thing I had imagined, thinking it would only be a fantasy that played out in my dreams, was coming true.

The elevator dinged, triggering both men to step away from me, leaving me feeling as though the very air was sucked from my lungs for a moment. Sal's breath was heavy as the doors opened, and I turned around to an empty hallway. It was just as long as the other guest floors I had passed by earlier in the day when we went to the room that Carmen had rented the night before and we used for hair and makeup this morning.

This floor seemed to only have a few rooms—only *suites,* as I came to discover as Adrian pulled a card from his pocket, stopping at the very last door around a corner. I took a long swallow of my whiskey sour as he pushed the doors open.

Never before had I been in a hotel room that was bigger than my apartment. There was a full-sized living room, a kitchenette, and more doors along the wall that I could only assume went to more rooms. The door closed behind Sal, and I tried my best not to act like this place was something out of a dream, but it was hard.

"Do you often stay in places like this?" I asked, managing to walk to the little bar top and set my glass down. It put a little distance between me and the men while I got my bearings.

"We rented out most of the hotel. For security," Adrian said.

"So that's a yes?" I asked, raising an eyebrow. This was easy, this was normal; instigating a fight with them was what we did.

"From time to time," Sal said.

Adrian shrugged his suit jacket off, loosened his tie, and threw them both over the arm of one of the plush chairs, while Sal slowly walked from the door to where I stood at the bar. It was deliberate, like a predator that didn't want to spook its prey, but I wasn't spooked. Remaining calm and trying to remind myself this was really happening? Yes. But I didn't want to run.

Sal moved past me, not without a heated glance as I sipped my drink, opening the glass cabinet that had bottles of hard liquor and snagging two little bottles of whiskey. Adrian, now only in his dress shirt, seemed to saunter to where I stood, only a few feet away, and took the bottle Sal offered him.

"Did you two have some plans I didn't know about?" I asked, watching them take their own sips of their new drinks. Two men, so very similar, but also so very different at the same time. Two men that I had lusted after for years, but never thought would come to anything, stood before me and beside me, brought me to this suite, and wanted *me.*

Adrian's more clean-cut appearance from earlier was a little shaken through the course of the evening. He had clearly run his hands through his curls, mussing the styling, but looking much more his usual self, while Sal still maintained his prim air, always put together. I liked that duality. I also wanted very much to see how much they would unravel for me.

"Not plans, so much as we knew there might be a possibility," Sal murmured, his hand reaching over and gently pulling the lock of hair that had fallen over my shoulder.

Adrian stepped forward, closing the small distance between us, and tilted my chin up so he could take in my full face.

"Ash, we want you. We've both wanted you for a long time." His words added fuel to the burning desire within me.

"You don't mind sharing?" I asked, internally damning myself for how quiet my voice sounded to my own ears.

"We share everything else," Adrian said, smirking a bit and glancing over to Sal.

"We don't want to push you if this isn't what you want," Sal said, his voice almost a bit sad, as if the prospect of me changing my mind here in this moment tore at him.

I slipped from between Adrian and the counter at my back, moving around to step farther into the room. Turning back to face them, I looked at their eager, yet hesitant faces, waiting to see what I'd do or say.

I didn't need to say anything. I reached behind me, unclasping the bracket that held the top of my dress in place at the back of my neck, before I slowly slipped my arms from the sleeves. With the most deliberate movements of my life, I pushed the dress past my hips, revealing myself to them in only the no-show thong I had on and the heels Carmen had gotten me to match the dress.

"I want," I said, watching as both men's eyes seemed to ignite further, both at my new state of undress and my words.

In a moment they had crossed the room to where I stood, Sal grabbing my waist and pulling me in for another searing kiss as Adrian grabbed my ass, his tongue immediately descending on my shoulder. They both pressed against me, sandwiching me between them, but enough that I could feel how hard they were for me.

I pulled away from Sal, turning between them so I could grab the back of Adrian's neck, bringing his lips to mine. Our tongues clashed for dominance as Sal trailed kisses down my back, hands grasping at my hips and sliding down my ass to my thighs. I felt so keenly the moment his mouth touched the fabric of my thong, teeth grazing against my skin as he snagged it between them.

My own hand slid down the length of Adrian's body until it grasped the thing begging for attention that was still restrained behind his suit pants.

"You're both overdressed," I whispered against Adrian's lips, just as I gave his cock a squeeze.

They both stepped away from me, breathing heavily, as they began to undress. Sal pulled off his jacket, unbuckling his belt with a speed I had never seen before; the belt whipping as he pulled it from his pants and threw it to the floor.

Adrian didn't even bother with the buttons on his shirt, popping a few off as he pulled it apart and threw it. Shoes were promptly discarded, and they seemed to drop their pants at the very same time. And then there they were, in all their naked glory before me.

Adrian was bulkier than Sal, his chiseled muscles standing out, adorned with tattoos, his long cock standing at attention for me. Sal wasn't any less impressive, still very muscular, but leaner. He too had tattoos, though I had never seen them. They adorned his chest and sides, and only a few were on his arms. His cock was thick and pulsing.

I swallowed, my mouth watering at the sight of both *my* men.

They want me.

It was odd, like I had to keep reminding myself this was truly happening. That both of these men wanted me. That they were willing to share, and that this wasn't just some fleeting thing. This had been a relationship built over years.

"We're undressed, Blue. Tell us what you want," Sal said, his hand finding his cock as if it were uncontrollable, squeezing it a little.

It was strange to see Sal deferring to anyone. He was the boss in every other situation, but here, in this moment, I was in charge. Knowing that emboldened me a bit more. I moved to the couch, laying down and running my hands over my breasts, down my stomach, and to my now completely soaked thong.

"Did you want to have your dessert?" I asked, rubbing my clit a little through the fabric and letting a shiver run through me.

Sal was there in an instant, kneeling between my legs and swatting my hand away. His fingers grasped the little scrap of fabric at my sides, sliding it down and gently helping me lift my legs so he could pull them free. Instead of tossing them away, he held them out in his hand, offering them to Adrian, who happily took them, curling them into his palm as he stroked himself and watched us with rapt attention.

"You smell like heaven," Sal said, his nostrils flaring as he leaned in, but he didn't immediately put his mouth on me. His hands slid up my calves and to my thighs, pushing them farther apart. "And already dripping for us."

Us.

With one hand, those fingers inched closer to my soaking center, each breath from my chest labored with anticipation. It had been so long since I had anyone to my bed, so long since I gave myself enough time to find my own pleasure, I almost felt like I'd fall off the cliff from one touch alone.

Adrian dropped down on his knees beside the couch, leaning over and kissing me just as Sal's finger brushed at my sensitive folds. The combination made me shiver.

"So fucking wet," Sal rasped out, just before I felt his lips at my hip, trailing kisses down farther until his tongue finally touched my bundle of nerves. My hips rocketed off the couch and a cry burst against Adrian's lips.

That must have been the tipping point for Sal, because his tongue became relentless, licking my cunt like a starving man. Adrian's hands got to work, grasping my breasts while he relentlessly kissed my mouth, grazing his rough palms over my hardened nipples.

I couldn't keep the sounds from spilling from my mouth, even if I had wanted to. The feel of them on me was exhilarating and wracking my body with wave upon wave of building pleasure. I opened my legs wider, my hips pressing against Sal's face with wanton abandon as he added two thick fingers to the mix, pressing them inside me. It felt so good. Too good.

Adrian lifted his head, moving his lips to one of my nipples and then the other. His tongue circled them, teeth lightly biting as I felt a tingle start at my belly.

"Don't stop!" I managed to say, panting as I looked down at the sight before me. Adrian's mouth on my breast, and Sal's head between my legs. Both their eyes on me, watching me.

"Are you going to cum for us?" Adrian asked, popping off my breast to look down at where Sal was fingering and licking me with brutal intensity.

"Fuck!" I screamed, just as the wave of pleasure peaked, shivers overtaking me as stars exploded in my vision.

Sal slowed his pace, still laving at my now pulsing core, while he took his fingers from within me, holding them up for Adrian to see.

"Taste?" Sal asked, surprising me a little, but what surprised me more was when I watched as Adrian took Sal's fingers in his mouth, sucking off my juices. Sal's eyes darkened, and I saw Adrian's cock bob against his stomach.

Realizing it was within my reach, I grasped his cock in my hand, watching the shudder that took his body over at my touch. So hard like steel under silk, I stroked, watching between the two men.

"I need a taste," I whispered, looking at the needy expression on Adrian's face, and the complete and utter desire on Sal's.

I sat up, steering Adrian to sit while I slipped off the couch, grasping his thighs for a moment and watching as his stomach flexed and his cock continued to pulse toward me. On my knees before him, I dipped my head down, keeping eye contact with him as my lips brushed the head of his cock, my tongue peaking out to lick the salty precum. His hands came up to my hair, pulling it over one shoulder as I opened wide, slowly putting my mouth fully around him, and letting my spit slide down his shaft with each bob of my head lower.

Adrian's moans were all the encouragement I needed, my mouth working, tongue sliding up that swollen vein on the underside, hands coming up to grasp his balls and stroke the base of his cock, now slick with my spit.

I felt Sal come up behind me, his body heat radiating first, before his hands came and grasped my ass, spreading my cheeks apart. I whimpered when I felt his fat cock press against my slick heat, pressing and grinding against it, but not going in.

"She wants you to fuck her while she sucks my cock," Adrian said to Sal while his hips moved a little in time with mine, his dick pressing farther into the back of my throat each time.

"Mm, is that what you want?" Sal asked, notching his head at my entrance and making me moan greedily around Adrian's cock.

"I-I think that's a yes," Adrian said, his breath hitching with the sensations I was bringing him.

Sal pushed forward. The feel of him stretching me, filling me no matter how agonizingly slow, was clearly worth another moan; not that I could have avoided it, anyway. Each slow thrust went just a little deeper than before, until he was flush against me, gripping my hips in his hands tightly.

He paused there, his cock pulsing inside of me, labored breathing, and I imagined that he and Adrian were looking at each other, especially when I felt Adrian's cock get even harder as I pressed the head of his cock to the back of my throat. Just the idea of that had my stomach clenching. I needed more. Now.

I pressed back against Sal as I used one of my hands to massage Adrian's balls and taint. The responsive groan and hip thrust from Adrian seemed to spurn Sal on, because in an instant he began thrusting within me. The feel of him moving inside was fucking heaven. But the slow pace quickly gave way to hammering. Each snap of Sal's hips against my ass sent my mouth farther and farther down Adrian's cock.

"Oh, fuck!" Sal exclaimed, pulling out abruptly, causing me to pop off Adrian to make sure Sal was okay.

"I'm not ready to cum just yet. I need more of that pussy in my mouth," Sal said, laying back on the plush rug on the floor. "Sit on my face, Ash."

"Fuck, that's hot," Adrian said, having taken over stroking himself.

"But—"

"On my face," Sal demanded.

I wasn't one to refuse, grinning as I crawled over to him, loving the way Adrian groaned, watching my ass as I did so. But instead of simply sitting on Sal's face as he had instructed, I turned around, giving him access, while being able to reach his thick cock.

As soon as I took him in my mouth, the taste of my own arousal only seemed to heighten my pleasure. His hands came up, pushing me down onto his mouth, his tongue. His lips and teeth were aggressive, ravenous. My second orgasm had already been building with his cock inside me, but now I could feel it growing bigger with each nibble on my clit.

I looked up to see Adrian, but he was no longer on the couch. A moment later, I felt another set of hands joining Sal's on my ass. His long, hard cock pressing against my ass crack.

"I can't resist," he ground out, notching his cock to my entrance while Sal continued to lick at my clit.

My breath hitched in my lungs as I felt him pushing in my wet center, Sal continuing to lick my clit. The very *idea* of this would have made me cum, but being fucked and licked by both of them at the same time set off my orgasm. It rocketed through my body, making me cry out around Sal's cock. My hand stroking at his base grasped at his balls, which were seizing up, about to blow.

And through the stars behind my eyes and the ripples of pleasure coursing through my body, I felt it the moment Adrian's punishing thrusts into me became erratic and brutal. The hot gush of his cum filled me just as Sal moaned against my clit and unloaded his within my mouth.

I pulled my mouth off, swallowing, and we all just froze for a second, our labored breathing the only sound in the room.

Adrian pulled out of me, and I crawled over Sal's body to his feet, standing on wobbly legs and looking back at them. I wasn't sure what I expected when I looked back, but it wasn't Adrian helping Sal to his feet, or the way they both immediately flocked to my side.

"Are you okay?" Adrian asked, his hand cupping my cheek on one side while Sal's fingers drifted over my hurt shoulder and ribs.

"Did we hurt you?" Sal asked, tenderly kissing my shoulder.

"I'm okay," I said, still tingling from the most explosive orgasms I had ever had and reeling from the show of affection. "Bathroom?" I asked, unable to help myself as I touched them too. One hand brushed down Adrian's chest, while the other threaded through Sal's hair.

Adrian took my hand, guiding me to a door on the other side of the room from the bar. The door opened to a massive king-sized bedroom, and another door on the side revealed a lavish bathroom with a huge walk-in shower.

"Take a shower, whatever you need. We'll be right out here," Adrian said, grasping my face in his hands before bending and pressing his lips to mine.

"Okay," I whispered when we finally parted. He seemed almost reluctant to leave me, but I honestly needed a moment to myself to fully process what had just happened. I just fucked them both. I just had sex with two men at the same time. My wildest fantasies had just come true, and it had been better than I had imagined.

CHAPTER 20

ADRIAN

I waited for a moment in the bedroom after I had closed the door to listen for the sound of the shower and make sure there weren't any other sounds to indicate she wasn't okay, as she had said. When it seemed like all was well, I went back out to the living room to see Sal pulling on his briefs. Somehow, the sight of him getting dressed was a bit of a disappointment. A fact that I quickly stuffed away to the back of my mind.

Snatching my briefs from the floor, I pulled them on and found Sal looking at me.

"She's okay?" he asked.

"She seems to be," I said with a nod, not bothering to put anything else on before moving to the bar once more, but this time for some water.

"Are *you* okay?"

I furrowed my brow, turning around to look at Sal again. This was a side of him really only I had been witness to in the last decade or so. The men in charge couldn't be seen as vulnerable. His expression was somewhere between worried and perhaps a bit fearful.

"I'm more than okay, Sal. You?"

A look of relief came over his face before he walked to me, grasping my shoulder and nodding. What I really wanted was to hug him, for the two of us to extend that intimacy we had while Ash was between us just a little bit, because I knew I would feel better, and maybe so would Sal. But instead, I opted to watch him carefully for the next fifteen minutes while we waited for Ash to come back out. Sal had turned the television on, and we were sitting side by side, as usual, when Ash reemerged. She was wrapped in the fluffy hotel robes they leave in the bathrooms for you. Her hair was wet, makeup scrubbed from her face, and her eyes bright.

Beautiful. More beautiful like this than she had been dressed for the wedding, that was for sure.

"Sit with us," I said, beckoning her to the couch with us. She quickly padded across the room, coming in front of us and seeing there really wasn't much space between us to sit. Sal grasped her hips and pulled her onto his lap, swinging her legs over to mine.

"So, what does this mean?" she asked as I turned the volume down. None of us were interested in the show that was playing on the television.

Of course, the first thing she does is ask a tough question to answer. Sal glanced at me. We hadn't exactly laid out the parameters of how we would share her. Quite frankly, we hadn't really discussed fucking her at the same time until I said something about it earlier this evening, but that worked out well.

"When I asked if you'd let us take care of you and be part of your life, we mean it," Sal said.

"And what we just did?" she asked, raising one defiant eyebrow.

"What about it?" I asked, seeing a glint of mischief in her eyes, her skin turning only the very slightest shade pinker than her usual. I grinned. "Would you like to do that again?"

"I'd like that," she said quietly, and Sal groaned a little at the very idea. My penis also got a little hard at just the prospect of having sex with her and Sal again. Watching them fuck and fucking her was so much more intense and more pleasurable than I thought possible.

"You need to fully move in with us," Sal said, and she stiffened in his lap.

"But I—"

"You are evicted from your apartment. Your stuff is in storage. You've already been living at the house with us, Ash," I said, already putting holes in her logic before she even began to lay it out.

"What about your families?"

That was honestly a good one. Trying to explain the unorthodox relationship between us with our mothers and siblings would probably be hard, but that was something to worry about another time.

"They love us, they love you. It won't be too hard for them to deal with it. And we don't have to tell them anything right away," Sal said, and I couldn't have put it better.

She was quiet for a long while, her eyes darting between us.

"Do you really want this?" she asked, her voice barely a whisper.

I couldn't contain the chuckle that came from my mouth. The sound clearly startled both Ash and Sal.

"Ash, from the moment I saw you fighting that night, I've wanted you, and I think the same goes for Sal." He nodded, a smirk forming on his face.

"And you really don't mind sharing me?"

"Did it seem like we minded?" Sal asked, gesturing to the couch we sat on and the floor where we all finished.

"I suppose not," she said, smiling a little.

"Move in," I said, squeezing her toes a little.

"Okay," she said quietly, smiling more. For a woman I had very rarely seen act like anything other than the tough fighter she was, it was oddly satisfying to see her snuggle into Sal's chest with her feet on my lap, seeming happy and contented.

My phone rang from the other room, waking me. I opened my eyes, delighting at the feel of Ash's ass nestled against my crotch, my feet tangled with hers and Sal's. If it hadn't been for the stupid phone, I might have instigated a repeat of our delightful night, since my dick clearly had ideas. With a quiet, but irritated groan, I untangled myself and walked into the living room to grab the ringing thing.

"Adrian speaking," I said, though it was Enzo calling.

"Ingrid found footage of Bernardo going to two of those locations. I bet if we do the hypnotist thing with Carmen, she might remember which one he took her to."

"Enzo, why are you calling me with this at—" I looked at the clock on the microwave. 8:30 a.m.

Shit.

I had planned on being back at the house in about thirty minutes to go over details with Enzo.

"Don't worry about it. We're still in the hotel too," Enzo said with a chuckle. "Late night?"

"Yes, actually, but that's really not your—"

"The whole floor heard you. Did Sal go back to the house or stay in another room?"

Shit, shit.

"Let's meet at ten," I said, before I hung up and grabbed the remnants of my clothes off the floor. Or at least what I had thought were mine, until the pants didn't quite fit, and I realized these were definitely Sal's. He came out a moment later, gingerly closing the door to the bedroom behind him.

"Who was that?"

"Enzo," I said, taking the pants back off and handing them to him. He smirked, amused, before slipping them on. "I was supposed to be meeting him in thirty minutes at the house with Travis."

"Why there?" Sal asked, not bothering with a shirt as he went to fill the coffeepot with water.

"Nora's there with the moms," I said, finding my shirt and sighing when I realized it was missing a few buttons.

"Travis is going with Joey and a few other men to talk to Cal. Now that we know about April Smith, he might have a way of contacting her or at least telling us when the next tournament she's hosting will be," I said. There were always more irons in the fire than I let Sal know. He always had to make the big decisions with or without me. I liked to take as much off his plate as I could.

"All I planned was going to the gym and then checking in with the moms," Sal said, sounding a little upset that he wasn't doing more.

I gave up on trying to button the shirt, choosing instead to walk up to Sal and wrap an arm over his shoulders.

"I'm your second. You don't have to do everything, Sal."

His arm wrapped around me, giving me a side hug as we watched the coffeepot dribble the first bits of coffee. This was what we needed the night before, but didn't do. It felt right to hold him. We needed each other.

"I'd feel a lot better about that if we didn't have O'Shea breathing down our necks trying to take Carmen, and Morelli's new condition to consider," Sal grumbled.

"Who is Morelli?" came Ash's voice from the bedroom doorway. Her blue hair was mussed into delightful, wavy bedhead, and she had wrapped the sheet around her. If I had time, I would have asked for that second round I thought about before I answered the phone.

I pulled my arm from Sal, sighing and grabbing a mug from the counter. I needed some liquid energy before I headed home and had to fight off the moms before I could wash the scent of sweat and sex from me.

"If I had time, I'd stay to elaborate, but I guess I'll leave this one to Sal," I said, taking the two gulps worth of coffee I poured into the mug and looking around for my shoes. Thankfully, it was much easier to tell the difference between our shoes visually, as my feet had always been about a size larger than his.

"Morelli is technically my boss," Sal said, filling my mug the rest of the way with coffee for himself and then pouring another for her.

"*You* have a boss?" she asked, walking over to him and taking the cup.

"Well, my father had a boss. We have been working very hard to make sure that I fill my father's shoes."

"What happens if you don't?" she asked. I looked up from my shoe-tying to see that Sal had looked at me. There was a question in his eyes.

Should we tell her?

My first instinct was no. Keeping her out of things would keep her safer, but then I realized that things had very much changed between us. She was now going to be living with us, in a relationship with us. She needed to be fully in the know, otherwise her life could be at stake. I nodded to him, standing and moving back to the two of them.

"I have to go," I said quietly, leaning down and placing a delicate kiss on her lips. She pressed up on her toes, lengthening that kiss when I started to pull away. With a smile I finally did part away from her, turning to Sal and clapping his bare shoulder. "See you at home."

ASH

Adrian left, and I turned to Sal, giving him my most expectant expression. He gave a heavy sigh, but smiled, gesturing for me to take a seat in one of the chairs while he leaned on the counter. He almost looked like it pained him to tell me, but this was the moment I had been waiting for. He was going to tell me everything I had wanted to know for so long.

"We would be taken out if we don't. A liability, especially because of *how* my father died," Sal said, taking a sip of coffee.

"And how did your father die?" I asked, my tone noting how obvious my next question should have been. He smiled, but then raised his eyebrows as if he were anticipating something bad.

"We killed him."

Those words hung in the air for a few moments. My mind was working on its own, trying to imagine and truly piece together what I already knew deep down, but never had confirmation of until now. They were killers, mobsters, criminals. I had known this, of

course, but I hadn't completely unpacked what that would mean.

"He tried to sell Carmen to the Irish, the O'Sheas. We stole her back and killed him for it."

I knew this. I understood it. What I couldn't wrap my head around was the fact that the people I had known for so long, the families that I had been included in, were full of killers. Fights, pain, and bloodshed I was used to, but I hadn't ever been in a world of death.

"How many people have you killed, Sal?" I asked, because even though his reasoning for killing his father was sound, and thank goodness they got Carmen back, the instinct within me to flee the dangerous predators was mounting.

"I have no way of counting," Sal confessed, scrutinizing my face closely.

"And Adrian?"

"If you count when he was in the Marines, would probably be more than me."

"So, all of you, Leo, Enzo—"

"Carmen, Benny, and Ingrid now too, yes," he said when I seemed to struggle to get the words out. "We were born into this. Adrian, Benny, and Carmen all tried to stay away, Leo too, but it was impossible for me and Enzo. Our father being the Capo, meant that we were obligated to follow in his footsteps. Adrian was forced in after he was discharged. Leo, Carmen, and Benny were forced back in after Carmen was taken. We made an oath to each other; the six of us would always have each other's backs, and we will."

Something about knowing none of them wanted to be part of the underground world of organized crime helped my fears settle, but only a little. These were people who loved passionately and would lay down their lives for the people they cared about, but they had also taken innumerable lives in the process. Could I handle being one of them? Could I deal with the knowledge that they had killed so many people, but wouldn't hurt me?

They wouldn't hurt me. That I knew deep in my core. Everything they had shown me throughout these years told me that was true.

As my mind settled, relaxing into the fact that these men were dangerous, but not to me, the word "Capo" stood out to me from the explanations Sal had been giving me. I had no idea what that meant. Suddenly I felt incredibly uneducated about organized crime.

"You're blushing?" he asked, standing straight again and walking over to where I sat.

"I just—" I stopped myself.

What was I supposed to say? Can I get a glossary?

I was raised in the gray area. My father had dabbled, fighting in illegal fights like I had, gambling, and other things too—clearly, since he owed such a huge debt to Marek when he died—but he shielded me from the bulk of that world. I had no real frame of reference for how the Mafia worked other than what I had seen in movies and television.

"You're embarrassed?" Sal deduced, reaching out and brushing his knuckles over my hot cheeks.

"I feel like I should know more about this than I do. More about you," I admitted, glancing down at the coffee cup in my lap.

"What do you want to know?" he asked as he settled onto the floor at my feet. For a man who exuded confidence and was the boss in almost every situation he was in, it seemed strange that he would submit to me, be an open book, put himself below me physically.

"I'm sure you have much more important things to do today," I said, moving to stand, but he put his hands on my thighs, stopping me.

"I am simply going to check on my mom and Maria and take you to the gym for your classes. That's all that's on the agenda until we get more information. So tell me what you want to know."

His voice was deep and warm, comforting in a way that I wasn't sure I had ever experienced.

"You're the Italian mob."

"Yes."

"What does 'Capo' mean?"

"It's short for caporegime. Literally, it means, 'head of the regime.' My father was essentially a lieutenant, governing this territory for the Big Boss. My uncle Romolo is the Capo in Chicago," he said.

"Do you speak Italian?"

I must have blushed again, and he grinned.

"Sì, parlo italiano. Per te farei di tutto," he said, his voice somehow becoming even more buttery. I shook a little, my body quivering with a need I didn't think I should have again after being so thoroughly satisfied the night before.

"Does Adrian?" I asked, my voice a little more breathless than I would have liked.

"We all do," he said, that cheeky grin sliding on his face. I leaned forward, narrowing my eyes at him.

"I just want you to know, if I didn't have to go back to the house and change before work, I'd make sure you were speaking Italian to me the whole time we were naked on that counter over there."

I could see it as the image flooded his mind, his pupils dilating with desire as he stared at my barely clad body.

"Now help me into that dress so we can get back," I said, standing and setting the mug on the table beside the chair so I could let the sheet fall to the floor.

CHAPTER 21

SAL

If I could have lifted her up on that counter and fucked her after telling her to spread her legs for me in Italian, I would have. I so wanted to watch that cunt glisten as it started dripping from my words alone. But she was right. We both had places to be, and her first class was going to start in an hour. Not much time for her to change and head to work, let alone eat.

I parked in the garage, coming around to take Ash's hand as she navigated in the dress and heels. Expecting that only Enzo would be there, and most likely either in the basement den or the office with Adrian, I went through the kitchen entrance, my arm wrapped around Ash's waist, and was shocked to see them all in the kitchen. The moms, Adrian, Enzo, Ingrid, *and* Nora. All of them.

The look on Adrian's face said exactly what I was thinking, as the whole room's attention seemed to focus singularly on us.

"Ash!" Nora said with glee, feet kicking as she stuffed her face with pancakes that the moms had prepared.

"Hi, Nora! I'm just going to get changed for work," Ash said, slipping away from me and through the kitchen quickly.

Enzo turned to Adrian, and then his eyes turned back to me standing in yesterday's suit with hair that didn't quite want to stay in its normal spot.

"I thought—" Enzo started, but Ingrid elbowed him in the ribs, effectively shutting him up for now. There really wasn't a zipper for that mouth of his, and I glared at my brother across the room.

"What? I thought Adrian had—"

"Present … company," Ingrid said through gritted teeth. As if the moms could hear nothing, they turned back to their cooking, though much more quietly than they normally would have.

"I'll just change, and I'll come back for food," I said, starting to head toward the kitchen stairs.

"It will be cold by then," Mom said.

"Five minutes at most," I tried to assure.

"It will take longer than five minutes to clear the stink from your skin. The food will be cold."

Mama was not a woman who minced words. Usually, she was an ever-kind and patient woman, so something didn't sit right with this interaction and I was desperate to know exactly what happened before I arrived. Adrian was showered and changed, his normal jogger sweats and t-shirt on, hair still wet.

"Is there a problem, Mama?" I asked as I moved back to the kitchen table, pulling out the chair next to Adrian and sitting down.

"I am confused about what I'm thinking occurred last night and a little tired. So I think maybe we talk about things when innocent ears are not in the room," she said, before walking over and practically slamming the plate in front of me.

I turned to Adrian and mouthed, "What the fuck?" He merely shook his head, though his face was solemn, like he *did* know.

Enzo was holding back chuckles, and Ingrid's face was red as a tomato. I picked at my food, feeling exceptionally uncomfortable with the quiet kitchen, the heavy silence only disrupted by the sounds of Maria doing the dishes. Now that I looked at her, her brows were drawn together, anger set her mouth into a pinch, and her movements were the sharp jerking movements that she used to make when we spilled something on her carpet as kids and she would silently scrub it while we apologized.

Why did it feel like I needed to apologize?

I got up, picking up the barely eaten food, and scraping it into the trash.

"And now you won't eat?" Mom asked, her tone dripping with whatever unsaid insult I had done to her.

"It's my house," I said, throwing this attitude right back in her face. She looked like I had slapped her.

"You are my son! And I won't have you behaving like anything other than a gentleman! That's not how I raised you!" she said, clearly trying not to yell since Nora was in the room, but her voice was not quiet by any means.

I wanted to yell at her, tell her how idiotic she was being, but I knew it would do nothing but make this situation worse. The night before had been a glimmer of joy I hadn't had in months, maybe longer, and whatever this was had dampened it. I stepped closer to her but didn't get in her face, making sure my hands were relaxed even though I wanted to ball them into fists of frustration.

"I don't know what you *think* is going on here, but whatever it is, you need to figure out a way to quiet that anger. We don't have time for this. Fights amongst ourselves will do nothing but hurt us right now when we have people outside who would rather us all be dead."

Mama looked up at me, the anger in her eyes still there, but it had softened, the ever-present worry coming to the surface in the set of her mouth and the crinkle in her forehead.

"I didn't want this for you," she whispered, tears in her eyes.

"Me either," I said, before turning and finally going up the kitchen stairs two at a time and down the hall to where my room was.

It had been my room for years, but until my father died, I had so rarely stayed there. There were no remnants of my childhood left over. It was "designed" by someone else, with cool, dark tones and sharp lines to embolden masculinity. Salvatore Lupo's son would be a *man*.

But Liliana's son was still a *man*, just a man who cared about the people around him. I hated to remind her of the reality. She was so much happier when she and Maria lived in their blissful bubble we tried to keep them in. The only things to remind her of the life we were forced into were their guards, specifically there to keep them safe and out of harm's way.

I looked at the room my father had designated as mine years ago. I didn't hate the room, but there was nothing here that felt personal. I didn't need it to be. This was the place I left behind who I was and became his son, his second, his heir. There were other safe spaces for me to be myself.

Since I wasn't going to be visiting the moms today apparently, given the complete hostility that was displayed there, and the fact that she would need some time to process the reality I had to remind her of, I was going to dress for the gym.

With a bag in hand and my joggers on, I stepped back out into the hall and saw Adrian leaning against the wall across from my door.

"What the fuck was that?" I asked in a whisper.

"Enzo said he heard *me* with Ash last night in the hotel. Apparently, he told the moms when he and Ingrid got here this morning. They wondered where she was, why I didn't bring her with me. I told them she was getting a ride with her guard for the day, hoping they would pack up and head back to Lee's Summit before you two got here, but they decided to make *breakfast* for everyone. Didn't you check your texts?"

I grabbed my phone from my pocket, finding that, yes, I did have numerous text messages, ranging from last night to all of Adrian's this morning, but my phone was still on silent from the wedding ceremony. I had never put the sound back on.

"Fuck," I grumbled, looking back up at Adrian. "So, what do they think is happening?"

"I'm not sure. Something not good," he said, running his hands through his curls.

Enzo came up the stairs at that moment, seeing the two of us at the end of the hall.

"Why does this feel like old times?" he asked with a grin. "The two older brothers in trouble for some *bravate* they got themselves into."

"What do they think is going on?" Adrian asked, ignoring the dig.

"That you two are taking advantage of Ash. And I have to say, it seems a little strange," Enzo said, crossing his arms and raising an eyebrow.

"Not being taken advantage of," Ash said, stepping out of the room down the hall she had been staying in.

She had opted to braid her hair, the blue twisting with the darker hair that hid underneath beautifully. In her standard black gym attire, she didn't look at all like a woman someone would think had been taken advantage of. She exuded confidence.

"Anyone care to explain then?" Enzo asked.

"Did we care for an explanation with Ingrid?" Adrian asked. The only thing I had wanted to know when Enzo decided to help Ingrid when she had been working against us, whether knowingly or not, was if he was sure.

"Well, come on," Enzo murmured, clearly uncomfortable with the script being flipped.

"If you need to know, you'll know," I said to my brother, narrowing my eyes and daring him to keep pushing. He liked to do that.

"I'll just go get some coffee," Ash said, watching all of us with restrained confusion.

"You have some things to go over?" Adrian asked.

"I do," Enzo said, still clearly torn between his curiosity over what happened with us and Ash, and trying not to pry.

I could have pried, as the boss, and forced my brother to kill Ingrid a month ago, or at least had someone take her out for us. She had been hacking into our information and keeping us out of O'Shea's. It had turned out that she was quite innocent, not looking into any of the information she was protecting or pulling for them, in fact, not even knowing that she was working for the Irish mob, but the threat she had posed would have been enough for a death sentence. I stayed that, opting not to take her out only because Enzo was sure. Enzo loved her.

"I have things to show you," Enzo said, bobbing his head toward the office and choosing not to go down the path I threatened him with.

"Let's see it," I said.

ASH

Aside from the very awkward morning and the strange speculations that the family had about what happened the night before, I felt good. Better than I had in a very long time. Strange that feeling wanted could change my perspective. I didn't love the opulent decor of the room I had been staying in, but I somehow didn't mind the idea of simply staying in the house with Sal and Adrian. I didn't love the idea of always needing to be driven places by *Joey,* of all people, but it was temporary, right?

I still didn't have the whole picture of what was going on with the family, but I got the impression, especially after that interaction with Enzo in the hall earlier that there was just so much to tell, it would be a while before I finally understood.

Instead of dreading going back to the house, I found I was eager for it, especially knowing that the rest of the people staying there were leaving for their own homes. We'd have the house to ourselves. My body heated with the idea of nothing standing in our way. That I could unabashedly touch them and kiss them if I wanted. Which I didn't feel like I could do this morning with everyone else in attendance.

Ingrid and Nora walked through the door, a little early for the three o'clock defense classes she was planning on taking, but I realized why when she grinned at me, holding a to-go cup of coffee out as she approached the counter.

"I thought you might need a little pick me up since you were up so late," Ingrid said with a mischievous smile.

"How do you know it was me?" I asked with narrowed eyes. The assumptions made by the family after Enzo apparently "hearing" Adrian and me having sex were going to continue to cause problems, I could tell.

"Enzo was getting ice and saw you in the hallway. Just a little glance, but—"

Well, fuck. I couldn't exactly argue that it could have been someone else, because I was definitely the only guest who had blue hair. Daph's hair was a vibrant shade of red, which complemented the red bridesmaid dress she wore, but those colors couldn't have been mistaken.

"Ash and Adrian! Nonna Maria said that Benny and Sal were going to be the only ones left without a wedding soon," Nora said, though she immediately followed it up with a high kick in the air.

"Oh? Wedding for you and Enzo coming up?" I asked, hoping to steer the conversation blissfully away from me. Ingrid's face turned red immediately.

"We're thinking about it," she said quietly, and I smiled behind the coffee she brought me, tilting my head toward the classroom we usually went in.

There wasn't much more time for us to talk, or for me to finish my coffee because soon after we made it in the room, the rest of the class filled in. Nora was my trusty helper for most of the class, and when it ended, I gave her a squeeze.

"Maybe I'll be a good fighter like you, Ash," Nora whispered in my ear.

"If you want, but I hope you don't have to," I whispered back. Those words had more meaning than sweet Nora's six-year-old mind could contemplate, but maybe someday she'd think back on it. Especially with the world she was going to be raised in.

Ingrid hugged me goodbye, and they left just as my next class was starting to file in.

I only had two more classes and then thirty minutes before we closed the gym down for the night. Joey went out for a cigarette as Benny was finishing up with a man who had surgery on his leg and was rebuilding his strength when I saw a car pull up at the front of the store.

It was a nice car, a blue sports car of some kind, but it wasn't the car that made me pause, it was the woman who got out of it that had my brows raising. April Smith got out of the car and came around to the hood, sitting on it and staring through the glass at me.

She continued to sit there, staring for the rest of the short time until close, even gesturing to me when Joey came and talked to her. When he came back inside, his lips were set in a hard line.

"She wants to talk to you, but I don't think the bosses will like that much," he said, standing in front of me and obstructing her view.

"Why?"

"You know how they are. They don't want weird outsiders talking to you guys unless one of them is there," Joey said, but I shook my head at him.

"I mean, why does she want to talk to me?"

"Oh, about the fights, I suppose," he said, leaning back against the counter and looking back out at her.

"I'll stay," Benny said as he walked over with his clipboard in hand.

"Roman is on his way," Joey said, since there had to be someone on site now, even when we were closed.

"I'll stay when she's talking to Ash," Benny said, setting the clipboard on the counter and raising an eyebrow at Joey. I knew Joey was oblivious and didn't see the potential threat that Benny did. While Benny wasn't an incredibly active member of the organization, he was raised in it, just like the rest of the Lupos and LaMartinas. "Once my patient leaves, you can show her in," he told Joey, who shrugged and went back outside to wait by the door.

"He's harmless," I said to Benny as soon as the door closed again.

"He's an idiot and a liability. I don't know why Sal and Adrian think he's good enough to protect you," Benny said with a grunt of irritation.

"I think it has less to do with his skill and more to do with charity."

"At the expense of your safety?" Benny asked. That was a good one I couldn't argue with. Not that I was incapable of taking care of myself, but when it came to Mafia dealings, I was not exactly skilled at seeing the writing on the wall. "They might not realize. He's lucky nothing has happened to you on his watch."

I glanced at Joey's back through the window he was leaning against and hoped that some sense came to his head before something bad happened. He may have been an idiot, but he was a kind idiot who had clearly gotten into the wrong business.

Benny's patient checked out with me and then left shortly after. I was counting the register when April came in, her heels clacking loudly on the tile floor, making me glance up at her before I typed the last number into the computer and closed out the shift.

"April Smith," she announced, holding out her hand for me to shake. Her perfectly manicured hand and tight smile made me uncomfortable immediately.

"Ashley Torres," I said back, grasping her hand with my calloused fingers. The black nail polish I had painted on to go with my dress for the wedding the day before was thankfully not chipped, but it was clearly not the same quality as hers. In fact, everything about us was opposing to me. Her blonde hair was again pulled back into a tight bun, her fair skin was nearly flawless, with only minimal wrinkling in a few places, and her dress was high-end and business class, while I was darker skinned, with wild blue hair, and still sweaty in my workout attire.

"You fought at my tournament last week," she said as our hands parted.

"I did. Didn't get very far though," I murmured, stacking the cash bags on top of the balanced register to go in the safe.

"But I hear you very much *could* have gone quite far, given your skill."

My brows furrowed, looking at her and trying to deduce her purpose for coming here. I hadn't been fighting for years. I was fairly unknown in this area too, but somehow, someone there had told her about my past, because there was no way she remembered me from my fights before I was released from Lewandowski's chains.

"Well, there's no way to know. She got a good one on my ribs and then dislocated my shoulder. I wouldn't have lasted any more fights even if I had won that one."

She chuckled as I rolled my shoulder. It was still very slightly sore, but nothing that I couldn't deal with. Taking a break from working and letting it heal properly had been a blessing, one that I wouldn't have taken if the men hadn't made that happen.

"I have a proposition for you," she said, leaning forward on the counter and setting her chin on her fist.

I could feel Benny's eyes on my back, listening and watching intently. Perhaps there was still a bit of doubt in my loyalty within the family. I was an outsider, and I was also, as far as they were all concerned, playing Adrian and Sal. Even if it made me bristle a little, I couldn't fault Benny's concern about my intentions.

"What's that?"

"I want you to fight in my next few tournaments. Even if you don't win, you'd cause quite the spectacle. Little thing like you taking on everyone. You'd get paid handsomely either way."

"What's in it for you?" I asked, narrowing my eyes at her.

"I need a draw to these fights. There's a bit of a monopoly going on in this territory. You might be just the thing I need to get more people coming to mine."

She meant Sal and Adrian's fights. They were the monopoly by design. This was their territory, and the only reason Cal had been able to start his own little operation was because he had held them in a more neutral zone with the intention that he might be folded into what Sal and Adrian had already created. She was talking about trying to take over, ripping a form of income from my men, and I already wasn't having it.

"I don't think I'm interested."

"I want you to think about it. You'll come to your senses when you realize how much more money you could be making partnering with me," she said, pulling an envelope from the purse at her side and sliding it across the counter to me. "Call me when you change your mind."

And with that, she turned, walking back out of the gym, getting into her expensive car, and driving away.

I looked down at the envelope only after she was fully out of the parking lot and her headlights were no longer visible. Benny came up and stood beside me as I flipped the lip of the envelope open and pulled out the contents. Five crisp hundred-dollar bills sat, with a business card and a single piece of paper with the words "$5,000 per event. Think about it," written on it.

"I don't like this," Benny said, taking the paper as I offered it to him.

"Me either," I said, looking at her business card, which had her name, her phone number, and a four-leaf clover in the corner.

"I'm texting Adrian and Leo about this," Benny said, pulling out his phone, but I stopped him, putting a hand on his arm.

"Don't bother Leo," I said. There was nothing I wanted to do less than interrupt the few days of peace that Carmen and Leo should have been getting following their wedding. This was not an immediate threat, and there was no need to get them involved unless it became something more.

"Fine, Adrian then," Benny said, proceeding to type out the message to his brother as I took the money and register to the safe. Entering the room, I suddenly remembered what had happened here the last time Adrian and I had been alone closing up. My mind flooded with the possibilities in this office now, and all at once, the curiosity over April Smith dissolved back into my complete and utter desire to get back to those men.

My phone dinged with a text message just as I closed the safe, and I pulled it from my side pocket to take a look at it.

[Adrian: April Smith, huh?]

[Me: An offer. I thought I'd talk to you two about it first.]

[Adrian: How much longer?]

[Me: Just finishing up. Joey will drive me back.]

[Adrian: Good.]

I shivered a little, and moved back out to the front room, turning off the office light along the way. Benny and Joey were waiting by the front door, and I turned the alarm on.

CHAPTER 22

SAL

I had come home from the gym after dropping Ash off and trying to get my mind centered with some punching bag therapy. I showered, found some leftovers of the moms cooking in the fridge, and found Adrian in the den watching something on the TV. I sat next to him, as usual, and we dissolved into a comfortable silence, watching the news, which had nothing of interest being talked about.

My mind started to wander, and I began thinking about the three of us together. All of our bodies moving so beautifully together, the feel of skin on skin, both of their scents filling my nose as I breathed raggedly. My cock started stirring in my pants and I so desperately wanted to rub it, put a little pressure there to relieve the need, but Adrian was just beside me. Just six inches of leather cushion sat between us on the couch. He would definitely notice.

There had been times, especially when we were younger, that we had jerked off in the same room. Usually because one of us stumbled on some porn and we got hard looking at it together. Side by side, we would jerk off, and I—though I hadn't wanted to admit it at the time—would usually finish watching him, not the video playing in the background.

I glanced at him, wondering what he was thinking. How could he simply watch the TV and not be remembering what happened with Ash just the night before? Never mind that she agreed to move in with us, and we could do that again.

My eyes dropped to the crotch of his pants. His hand was already resting there. Just before I flicked my eyes away, I saw him squeeze himself.

Hmmm, maybe he was thinking about it too.

I shifted, pushing my hips up and leaning back a little farther on the couch, my hand moving to cup myself more discreetly, but apparently not discretely enough, since Adrian's eyes darted to watch my movements.

"Ash is on her way?" I asked as Adrian's eyes turned back to the TV.

"Yeah, she should be here in a half hour, maybe forty minutes," he murmured back. A half-hour was not fast enough. I wanted her here now. I wanted to lick that sweet pussy and watch as she sucked Adrian's long cock. I wanted to lick her nipples until she was moaning incoherently while Adrian's fingers rammed inside of her.

I got harder—*damn it!*—my hand now unconsciously squeezing and stroking myself through the fabric of my sweats.

"I can't wait an hour," Adrian groaned, his own hand moving over his length.

Thank goodness he was on the same page. I was going to have to come up with a reason to leave the room and, for some reason, the thought of leaving him wasn't ideal. Like whatever this was with Ash and us meant we had to do it together.

"We'll lick her first," I said, sounding a little breathless to my own ears.

"Bend her over the arm of the couch, I'll take her clit while you spear her with your tongue," Adrian said in a groan, clenching his left fist while his right picked up speed rhythmically pressing down on his throbbing tent in his sweats.

"I'll have her wet my dick with that mouth so I can jerk my cock while you fuck her relentlessly," I said as my hand slipped into my sweats, fisting my cock, which was so hard it was almost painful. Picturing it and talking about it with Adrian while I could smell his heady male scent made all of this so much more intense.

His eyes turned back to where my hand had disappeared beneath my pants, and a choked sound seemed to come from him as he squeezed himself through his sweats one more time. A moment later, he simply lifted his hips and pushed the pants down to his knees. Legs spread, he fisted himself at the base, his long cock standing at attention as he began slowly stroking himself.

"She'll take you in her mouth, while you lick her pussy again. My dick and your tongue will make her so wet she'll be dripping," he said roughly, swirling his thumb over the head of his penis and spreading his precum down his shaft.

Oh fuck.

I did the same, pushing my sweats down and releasing my cock from its confines, spreading my legs as I took it back into my hand, my knee pressing into his.

For a few moments, it was silent, except for the sound of our breathing and our fists working, the slap of skin.

Adrian kicked his sweats the rest of the way off, now sitting completely naked beside me, though he had inadvertently scooted closer to me, our thighs now pressing closely, the arm I was using to pump my cock, rubbing against his arm with each movement.

I watched his hand move up and down his cock, his other hand moving to cup his balls, but his reach was inhibited by our thighs pressed together.

I stopped working myself, boldly grasping his thigh and slinging it over mine, letting his legs part wider for better access. He didn't move away or stop. He simply used the new space to do exactly what he wanted, cupping and rolling his balls in one hand as he worked himself with the other, groaning at the new sensation.

I didn't move my hand from his thigh, instead using my other hand to take over jerking, while the hand that remained grasped his flesh there.

It was Ash who we had been thinking of that started this, but I realized that she wasn't who I was thinking about now. No, I was definitely hard and leaking precum, my lower body tingling because I was watching Adrian. I was touching Adrian while he touched himself.

And I wanted more.

Adrian's eyes were also fixed on my hands, my cock, his thigh, before they met my eyes.

"Fuck," he whispered, bucking his hips slightly and causing my hand to slip farther down his thigh, my fingers now so close, his knuckles brushed them as his hand moved over his cock.

He pulled his hand away from his balls, his eyes closing for a moment as my fingers pressed in on his skin, before sliding, reaching until I was the one holding his sac. He took in a sharp breath, but he didn't stop moving his hand over his cock. In fact, it went even faster, his balls starting to draw up as I massaged them with my fingers.

I couldn't resist as I released my own cock, from its hold, drawing my whole body to his so his leg was draped fully over my lap. I continued massaging his balls, but now my other hand joined his on his cock. He released his hold, letting me take over. The silky feel of his erection in my hand, so hard, leaking precum so regularly it slicked and lubed each jerk I made.

My hand on his sac splayed, fingers playing with his taint and making him groan loudly. I spit on the head, then looked up at his face. His eyes met mine. I kept pumping him, licking my lips while my fingers still massaged his taint, moving them to just touch lightly on his puckered hole.

His breath caught, his left-hand splaying over my chest and down my abs, until his fingers brushed the head of my cock. The feel of him touching me, those calloused fingers on my most sensitive skin as he grasped me, had my head spinning. There was only one other person who lit up my body at just their touch, and that was Ash.

His strokes matched mine. The only sound was our labored breathing, the muffled sound of the news that we no longer cared the slightest about, and our skin slapping. His hips bucked, pressing my finger, which had been lightly circling his ass a little farther in. The resulting groan from him gave me courage as I pressed farther, pushing one knuckle past the tight ring of muscle.

"Sal," his voice came out like a whine, leg muscles flexing and his hand pumping my cock, squeezing a bit more.

I leaned over again, spitting over my fist. As I did so, he pulled his leg from my lap, placing his foot on the couch and therefore widening his legs. In the process, my finger went deeper within him. The feel of his tight heat surrounding my finger made me let out a groan; his fist tightened again on my cock.

I love anal almost as much as I love pussy. I had licked Ash's ass a little and considered slipping a finger in there when I was eating her out, and suddenly I wanted to do that with Adrian.

I pulled my finger from within him, his eyes snapping to mine as he watched me stick it in my mouth, wetting it thoroughly before putting it right back in, this time pumping in time with my hand moving over his long cock.

"Oh god," he said, his hand falling away from my cock as he slumped back on the couch, bucking his hips and meeting my hands as I worked him.

"You like that?" I asked, pushing another finger in and watching in awe as he pushed back with his hips as if he wished I could go deeper within him.

My cock bobbed, a new desire licking within me. I wanted to fuck my best friend. I wanted to press my cock into the tight hole I was fingering.

"Tell me what you want, Adrian," I murmured, my voice coming out like gravel as I watched him continue to writhe against my attention, more precum leaking from his tip like he was almost ready to blow.

I could see it in the way his hips moved in time with my fingers. What he wanted was exactly what I wanted. And I wanted to spit on my own cock and slide it right in where my fingers were stretching.

"Next time you're licking Ash's pussy while I fuck her, I'm going to pull out and have you suck her cum from me before I put it back in," Adrian said, his voice coming out more like a growl.

My dick twitched at the suggestion. That stream of precum coating my hand was begging to be sucked off, but something inside of me want to assert some dominance with him, especially after that growl that came from his lips. I released my hand from his cock, thrusting inside of his ass one more time and giving a good rub to his prostate, before pulling out. I stood, pulling his legs so he was back to sitting normally on the couch. His face dropped, almost seeming hurt by my actions, until I stood in front of him, my cock just at level with his face.

"You first," I said.

There was a pause where we just stared at each other, the words we just said hanging in the air before he shifted and sat up more.

I had just touched him, finger fucked his ass, and I very much wanted to do more. He had jerked me, but in comparison, it was quite the leap to expect him to readily suck my cock. There was no way it was going to happen.

But then he reached out, hand grasping me at the base and scooting closer to the edge of the couch.

"I don't know what to do," he whispered, looking up at me, his blue eyes looking so vulnerable at that moment I couldn't help but reach out and brush my fingers down his cheek, loving the way his soft skin transitioned into his beard.

I had no idea what to tell him. I hadn't sucked a man's dick before, only been on the receiving end of a woman's mouth.

"Just try and do what you feel me doing to you," came Ash's voice from behind me. I looked over my shoulder, watching as she walked over, her clothes mostly discarded behind her, except for her sports bra and thong.

The heat in her eyes immediately took away the momentary panic I felt at hearing her voice, having caught us doing this without her. She liked this. It was obvious in the way she hungrily took us in as she moved over toward us.

Both of us were enraptured as she crawled between my legs, popping up so her face was level with Adrian's dick. She licked him root to tip, swirling her tongue over the little slit and dripping drool all down his long shaft to slick the way for her hand to come up and stroke him. He watched for a moment or two longer, engrossed in what she was doing, just as I was, before he turned back to me, squeezing lightly at my cock he still held in his hand and tentatively moving his head forward, thick lips parting.

His hot breath hit the head of my erection first, before his lips closed over the tip, tongue snaking out to caress it.

"Oh fuck," I grunted out.

The feel of his mouth on me, the knowledge that it was him, his tongue moving over the vein on the underside, his grip on my cock as he pumped me, his lips gliding up and down. It was *his* throat that I hit when my hips snapped forward of their own will. I couldn't help it. It felt too fucking good.

It earned me a swift slap on the ass. I looked down, expecting anger there, but his eyes were eager, fiery as he looked up at me. His cheeks hollowed out, sucking, tongue swirling, moaning, and swallowing when he took me to the back of his throat. His hand, which had gotten slick with his spit, slid down, his other hand taking that spot, as he moved his thick fingers to massage my taint and ass. Just that gentle rimming while he relentlessly bobbed his head over my erection had my stomach clenching with that familiar feeling.

I wanted to cum in my best friend's mouth, but I also wanted to cum inside Ash.

I wanted to cum inside Adrian too.

Oh god.

I propped one foot up on the couch, opening my legs more for him.

He moaned around my cock, the vibration in his throat making me thrust again, but he didn't choke. It was like he was waiting for it. Like he wanted it. My thrust into his throat made his finger slip right over the ring of my ass, going in deep.

Fuck, that felt good.

I was fucking Adrian's face, as he fingered me in the ass and Ash sucked him off.

It was too much. The pleasure, the knowledge, the rightness.

"Adrian," I said, grunting as I tried to back away, but he just kept his relentless pace, moving his hand from the base of my cock to my hip, holding me tight to keep me there. Something Ash did to him must have tipped him over the edge too, because he moaned deeply, taking me even farther down his throat. I exploded, grasping his head as I pulsed in his mouth, spilling rope after rope of cum into him.

He finally popped off, licking his lips and groaning loudly as he looked up at me, his ab muscles trembling as Ash took his own release down her throat.

"That was so fucking hot," Ash said, still on her knees between me and Adrian. I reached out a hand to help her up, and she took it, standing to discard the last shreds of her clothes. "I am dripping," she said in a moan as soon as her tiny thong had dropped to the floor at her feet.

I watched in awe as her hands came up to squeeze her own breasts, before one of them snaked down her stomach, dipping between her folds for a moment before she reached out her fingers to show off the glistening liquid that literally dropped from the digits.

My mouth watered as I leaned forward, sucking them into my mouth and tasting the sweet tangy taste that was Ash's pussy.

She watched my mouth, enraptured, and it was long enough for Adrian to snatch her around the waist, pulling her toward him. She seemed confused when he didn't sling her down onto the couch or pull her into his lap, but instead lifted her, putting her legs over his shoulders, pussy directly in his face.

With Ash clinging to the back of the couch, Adrian relentlessly went to town on her cunt, making her gasp and moan. I needed a taste. I needed to help her make those sounds too.

I climbed onto Adrian's lap, focused on the need to pleasure Ash. I wanted her to cum at least three times.

Adrian's hands came out, grasping her ass and pulling her cheeks apart, giving me more access to witness his tongue lapping at her vagina, juices and his spit were coating him from the chin down. I slipped two fingers into her hole, his tongue touching them and joining in as we fucked her together, before his lips and tongue moved to give attention to her sensitive bundle of nerves.

While I fingered her and he laved at her clit, I gazed at the puckered hole that was fluttering right before my face. My mouth went there, licking and teasing it as it continued to flutter. It wanted my attention, just like Adrian's hole wanted me to fuck it.

There it was, my cock hardening again. I could feel Adrian's hardening against my thigh. Ash's moan as my fingers started curling to touch that perfect spot within her, setting up her first orgasm, had my cock bobbing and my hips moving just a little. It was enough that my thigh rubbed against Adrian's cock, and he moaned too, his hands pulling Ash's cheeks apart and gripping a little tighter.

My tongue slipped into Ash's hole, pushing past that ring and then it was mine, I tongue fucked that ass, adding another finger to her pussy, while Adrian's cock slipped between my ass cheeks, his cock rubbing against my taint and asshole with each gyration of my hips.

Ash's first orgasm ended with a huge gush of liquid that coated my arms and both mine and Adrian's chest. I slipped my fingers and tongue from within her, being sure to spread some of that cum juice right on her asshole. One of us was going to be in that ass. It was a certainty, especially with how well she could take us.

"You want more?" Adrian asked as I moved to get up and let her have some room.

"I need someone inside me. Now," she snapped.

"Both," I said, pulling her down to Adrian's lap and grabbing his cock to line him up at her silken and dripping core. She sank down on his cock, groaning loudly as she did so. I came back to Adrian's lap too, our eyes locking as I spit in my hand, thoroughly coating my cock, before I lined it up with her hole.

"You ready for both of us, Ash?"

"Oh, fuck yes," she said, clearly trying not to ride Adrian's cock so soon when I wasn't even inside her yet.

I pushed the head of my penis against it, going past the little ring of muscle and eliciting a gasp from Ash.

I pulled out, and then went in, farther this time. I had fucked women in the ass before, but with Adrian's cock already inside her, it was so much tighter.

"So tight," I managed to grunt out, as I pulled out one more time, this time slamming back into her, my balls slapping against Adrian's.

We all just stayed still for a moment. It was a strange feeling of oneness. We were all together. One pretzel of limbs, both of us truly inside her. Then I started pumping.

"Oh, fuck!" Adrian cried, his hands on her hips as he started moving in tandem with my thrusts. Ash's moans turned to feral cries of pleasure. The feel of her second orgasm rippling through her and squeezing us even more tightly had me wanting to pick up the pace.

I was going to cum soon, but I wasn't going to do it without them.

My eyes met Adrian's, and I could tell it wouldn't take much to push him over the edge.

"Rub her clit," I instructed him, licking my own fingers and reaching behind me to find Adrian's hole.

I could tell the moment he started rubbing her. Two holes full, her clit being rubbed, it took no time at all before I could feel her body coiling tight, ready for release. It was then that I pushed my fingers into Adrian's ass, finding his prostate and rubbing it as I fucked Ash's ass so hard.

Adrian let out a sharp cry, Ash screamed in ecstasy, and the whole world went white for a moment as my second orgasm exploded from me.

CHAPTER 23

ADRIAN

Ash's lips were on mine as soon as our breathing started to go back to normal. The kiss was sloppy and tired, but happy. I felt it when Sal pulled out of her. A moment later, she parted from me, smiling, before she turned her head and pulled Sal into a kiss as well.

All of the sudden, the fact that this was real seemed to come over me. What had just happened was not a fantasy or one of the dreams I woke from alone in my bed just across the hall from Sal. This was real. As much as I had shamed myself for years for these thoughts, I felt relieved and also scared of what just happened.

But at this moment, I couldn't wallow about my strange feelings. Ash was wobbling on her feet as she got up off my lap. Sal immediately scooped her up in his arms.

"I'm going to take her to shower," he said to me and turned to leave the den.

Fully naked and crossing the room, the two of them looked … *right.* How could I fit into that? But then Sal stopped at the door, turning around and looking at me with a quizzical expression.

"Come on," he said, tilting his head to indicate I should follow. I got up, following him up the two flights of stairs and to his bedroom. We went through the room and into the bathroom before Ash said, "I can walk."

"We're already here," Sal said with a chuckle, setting her on the counter by the sink before moving to the walk-in shower to turn it on.

"Adrian," Ash said, her expression also questioning as she beckoned me over to her. I moved to stand between her legs, feeling much more grounded and not like I was floating in a cloud of uncertainty like I had been once I touched her. She cupped my cheeks, looking at me with those gray eyes. "Are you okay?"

Was I okay?

I wasn't sure.

How was Sal?

Was he okay? Did he regret what just happened?

I glanced up into the mirror, looking at Sal through it. He stood behind us, watching me from the mirror. His face had slipped into that classic stoic mask he put on. Not letting me see what he was really feeling. For the first time in years, I couldn't predict it like usual. Where there had been nothing between us, moving in sync without words, now felt like an ocean.

"I—"

But what was I going to say?

I've been in love with you for years, Ash, but I'm in love with Sal too?

Because that's what I realized when I was touching him, and he was touching me. When I watched Ash kiss him, and wanted to kiss him too. I had been in love with Sal for a very long time.

"I'm happy for you two and for us," Ash said, her fingers petting my beard with one hand as she put her hand on my chest. "Are you not happy?"

"Just leave him be, Ash," Sal said, turning around and stepping into the shower.

"Go on," I whispered, pulling away from her before helping her down to join him.

She reached out her hand to me, and even though I wasn't sure of how Sal felt, the idea of being without them was too terrible for me to handle. I stepped into the shower stall after her, and there we were again, the three of us. Sal on one side of her, and me on the other.

We washed silently, Ash yawning every few minutes as Sal washed her hair and I soaped her body. It was pretty clear she wasn't long for the waking world by the time we all got out of the shower and toweled off.

"In my bed," Sal said, and we moved back to the bedroom, pulling back the sheets and watching as Ash and Sal crawled in together.

"Adrian," Ash said, patting her other side, but I shook my head.

"I'll come back," I said, even if I wasn't sure that was true, heading out of the room and back down to the den to grab my sweats.

I went to the garage after that, rummaging through the old toolboxes for the pack of cigarettes Sal and I put there for emergencies. This felt like a moment I needed the artificial calm nicotine gave me.

My hands shook as I made my way out to the back patio, pulling a cigarette from the pack and lighting it.

"Having one without me?" came Sal's voice, causing me to whip around to look at him.

"I thought you'd be asleep," I murmured as he approached, also in only a pair of sweatpants.

"I had to see what was going on with you and make sure you were coming back to bed," Sal said, snagging the cigarette from my fingers and taking a drag.

"Coming back to bed" sounded like he wanted me there, but I wasn't sure. I felt so stupid for being this way. We couldn't fall apart now. There was too much at stake for our closeness to crumble. We had to be able to rely on each other, and yet I felt so strangely adrift.

"Are you okay?" I asked him as I took back the cigarette. Sal narrowed his eyes at me for a moment before stepping closer and putting his hand on my shoulder. The simple gesture was the same one he had done for years, one of the only things that seemed to calm me in some of the worst times. But he didn't stop there. His hand slid up to my neck, fingers curling around to the back of my head before he moved even closer and brought my head down to his, our foreheads pressed together.

"You are my second, my best friend, and I have loved you for years. I already want to share everything with you. My home, my work, my family, Ash. And I also want you," Sal whispered, looking into my eyes. The relief that flooded me first and then the elation was like nothing I had ever felt before.

Before I could think about what I was doing, my face came forward, lips pressing against his. He seemed to melt against me, lips parting as he kissed me back, softly, sweetly. With love.

I startled awake. The sound of knocking at the door was loud, too loud for it to have been the front door. Opening my eyes, I looked over and realized I was still in Sal's bed, Ash between us.

"Sal! Wake the fuck up!" came Leo's voice.

"Just go in!" Enzo said, his tone clearly exasperated.

"Fuck!" Sal said under his breath, flinging the cover off and moving to the door. I got out of bed too, with Ash stirring and opening her eyes. Slipping behind the door, I nodded at Sal before he opened it.

"What the fuck?" Sal asked as soon as the door opened.

"Ingrid found something," Enzo said, his voice breathless. "Oh! Good morning, Ash!"

"Fucking move!" Sal growled, shoving whichever brother of his was closest to the door and stepping out into the hallway, slamming the door behind him.

"Shit," Ash mouthed at me, and I gave her a reassuring smile, heading to the dresser on the far wall and grabbing a t-shirt and some of Sal's gym shorts for her to put on.

"What is it?" Sal asked from the hallway.

"Where's Adrian?" Enzo asked.

"Just tell me what it is," Sal said, clearly trying to avoid having to reveal I was in his bedroom with Ash. Protecting me. I liked that, but it wasn't going to be able to last forever. Not in this family.

"He should really see it too," Leo confirmed. "That and Carmen remembered something else. I talked to her about the hypnosis. She's willing."

My heart rate skyrocketed.

"No, no!" Ash whispered, seeing the look on my face and knowing exactly what I was going to do.

"It's fine," I said, stepping over to the door and flinging it open. "What did she remember?" I demanded.

For a moment, everyone froze. Enzo and Leo's eyes slid over to me, shocked expressions written all over their faces, Sal's expression sliding into his stony, stoic expression, in preparation for whatever was about to come next.

"Were you…?" Enzo trailed off, looking between me and Sal and then through the door at Ash.

"What did Carmen remember?" I asked again, not interested in whatever mental breakdown Enzo was going to have about this.

"You're *both* fucking her?" Leo asked. It somehow felt eerily reminiscent of what I had asked when I realized he and Carmen were together.

"Yes. Can you answer my question now?"

"Together? At the same time?" Enzo asked.

"*Incazzato!*" Sal exclaimed, shoving Enzo and Leo farther down the hall. "Get to the fucking point. Did you come here to tell us something or ask about our sex life?"

"'Our sex life,' brother?" Leo asked, a grin spreading over his face. Apparently, Leo was no better than Enzo if pushed to it.

"For fuck's sake! You two are fucking children. Get it out of your system," Sal said, throwing up his hands in defeat and glaring at them expectantly.

"You two are both sleeping with Ash," Enzo started, holding up one finger. "At the same time," holding up another. "Are you two … sleeping together too?"

Sal bristled a little, stretching his neck and glancing at me.

"Yes," I said, leaning against the doorway with as much nonchalance as I could muster. Sal seemed to relax a little, a faint smile edging at the corner of his lips.

"How long?" Leo asked, eyes darting between us.

"Very recently," Sal said, now reaching and rubbing his forehead with frustration.

"Is this a…?" Enzo didn't seem to be certain how to ask the question, but I deduced what he wanted to know.

"Do we plan on being a throuple? That's how we are proceeding," I said. "Is that all? Want to tell us why you woke us all up now?"

"I think I'll make some coffee," Ash said, squeezing past me through the doorway and heading down the hall to the kitchen stairs. Thankfully, Leo and Enzo's eyes stayed shifting between me and Sal.

"Sal?" Leo asked.

"Yes," Sal said with finality, his stoic, frustrated demeanor giving way to anger now.

"You're sure?" Enzo asked.

"Do we need to kiss in front of you perverts?" he yelled. But before they could respond, he took the two steps toward me, pinning me against the doorframe with a hand at my waist, and yanked my head to his with the other, kissing me hard and biting my lip a little, before releasing me. For a moment when we parted, we stared into each other's eyes. Strange how doing this to prove a point to his brothers felt oddly right.

"Good now?" he asked, turning back around to his brothers without releasing his hold on my waist.

"We'll meet you in the kitchen," Leo said, pushing Enzo toward the stairs.

"I guess the family knows now," Sal said once their footsteps faded.

"I guess so," I said with a sigh, pushing off the doorframe and heading toward my bedroom to grab a shirt.

CHAPTER 24

SAL

Adrian and I came back down the kitchen stairs to find Ash sitting on the counter, mug in hand, while Enzo and Leo sat at the island stools with their own mugs of coffee.

"And you're okay with that?" Enzo asked, though his tone wasn't accusatory, only curious.

"I'll be honest, everyone kept asking me which one I was going to choose since I obviously liked both of them and them me, but I really didn't want to pick one," she said with a shrug.

"I don't know how Ma's going to take this," Leo said.

"She'll be fine," Enzo said, leaning back in his chair and noticing us at the bottom of the stairs and grinning. "She told me she had suspected they were a couple for years secretly. Even tried to have me ask them a few years ago."

"What?" I asked, shocked. "That's not true."

"It is. Just wait until I tell her she was sort of right," Enzo said, wiggling his eyebrows with glee.

"Did you already text Carmen?" Adrian asked Leo as he crossed Ash to get to the coffeepot.

"Did you expect anything else?" Leo asked, his own smile spreading over his face.

"Alright, what's your urgent news?" Sal said, waving his hand as if it would shoo the cloud of the topic of our relationship away.

"I was talking to Carmen this morning as we were packing up to come home about the possibility of hypnosis. She mentioned a sign when they got to the place she recalled before that mentioned something about storage," Leo said, his voice a little excited as he turned to Enzo.

"Leo texted me. Ingrid had already pulled lists of potential places, but she found old, archived footage of Bernardo taking Carmen to a storage place that was not included in the spaces owned by Salvatore in the four months before his death. She went digging into Bernardo's finances and discovered he had numerous storage units in his name. Six of which are still being paid for from an account under a trust."

"Six?" I asked, wondering why Bernardo would have storage space of his own. We utilized long-term storage facilities to hold some of our more valuable items until we had a buyer. Sometimes it was just space we saved for *other* uses, like torturing someone, if we weren't confident about the warehouses being clear for such a thing. For Bernardo to have his own, secret and separate from my father was odd, but definitely promising as far as our purposes of finding this thing before O'Shea.

"Six. One that April Smith just so happens to have visited since she's been back in town," Enzo said with raised, suggestive brows.

"What does that woman know?" Adrian asked, though it was more rhetorical to the group.

"She approached me at the gym," Ash said, slipping off the counter and going to the table where her bag had unceremoniously been left.

"Benny texted about that, but didn't say what it was about," Adrian said, watching her, like the rest of us.

"She offered a partnership. I fight in her tournaments; it draws more people somehow. I assume because I'm a woman. Proposed it would be a win for me either way," Ash said, coming back over to us and handing over the envelope to Adrian she had pulled from her bag.

"Well, that's not happening," Adrian said, flicking the envelope to me without even looking at it.

I took it, opening it to find its contents. We had her number now, which I slid across the island counter to Enzo after reading the note she had left.

"Maybe it's an opportunity," Ash said, nodding her head while Adrian shook his. "You need a way to get close to her for information. I don't know how much we can get, but it will give us access to her, at least."

"She's not wrong," Leo said, shrugging. "We might get something we can use, maybe find out what she told the Irish, or if nothing else, we'll be able to grab her easier if Ash is on the inside."

I didn't like it, but it felt like we were running out of options.

"You sure about this, Ash?" I asked, watching her expression closely as she hopped back up on the counter, snagging her mug. My sweatpants and t-shirt were far too big on her, but I loved seeing her in my clothes. With her eyes full of mischief and a smile on her lips, she raised the coffee back to her lips, taking a sip.

"Absolutely," she said.

ADRIAN

I pulled up to Liliana's house, waiting for the others to come meet me. Once Carmen had agreed to the hypnotism, Mom hadn't wasted any time in contacting the person she had gone to before and set up an appointment. Thankfully, the haste with which we had to plan it all meant there hadn't been much time for the families to try to discuss the development of the relationship between me, Sal, and Ash that had been thrust out into the open.

Carmen came out of the house first, dark curls bouncing as she jogged out and slipped into the back seat.

"I still haven't told her," Carmen said, catching her breath as she buckled herself. Later that morning, after Leo and Enzo found us in bed together, I had looked at my phone and found a text from Carmen saying she wouldn't tell until I was ready. Apparently, that hadn't changed, even though I was expecting it to.

"*You* haven't, but that doesn't mean someone else didn't," I murmured, watching Leo and Benny come out with Mom.

"I think everyone's keeping it quiet until you're ready," she said softly. I glanced through the rearview mirror and saw her green eyes looking into mine.

I wanted to ask about Enzo, but the doors opened and the three of them climbed in.

"Good morning my *mimmo*," my mom said, reaching over and patting my cheek after she got in the front seat.

"Morning, Mama," I said with as much of a smile as I could muster.

The ride was quiet as I drove to Blue Springs. Off to the hypnotist, we went. I was still unsure if this would work. For a long time, I thought this sort of thing was all a bunch of crap, that people couldn't really be hypnotized, but if Ma thought it would work, I figured we might as well give it a try.

Carmen was clutching at Leo, Benny's arm resting over her shoulder, like two guardian angels, except maybe more like guardian demons with the solemn looks on their faces.

"How long will this take?" Benny asked Ma as I pulled into a neighborhood. This wasn't a doctor's office or any sort of medical building, it was a house.

"As long as it takes," Mom said, pointing at a spot that was open in front of a house halfway down the block. The houses were spaced farther apart than most of the neighborhoods here. It was quiet, like we were plucked out of the loud city sounds and plopped into some little hidden village.

We all got out, following Mom until we got to the front door. The whole house was painted cool, calming colors; a little trickling pond was in the front yard. She knocked at the door, and I turned around to look at Carmen. She was nervous, that much was clear, her lip being worried by her teeth, fingers clenching and stretching in Leo's hand.

The door opened and a man appeared. He was short, his hair a wiry poof of white atop his head, but his eyes looked soft and kind as he smiled at us.

"Good morning, Maria! I haven't seen you in so long," he said, stepping aside and gesturing for everyone to enter.

"Good morning, Richard," she said, stepping in and the rest of us followed. As soon as the door closed, I looked around more closely. The interior was much like it was outside. Calming colors, nondescript, but there

was a nice scent to the home, nothing that could be considered triggering.

"These are my children," Mom said. "Adriano, Benito, and Carmen," she said, gesturing to each of us. "Leonardo is Carmen's husband."

We each shook his hand as she announced our names.

"Please come sit. I have a few things I want to go over with you before we begin."

The living room had plenty of seating, subtle lighting, and lots of space. It looked like this had once been a great room with space for the living and dining room, but he had furnished it for only this purpose.

Carmen and Leo sat on a small two-person sofa, while Benny and I perched in two of the armchairs available, Mom finding a place on the long couch.

"I am remembering correctly that it is Carmen I am working with today?" he asked, gaining nods from the rest of us. "Alright. Carmen, I am going to put you in a relaxed state. This works best if you are willing to follow my suggestions. Does that sound like something you can do?"

Her brows pushed together, shoulders coming up to shrug with uncertainty.

"I will try," she said quietly. This might have been the quietest my little sister had ever been, and perhaps even the most nervous. Richard smiled kindly.

"That's all we ask, my dear," he said, turning now to look at the rest of us. "This only works if I am the only person guiding her, which means the rest of you must remain silent. If you can't, I will ask you to leave before we begin."

"Is she going to be okay?" Benny asked, glancing at her and back at Richard.

"We are trying to resurface a memory. It has already happened. There is no fear of anything actually harming her, but it may not seem that way to her. If there are moments of distress from that memory, she will again have some panic. As long as I am allowed to guide her back to us without interference, there should be no problems," Richard said, and I found my knees bouncing as I thought of all the possibly disturbing things that could be present for Carmen in her mind. None of us had grown up with ideal circumstances, and I hoped this wouldn't do more harm to her than was necessary.

We all agreed, and Richard rearranged our seating so that Carmen was lying on the couch, Mama and Leo were sitting together on the sofa, and I was like a tree that fixed its roots, feeling trapped in the chair, but also unwilling to move and leave. I wasn't going to let my sister go through this without me. She already had to go through enough before.

Richard set a metronome on a steady rhythm, then sat in a chair he had placed only a few feet away from the couch.

"Carmen, as you hear my voice, you will follow my instructions," he said, his voice somehow softer and more soothing than it had been even minutes before. "You can feel the calm relaxation drifting from the top of your head down, slowly, slowly. It's cascading over you, covering you in a soft, warm blanket. Slowly, slowly. Your eyes are heavy, your breathing is even. Slowly, slowly. You can feel each part of your body getting relaxed, from your fingers—slowly, slowly—to your toes. Slowly, slowly."

I watched as my sister's body began to visibly relax with each calming prompt. He went on for what seemed like forever, until Carmen's eyes were fully closed, her breathing even.

"Carmen, you are eight years old," he said, glancing at the page of information Mom had given him in advance. "Are you eight?"

"Yes, it's my birthday. I had a princess party," she said. Her voice was off, strange and higher pitched than usual, and monotone.

"Good. Is your dad there?" he asked.

"Papa is talking to Salvatore, but I want him to play," she said, her voice a whine as her face turned to a bit of a frown. "Adrian is playing instead."

My heart fluttered a little. I remembered that party. Papa kept trying to excuse himself from Salvatore, but he just kept getting pulled back into whatever conversation they had been in. Carmen cried at bedtime when Papa left with Salvatore and couldn't at least read her a book before bed. I played at every party there was after because Papa wasn't there to play anymore.

"Carmen, do you remember when Papa would take you places, just you two?"

Carmen's eyebrows furrowed, her lips turning down.

"I'm not supposed to tell. Papa said it's just for us," she whispered.

"It is just for you. Just remember what it was you and Papa used to do," Richard prompted.

"Papa would drive. He would tell me special things," she whispered, her arms coming up to wrap around herself.

"What special things?"

"Papa said there were bad men, worse men than him. He said to keep a secret, he had to get my help because I was his special girl."

"How did you help your papa?"

"He took me to a place, lots of doors. It smelled weird, and it was quiet." Her fingers were ringing together now.

"What did you do there?"

"We went to more than one. He put something in a box and used my hand, my eyes, and a prick," she said. I glanced at Mom. She looked like she wanted to sob, but was somehow keeping it in.

"What does that mean, Carmen?" Richard asked.

"He said my fingers were special, like no one else's, my eyes and blood too. It would keep it protected when I touched the plate. The light shined in my eyes, and it hurt. But it didn't hurt as much as when he poked my finger."

I glanced at Leo. He looked pissed and mouthed "biometrics" to me.

That made sense.

"Okay, Carmen, that's good. Can you tell me what you saw at the places with lots of doors he took you to? What was outside at the first one?"

For a moment she lay there, shaking her head before her hand reached up as if she were trying to hold someone else's.

"Papa, can we get a milkshake after?" she asked.

"Where?" Richard asked.

"Winstead's, it's right there, across the street!" she exclaimed, exasperated.

"Not this time, Carmen. What do you see outside another one?"

"It's just the highway. I don't like how the cars sound. It's too loud," she said, putting her hands over her ears. Richard gently tugged on her sleeve, careful not to make contact with her arm, and she dropped her hands from her ears.

"Do you see a sign?"

"The one blue one says, 'E to St. Louis.'"

"Good," Richard said with a smile. "Any other stops with Papa?"

"I don't like this one," she said, her voice getting quiet and concerned.

"Why not?"

"This one is where the lady was," Carmen said, her arms crossing over her chest again. I leaned forward in the chair, feeling like this was going to be monumental somehow.

"What lady, Carmen?"

"Papa called her April, but he was mad," she said, her voice getting small.

"Why was he mad?"

"She wasn't supposed to be there. He said she followed us."

My heart was racing.

"What else happened?"

"He yelled at her, and we drove away. I could see the roller coasters," she whispered, tears streaming down her cheeks.

"Did he take you to another one, Carmen?" Richard asked, his voice still soothing and quiet, never changing.

"No. Papa and Mama fought and then he was gone!" Carmen cried, curling up and turning to the back of the couch, her body shaking as sobs wracked her. "My fault. They wouldn't have fought if I didn't go on special trips."

I almost stood up, going to her, but I saw Leo do that as well, making Richard fling out a hand to stop him, shaking his head.

"Carmen, when I count to three and snap my fingers, you are going to come back to us. You won't be eight anymore. One, slowly, slowly," her sobs began dying down. "Two, slowly, slowly." Her shaking mostly stopped. "Three." Richard snapped his fingers, and Carmen stiffened, still not moving from the position she was in, curled with her back to us.

"Carmen?" Leo asked, slowly standing and moving to kneel by the couch.

"Is it over?" I barely heard her whisper.

"It's over," he confirmed. She turned, immediately wrapping her arms around Leo, muffled cries the only thing we heard for several minutes.

CHAPTER 25

SAL

[Adrian: Meet us at the Moms.]

The text message came about two hours after Adrian had left to pick up everyone for Carmen's appointment. I had already headed there to go over possibilities with Enzo and Ingrid of the storage units Bernardo had, as well as see what they came up with as far as the man who took Bernardo's eyes.

[Me: Already on my way.]

Ash was in the car next to me. Her first tournament under April was tonight, and it was closer to get there from Lee's Summit than it would have been from the Kansas City house. Bonus that I didn't want Joey taking her, since Benny let us know what an idiot he had been when April approached Ash at the gym.

I hadn't seen my mom since I snapped at her the morning after Leo's wedding, and I hadn't spoken to her since I made it abundantly clear to Leo and Enzo what kind of relationship I was in with Ash and Adrian, so I wasn't sure what to expect for us when we pulled up to the house.

Ma was on the porch with Nora, watering the flowers when I got out, and she looked up at me, her smile faltering a little. It was the same thing that used to happen when my father came home after a long absence. A look I had hoped would never be directed at me, but it was.

"Ash!" Nora called happily, racing down the stairs and jumping into Ash's arms.

"Hey, Nora! Man, that jump was awesome! Have you been practicing?" Ash asked the little girl as she settled her on her hip. Nora kept babbling, talking about how she had been working on her skills on the playground, while I went up to the porch.

"Hello, Mama," I said, stopping in front of her and kissing her cheek.

"Mio figlio," she whispered, wrapping her arms around my neck and holding me tight.

When we parted, Ash and Nora were finally on the porch and I went inside, unsure of what my mother knew, but figuring one look at Enzo would tell me. He immediately threw his hands up, shaking his head as if to say he didn't tell.

"Show me what you have," I murmured, giving him a skeptical glance as I moved around to stand behind him to see what they had been working on.

"Dr. O'Neill predominantly works in Chicago. On Stately Enterprises' payroll for the last thirty years," Enzo said, pointing to the blown-up still frame from Bernardo's death footage of the man who had pulled out his eyes. "Also happens to be an investor in April Smith's little tournaments, since his name is all over her bank account information."

"What about her?" I asked, pointing to April's photo.

"You know this organized crime shit is so incestuous, right?" Ingrid asked, rubbing her hands over her face. "I looked into the bank accounts, not that it's accurate," she grumbled, turning her laptop so I could see.

"Seventeen years ago, there were some interesting things on Bernardo's solo account. Six recurring payments to various storage units that are still being paid from the account, a large payment from this organization," Ingrid said, pointing to a name that I had definitely seen before. It was one of the companies that Morelli's money was laundered through. Moreland Markets, an umbrella for his outward-facing company, Nova Tech. "And of course, a payment to none other than April Smith."

"Any old footage of Bernardo at those units?"

"I got footage on four, but we'll see what Carmen came up with in this session," Enzo said.

"So he paid April?" I mused to myself, turning to pace a little.

"Maybe it wasn't an affair?" Ingrid suggested, to which Ash snorted as she walked from the porch, having gotten Nora back to watering plants with my mom.

"There's plenty of men who pay off their mistresses."

I looked at her, my brow raising.

"Marek is married. I saw plenty of transactions with his various lovers. Some happened right after I won him money from my fights. Like he was hanging on my winnings to keep his little secrets at bay," she said with a disgusted look on her face.

"Benny and Carmen were pretty convinced Bernardo hadn't really cheated on Maria," Enzo said, though his face looked grim.

"It really doesn't matter now," I said, wondering about all Bernardo's mysterious activity.

What was this secret that Bernardo held that O'Shea would have still been pursuing seventeen years after his death? It was baffling, but it had to mean it was incredibly important or life-altering, whatever it was.

"They're here!" squealed Nora from the front porch, and the energy in the room went from contemplative to anxious anticipation.

I wanted to burst out of the house and see them. I wanted to look at Adrian's face and know how he was feeling, but I waited where I stood, rooting myself to the spot as we heard them be greeted by my mom and Nora, then begin coming into the house.

"Is she okay?" Ash asked as Ingrid stood up, coming around the table.

I turned, Leo was settling Carmen on the couch, while Benny and Adrian sat on either side of her.

"Three locations. He took her to three different storage places," Adrian said, looking up and finding my eyes first. Confusion and fear were hiding in those blue orbs. Nothing I hadn't seen before, but I knew Adrian took Carmen's well-being personally. Oldest son and youngest daughter. They were the opposite and the same.

"Enzo, look up storage places that had a Winstead's near them seventeen years ago, another close to I-70 east to St. Louis, and anything around Worlds of Fun," Leo said, without looking away from his wife.

Winstead's was a local burger chain that had dwindled down to its original location, but the distinctly shaped buildings were still scattered all over the metro area, and Worlds of Fun was our local amusement park up in northern Kansas City.

"See if any match with the ones he was paying for," I said, gaining a "you think I don't know that?" look from my younger brother.

"Got it," Enzo said, his hands immediately moving over the keys of the laptop in front of him.

"What now?" Benny asked, and I caught Adrian and me running our hands through our hair simultaneously.

"Now I go to a tournament, and we find out what April Smith has to do with all of this," Ash said, and everyone's eyes shot to her.

ASH

"What the fuck? No!" Carmen said, shooting up off the couch and nearly knocking Leo over.

"It's already set. I need to be leaving in ten minutes to make it there," I said, glancing at the large clock on the wall over the fireplace.

"Text me when you have the addresses," Sal said to Enzo, pulling his keys from his pocket.

"I will," Enzo murmured, brows furrowing as he dug into research.

"I'm going," Carmen said, standing immediately.

"No! You just got hypnotized and look like you've been traumatized. You are *not* going anywhere, least of all to a freaking fighting tournament," Benny said, trying to push her back down by the shoulder.

"Shut it, Benny! We'll get some food on the way, and I'll be fine," Carmen insisted, shoving his hand from her shoulder and pushing past Leo.

"Adrian, help me," Benny said, looking at his brother as if that would make Carmen change her mind.

"I'm not arguing this one. She wants to go. Maybe we all should," Adrian said, shrugging.

I was a little shocked at that. The idea of all of them coming with, watching me fight, was a little daunting. But Adrian agreeing that Carmen should come along seemed like it was against his natural inclination. He was usually so against putting her in danger.

"What do you mean?" Benny asked, clearly fuming.

"I mean, if we get the information we need, this is the closure we all need. Not just me and Sal. Carmen is who they're after. If she wants to come with us tonight, then she should come," Adrian said, and it made so much sense. Closure.

They all needed it. The mystery surrounding all of this has been like a parasite, sucking the life from all of them for nearly a year. No one in my life had ever supported me in what I wanted to do like Adrian was supporting his siblings and the Lupos in all of this. No one until Sal and Adrian, that is.

"Enzo and I will stay. We'll narrow it down," Ingrid said, pulling Carmen into a hug and then coming around to me and doing the same.

"I guess I'll be there to put your arm back in place if you pop it out again," Benny said, a little defeated, but clearly conceding his older brother's point.

"What? I don't want to miss that!" Enzo said, looking up at me from the screen with a wide grin.

"Next time," I said, moving toward the front door.

I stepped out to the porch before anyone else. Maria had taken Nora to the bushes toward the sidewalk, and Liliana was standing just at the bottom of the steps. I stepped down and stopped beside her, looking out at the other two as she was.

I wasn't sure how much the moms knew about the new developments in my relationship with their oldest sons. Last I heard, they were both very confused, but what Enzo had said about them thinking Sal and

Adrian had been secretly together for years made me think that *maybe* these women wouldn't take the news too harshly.

"My son may have been brought up by his father for this life, but he was raised to be a good person by me," Liliana said quietly after a moment.

"He is a good person," I said to her, turning to look at her face, which was clearly worried.

"He and Adrian…" Her voice trailed off, hesitantly, her eyes snapping to look at me for a moment, before returning to Maria and Nora.

"Sal and Adrian both are good to me," I said delicately. Slowly she turned her gaze to me, her eyes narrowing as her brain seemed to try to work it out.

"I wondered for a long time if either of them would find a good woman," she said, and my heart hammered, unsure of what she would say next. "They found you?"

The fact that she said "they" as if it was already some sort of known was a relief. Maybe it wasn't completely clear to her the situation between the three of us, but something about how the two of them were together had already planted some seed within her. I nodded.

"Maria wondered if they would just be together. If they would ever just take that step. I think they were missing a piece of the puzzle."

Her hand came out, grabbing my arm tenderly just as Sal and Adrian came out of the house and stopped on the porch. Both looked a little fearful, clearly concerned about what Liliana was saying to me.

"Make sure nothing happens to your Ash, boys," Liliana said, glancing back at them, before she released me, stepping through the yard to join Maria and Nora.

CHAPTER 26

ASH

There wasn't enough time to process what Liliana had said to me fully, before we all piled between Adrian's and Sal's cars, driving up north where the fights were being held, per the text message I got from April's number.

I had already dressed in the clothes for my fight, braiding my hair down tightly on my head as the car zoomed down the highway.

"We just need to get her alone, so you don't have to win all of them," Sal said as he glanced in the rearview mirror at me.

"Fuck that. You know she wants to win it all," Carmen said beside me as she prepped the tape for my fingers. I gave him a smirk, nodding in agreement with Carmen as he continued to drive.

"What did Mom say to you?" Sal asked once Carmen's laughs of victory died down.

"She said I was the missing piece of your and Adrian's puzzle," I said, letting my face show the surprise I still felt about that. His eyebrows rose in shock and Leo actually turned around in the front seat to look at me.

"She did?" Leo asked.

"Has it not been obvious to you for years, Leo?" Carmen asked, looking at her husband like he was an idiot.

"What's been obvious?" he asked, exasperated.

"I'll give you a pass since you were overseas for most of it, but Sal and Adrian have been pining over Ash, yes; but they love each other. No action, since they were both wound so tight you could have launched a Roman candle, but that didn't mean they hadn't thought about it, wanted it," Carmen said, starting to hand over pieces of tape to me now that I had finished my braids. Now that Carmen said it, it was far more obvious. I had been blinded by my own connection to the two of them, but it was pretty clear the way they felt about each other, that they also wanted one another for a long time.

"I'm sorry… what?" Sal asked, his fingers tightening on the steering wheel.

"Sal, I knew. I just didn't call you two out for it," Carmen said with a grin as he glanced back at her, eyes looking like he wanted to be enraged, but he was just flabbergasted instead.

We pulled up to the large industrial barn just off the highway with nothing but a gas station and farmland surrounding it. Cars were already parked, the famil- iar-looking bouncers that were usually at Cal's fights were waiting at the back entrance, and I got out of the car, taking a deep breath of the country air as I pre- pared to walk over there.

"Where are you going?" Adrian asked as he got out of his car parked beside Sal's.

"Inside?" I said, confused. That's why we had come after all. But he took two steps, grabbing me by the waist and ducking his head to kiss me. The breath seemed to spill from my lungs with the suddenness, but I quickly wrapped my arms around his shoulders, kissing him back. It only lasted a moment though, before Sal took his place, soft plush lips moving against mine for a moment, before he parted from me, and I found myself wrapped in both of them, pressed against Sal's car.

"Don't push it, Ash. If you feel like you will get hurt, forfeit," Sal said.

But Adrian, much more a fighter like me, raised an eyebrow at him and then whispered, "Not *too* hurt."

They released me, and I walked alone toward the back doors, inside, and through the short hallway to the locker area. Many of the same faces from a few weeks ago were there, and Hurricane herself stood up when I came into the room.

"I didn't think you'd come back," she said, her voice sounding more like she had been concerned for me since our last fight. I was a little surprised but could admit to myself that she had grown on me too.

"Afraid I might beat you?" I asked with a smirk. She said nothing but watched me as I went to the tournament lineup posted on the wall. I was matched up with Didi, like I had been for the first fight since I'd come back to this, and I knew I'd be able to get us a solid few hours to have someone approach her before I lost.

The Tank was in attendance, looking at me now. I was surprised he was here without Sal and Adrian knowing. In fact, Elio wasn't in here with him as he usually was, which was unusual. Seeing me, he said with the look in his eyes alone that he hoped Sal and Adrian wouldn't find out. I couldn't help the sympathetic expression I gave him as I shook my head, telling him they were here.

Thirty minutes passed, several more fighters entered, and the door opened and slammed, alerting me to the person I came here to corner, even if I wasn't going to be the one doing the actual cornering.

"Ladies and gentlemen! So glad to have you here this evening. Some familiar faces, some new ones. Thank goodness Cal keeps letting me in on his fights. I'm so very pleased to be organizing this for our guests waiting out there. As it has been with the last few, it's tournament style. I'm happy to see so many of you are enjoying this as much as I am," April said with a grin, eyes scanning over the room until they landed on me.

"Five minutes until the first fight," she said, before turning around and leaving the room.

I knew mine wasn't first, but I still felt nervous, more nervous than I had been for a very long time. It struck me then, as the images of the people I cared about flashed through my mind, the knowledge that many of them were right out there in the audience, watching, waiting, needing me to pull through to make this mission successful, that I was scared because I had something more to lose than myself this time around.

And it wasn't just in these past few days that I had these people.

The LaMartinas and Lupos had been my people, my "tribe," as Rory and Daph said, for the last four years. It was my fault it hadn't been more until recently. My distrust of others, my hyper-independence made me keep them all at arm's length.

Like a shock ran through my body, I felt a strange sense of purpose. They were counting on me, and I could count on them. I had never been more excited to get out in that ring than I was now.

SAL

We watched Ash walk away and into the building, and I wanted nothing more than to feel the comfort of Adrian's hand in mine, but I still wasn't completely sure about that, with most of our siblings standing behind us.

"You need to change," Carmen said, grabbing a hoodie out of Adrian's back seat and throwing it at me.

"Why?" I asked, holding it up to find it was actually *my* Kansas City Chiefs sweatshirt that had been missing for about two years now. I shot Adrian a glare, to which he merely tried to hide his smile and look away.

"Because you look like … you," Carmen said, gesturing to me. I was wearing my usual suit.

"Is that a problem?" I asked, still confused.

"You look like you could either be a mob boss—"

"Which he is," Benny interjected.

"Or an FBI agent," Carmen finished, glaring at Benny. "And *you* look like a frat boy. Untuck your shirt," she snapped at him. He did, his polo shirt was tucked into slim-fit gray pants and a black belt. He'd fit right in at the country club.

"Jesus," he hissed under his breath, untucking his shirt. I pulled the shirt jacket off and unbuttoned my dress shirt, leaving them in the back seat of the car.

"What about you?" Benny asked Carmen. She was in yoga pants and had a sweatshirt on. It was all black.

"I look like I can fit in most situations. Thankfully, an illegal fight tournament where we don't want to stand out, this is probably just fine," she said with a smug little smile.

She had a point. I wasn't here to be Sal Lupo, I was here to be unnoticed and snag an opportunity to corner April Smith.

"Two at a time. Benny and Carmen, Adrian and Leo, I'll go alone," I said as we turned to go around the parking area toward the front.

"Benny, you have cash?" Leo asked, and I realized that of all of us, Benny was definitely the one who carried the least cash, given he had a legitimate job for so many years.

"I've got him," Carmen said, pulling up her sweat-shirt to reveal not only a small flat wallet secured at her waist, but also a tiny, concealed gun.

Leo seemed pleased seeing the gun as she pulled out a good amount of cash and palmed it before grabbing Benny's arm and leading the way to the entrance.

"She seems to have shaken it off," Adrian said to Leo as they slowed in front of me to let a few more people get between them. Carmen did seem to have rallied rather quickly, but I saw the signs. Like all of us, she could compartmentalize things for a little while to do what needed to be done.

"She's good at action. If there's something she can help or fix, she can put her own things away for a little while," Leo said, a little sadness in his tone as he watched her disappear into the entrance of the barn. At least they had each other as an anchor. They both needed it.

"You'll be there later," Adrian said, putting an arm over my little brother's shoulder.

"I will," Leo said.

The two of them moved forward, and I hung back, ruffling my hair a little, and looking over everyone who was piling in. A dark sedan pulled up, and the sea of people entering parted just after Leo and Adrian stepped inside. The back door of the sedan opened and two people who I most definitely didn't want to see got out.

Freddy and Marek.

My lip curled involuntarily as I watched them step through the entrance, and I found my feet had a mind of their own, since a pit formed in my stomach.

Was this a trap?

Suddenly I wasn't so sure.

I pulled out my phone after I handed over a wad of cash far larger than the sum the man at the entrance asked for.

[Me: You got eyes on Carmen? Freddy and Marek are here.]

[Leo: 4:00.]

[Adrian: I see them.]

I looked up, hoping to see the people I cared about in this room, but I was too close to the entrance still, caught in the crush of the crowd. I pushed through, heading to the four o'clock spot by the ring where Leo said Carmen and Benny were, and saw them. Relief at seeing half of my people ran through me, enough that I found a spot on the wall, leaning against it with eyes still on them.

It smelled like barn animals, waste, and wet earth, but soon it would reek with the scent of human bodies, blood, and cigarettes, like it always did.

[Adrian: I see you.]

The text came through just as admission seemed to be cut off. I was glad he could see me. At least Leo and Adrian had eyes on everyone. I just had Benny and

Carmen in my sights still. And then, of course, my eyes fell on the loft on the other side of the structure from me.

Up high above everyone else was the VIP. Funny that I hadn't received an invite from April this time around. It was clear where her alliances were, given the sheer amount of Irish up there in the loft.

Doors to my right and a few yards away opened, and the blonde woman in question appeared. Head held high, she walked to the ring, completely put together, not a hair out of place, as she stepped up, taking the proffered mic from the ref, and waving at the now cheering crowd.

"Good evening! We have quite a show for you tonight. Some of you remember that tiny blue-haired girl that made such a splash a few weeks ago—" The cheer was overwhelming, cutting off her speech. "We have her back tonight with us, and it's going to be a glorious tournament. Don't forget to place your bets and let the fighting begin!"

She stepped off the ring, and my eyes followed her, instead of watching whoever was coming from the back. She slipped through the crowd, two guards clearly trailing her movements, but not very close by. She finally stopped at a tall table that seemed to have been saved for her. Interesting that she wasn't going up to VIP, but it worked in our favor. We could keep eyes on her and hopefully find an opportunity to get her away from the crowded room without others noticing.

The first fighters were announced, and I barely paid attention as they began. There were no rounds, one fight between the two to see who would move on. The crowd cheered, Carmen and Benny stood watching, and I felt eyes on me from the bar.

Finally, I spotted Adrian, his gaze like an invisible tether, holding me in place for a moment as we locked eyes across the smokey room. He would have preferred to take Ash's place and fight tonight to get this done, but he didn't have an invitation. His name was too known, too associated with me to take her place here. There was fear in those eyes, and if I could have, I'd have been right there beside him, giving us both the comfort we needed right now, knowing our girl was going to be in that ring soon enough.

The bell dinged, first fighters done, with the man who won panting as the ref held up his arm, blood soaking his face from the smashed nose he'd received. His opponent was on the ground, out cold and being dragged off by bouncers.

I almost knew before it was announced who was going to be fighting next. My heart rate spiked, my eyes finding Adrian's again through the crowd, and I felt it in my bones as the door to my right opened again. Walking behind a girl with a buzzed head was our Ash. Her braids were now threaded through her hair on top of her head, a number painted in red on her bare stomach and back, and she walked with confidence to the ring.

She found me as she passed by, a hint of tension there. I was trapped in her gaze, watching her move through the crowd and step up into the ring as she was announced. The crowd went wild, everyone screaming for her, but the adoration or hatred from the audience didn't seem to faze her. She looked only at her opponent, gray eyes assessing and calculating every little nuance of the other woman before the bell dinged.

Ash was good. This wasn't a fair fight. Sure, she still had healing to do in her ribs, but she moved like she didn't know pain. It was quick. Too fast for a good show, but she wasn't trying to put on a show, she was trying to win. With an easy swipe of her leg, the other woman went down, and Ash's fist was immediately on her face, knocking her out cold with one decisive punch.

"Winner!" the ref called, making the crowd scream with praise as he held up Ash's arm.

I wasn't sure how many were in these first rounds of fights, but I needed to stay focused, to see if there was a way to get April alone, even for a brief time. The first round of the tournament fights continued, my focus flittering between April, Adrian, and where Benny and Carmen stood. But when The Tank was called for a fight, my eyes darted to the ring, looking to see that Vallo was, in fact, climbing in the ring, his menacing form towering over the man who would be his opponent.

My fists clenched at my side, the betrayal like a hot poker. I shouldn't have been surprised, Vallo lived for the fight, and these appeared to be quite lucrative, but something about anyone getting their hands on what was *mine* was a greater insult than many things. I watched his fight, which was easy for him, nearly insignificant in how few hits it took to put the other man down. But I should have been watching the enemies in the room, because when I looked out at the crowd, scanning to get to April, I saw the familiar sleazy head of Marek Lewandowski, moving with strange purpose toward the very spot where Carmen and Benny stood.

[Leo: Carmen, move!]

Came a text message to the group chat. She didn't seem to see it, but Benny did, grabbing Carmen's arm and pulling her back away from the side of the ring where they had been standing, until they were pressed into the shadows near me.

Benny said something to Carmen, and she gave him a seething look before she glanced over and noticed me only a few feet away from them.

[Leo: April's moving.]

I looked over at the table where April had been seated while the first round was going on. She was no longer there, her blonde head now pushing through the crush of people ready for the next rounds now that Vallo had closed out the first rounds with a bang.

I thought April would be going to the ring to make another announcement, but no, she was heading to the back. My heart hammered in my chest. This might have been the opportunity I needed. If it weren't for her guards, I would have just slipped in behind her and dragged her somewhere, but as it was, they passed me by, the door snapping closed behind them.

[Adrian: Round 2 is starting soon. I don't want Ash fighting much longer.]

I didn't either.

"First fighting round two, number 42 and number 33," the ref said into the mic, as the doors opened once again. April didn't come out, but Ash and the winner from the first fight did.

I didn't want her fighting him. His swollen taped nose did nothing to diminish his obvious advantage over her as far as bulk. He was built like Adrian and as tall as Leo, the combination of which made Ash look like a matchstick rivaling an inferno.

The crowd went insane, bloodlust clear in their screams as they saw the obvious imbalance between our Ash and this brute. She didn't look at me this time, going up the steps and into the ring, head held high.

"This is fucking bullshit," Carmen said, though I could only barely hear her over the screams and jeers from the people around us.

I found Adrian again, but this time he was pushing through the crowd, Leo on his heels, and headed to me. The bell dinged, and I looked up in horror as Ash and the man with a 42 on his chest started circling each other.

"Oh my god, that's Mickey," Carmen said beside me.

Almost a year had passed since Carmen had been in the clutches of Freddy O'Shea, and apparently one of his cronies was this fighter. And then I realized this was the *kid* I had spared just a month ago. Clearly, the over-sized suit and innocent look in his eyes as he had been sprawled on the ground with his injury had masked his body enough that I hadn't seen him as a threat, but that boyish look had been diminished with the way his head had been buzzed, and now the blood and tape on his face.

I watched him as he circled with Ash, and I noticed the obvious scars on his back. Beatings and torture were the only things that could have caused those marks. Either he was abused by his parents or O'Shea didn't just save the torture for his victims, he did it to his soldiers too.

"He was a scrawny thing last time I saw him," Carmen continued, now having slid closer to me along the wall. That was nearly a year ago; plenty of time for him to have bulked up to be the fighter he was. Maybe the warning I sent back with him a month previous took him away from the guard. At least I felt like I could maybe save him now, if nothing else, potentially get him away from O'Shea.

Adrian got to me as Mickey took his first swipe at Ash. She ducked it easily, moving under his arm and delivering a swift blow to his ribs, before moving out of arm's reach. My hand reached up to grab Adrian's arm, but his hand caught mine, our fingers threading together, squeezing as we watched.

Mickey recovered from the blow she landed, turning to face her yet again. He may have been bulky in comparison to her, but I could tell he was light on his feet. He bounced back and forth, moving quickly around her, but she seemed unperturbed, watching and adjusting from his movements with expert eyes. This was what she did, what she trained people for.

"Oh, look at that," Carmen said, now safely encapsulated within Leo's arms. "He's weak on that left side. His leg and arm."

I couldn't see what Carmen was seeing, but clearly Ash did. She waited for the perfect moment, when he went down on the left leg alone as he jumped from foot to foot. Her leg shot out quick, hooking around his knee. Her whole body seemed to twist around in midair as she torqued the joint, an unmistakable snapping sound resounding through the other noise, followed by a gut-wrenching scream.

Like time stood still, I was in awe as she swiftly climbed back to her feet, kneeling over him and ready to start punching, before the "tap, tap," of his heavy hand on the mat signaled his forfeit.

CHAPTER 27
ADRIAN

"During the next fight," Sal whispered in my ear, giving my hand a quick squeeze as we watched Ash walk past us. The man she was fighting hadn't even landed a hit on her. Her eyes sparkled with her victory as they looked into mine.

Just like the first round, the next round of fighters came out only a few minutes later, the doors opening and closing and the new set walking up to their fate.

"We'll go when the action starts. Us three. Benny and Carmen will get the cars ready," Leo said, leaning closer to Sal.

It didn't take long, one of the fighters almost immediately striking out and landing a blow to the other. I turned, slipping along the wall as people cheered and pushed farther toward the center of the room, pulling Sal behind me. As I opened the door to the back area, I glanced and saw Carmen and Benny making their way to the entrance.

I hoped she wasn't noticed. I hoped my sister would get out of there without a problem, but if there was one, I hoped she and Benny took care of it. Fuck the Hippocratic Oath. Benny would put down anyone who tried to take Carmen.

The door opened, and as expected, there were men stationed there to keep people out. Two of which were low-level soldiers of ours. There was enough hesitation and realization there in their eyes; they knew they'd fucked up. The other two immediately lashed out. My elbow went into one of their noses before our soldiers figured out which side they'd rather be on, taking over and subduing the other guards before Sal or Leo even had to raise a hand.

"April Smith," Sal said once one of them had successfully choked out his fellow guard.

"Across from the fighters," he said. "Are you—"

"Vinny and Nate, right?" I asked, glancing as Sal and Leo kept moving down the hall without me. When I looked back, he was nodding, worried eyes clear on his face as he watched me.

"We may be having a talk about loyalty. Or maybe a demonstration, depending on how you behave the rest of this night," I said, tapping my temple with the gun I had pulled from the back of my jeans.

"Yes, Sir," they both said, before I turned, racing down the hall to where I saw Leo and Sal disappear. The clear "pop pop" of a silenced gun going off before I reached the door.

April's two guards were on the ground with holes in their heads, Leo's gun drawn and now pointing at April, who was watching everything from a crude and hastily set up monitoring station.

"To what do I owe this pleasure?" she asked. She was clearly trying to remain calm, though the twitch in her eyebrow gave another story about how she was feeling. There was nothing between us and killing her now.

"Bernardo LaMartina," I said, my lips involuntarily curling as I spoke my father's name.

"What about him?" She was trying to play for ignorance, but the embers of recognition were burning in her eyes. She knew exactly who my father was.

"You told Colin O'Shea something. It led to my father's death. I want to know what it was," I said, stepping closer, my gun at her neck. She swallowed. Those eyes went from attempting to remain cool and collected to now filling with fearful tears.

"I partnered with Bernardo for bigger fights. He invited Morelli to one," she started, glancing at my arm and then at my face, before looking toward the hall, as if that would help her. "I heard something. That Bernardo had some information, some evidence. Morelli was instructing him to get rid of it."

"But he didn't get rid of it?" Sal asked.

"I had eyes on him. Information about Morelli would just be too hard to pass up. Joel needed to get a better position. I had the means to do that for him," she murmured, her face seeming to flash with a bit of anger. "Didn't do me much good though. My brother is dead because of you."

"I don't care about what your brother did or didn't do. I wanted to know what you found," I demanded, pressing the gun harder against the skin in her neck, right where her jugular sat, beating with fear.

"I caught him at a storage place. He was hiding it there," she whispered, whole body shaking now.

"And you told O'Shea," Sal said, nodding.

"What do you think was so special about this information?" I asked, even though the question that burned on my tongue was not anything to do with what my father hid.

"Morelli was angry. He didn't want that information out. Said it would 'ruin him and the whole of the Italian power in the country,'" she whispered hoarsely, my gun pressing too hard on her neck now for normal speech.

My phone buzzed in my pocket with an incoming text, but I couldn't be bothered. Anything other than this wasn't as important. Not now.

"Why didn't you just ask my father what it was?" I asked, thinking back to the tape of her kicking his dead body, to the coldness in my mother's eyes when she told us this woman was his lover. A woman who basically spit on his body when he died, when my mother sacrificed so much to be with him.

April's eyebrows furrowed as she looked up at me, confusion written all over her face.

"What makes you think I could have just asked him?" she whispered.

"Weren't you sleeping with him?" Sal asked from behind me as he slipped his hand on my shoulder. Her brows shot up in surprise, a faint nervous smile sliding over her lips.

"I tried, but no one could tempt him from Maria."

The world seemed to right itself again, the pressure of my finger on the trigger loosening with my grip. I stepped back from her, my breathing slowing and the sounds around me coming back as if the blood wasn't pulsing in my ears anymore.

"Enzo texted us," Leo said quietly, but urgently.

"I'll get Ash," Sal said, his hand leaving me, but my shoulder still tingled as if it were still there.

"You're not going to kill me?" she asked, clear surprise taking over her features as I backed up from the room after snagging her phone, which was on the desk in front of her.

"We don't kill women if we can help it," I said as I took one step into the hall. I gestured at Vinny and Nate, who came to mine and Leo's side in an instant.

"You hold this door until the next fight starts, then you leave. Anyone else here that's ours, you take them with you," I ordered them, waiting until they stepped in front of the room before I turned away from April and let my hand drop.

The other door opened a moment later, Sal and Ash coming out of the room with haste.

"We need to go now," Sal said, pulling Ash behind him and taking out his phone.

"Benny, you two moved the cars?" he asked when Benny picked up his call.

"Right out back," I heard Benny say as we raced down the short hall to the back door. The bouncers stationed outside looked bewildered when the four of us burst through, but we didn't give them time to comprehend what we were doing, because the two SUVs we came in were just a hundred feet away. Carmen in the first car and Benny in the second, we piled in them quickly.

Ash and Sal were in Benny's car, and Leo and I were in Carmen's, racing out of this gravel parking area, rocks and dirt flying until we hit the main road once more.

"Enzo and Ingrid figured out the locations. They sent them," Leo said to me as we got on the highway and he immediately started a three-way call between us, the other car, and Enzo.

"How were the fights?" Enzo asked as we headed back toward Kansas City. "Does Ash still have an arm?"

"Where are we going first?" Carmen asked, her voice snapping as she weaved in and out of traffic.

"First one is in Kansas. Shawnee Mission Parkway. There's a storage space not far from where the Winstead's used to be. Barely missed being bulldozed when they built the Ikea," Enzo said with a chuckle.

"Where that IHOP used to be?" Leo asked, piecing it together.

"Yeah. There are warehouses and storage spots all behind where the Ikea is," Ingrid said, clearly the one looking at the map. She proceeded to give an actual address, which helped so Leo could pull it up in GPS, and I took the opportunity as we flew down the highway to toss April's phone out the window.

"Benny, Carmen, she wasn't sleeping with Dad," I said when the chaos seemed to die down a little now that we had about fifteen minutes longer on the highway to go.

"What?" Carmen asked, briefly glancing at me in the back seat, before her eyes went back to the road. It was long enough for me to see the pained look on her face.

"She wasn't?" Benny asked over the speaker.

"She said, 'no one could tempt him from Maria,'" Leo quoted, grinning at her from the front seat and pressing his hand on her thigh.

"Maria, did you hear?" Enzo asked from the line. For some reason, it hadn't occured to me that my mom would be around to hear this, though Enzo and Ingrid had been set up at the moms' house when we left.

"She said that?" my mom's quiet voice asked from a bit of a distance. I could hear the wobble of emotion in her voice, imagine the way her eyes were filling with tears.

"I knew he wouldn't have done that to you, Ma," Benny said. I couldn't agree more. If there was one thing I had been certain of all these years, up until she said that to us, it was that our dad loved our mom.

"This exit, Carmen," Leo said, and we were turning off the highway to Shawnee Mission Parkway, the bold blue and yellow sign of Ikea nearly as blinding as the car dealerships' lights there.

Carmen turned the car, and we made it down the winding road, passing warehouses and service vehicle lots, until we pulled up to an old-style storage place. Carmen parked the car outside the chain-link fence closing it off from the rest of the world via a keypad, her hands shaking as she took them off the wheel.

"This is the one, huh?" I asked her, but I already knew it was, even before she nodded slowly.

"How are we going to get past this gate?" came Benny's voice as he pulled his car up next to ours.

"Leo," was all Sal said, as Leo leaned over, kissing Carmen on the head, and climbing out of the car.

"Carmen in the back seat," I said as I got out too, moving to the driver's door.

"I'm okay," she said, but she was shaking like she had been after the hypnotist.

"I'm going to drive now," was all I said, bringing her into my arms and hugging her tight.

"All this for me," she whispered in my chest.

"All this because Papa couldn't let something go. I guess we'll find out why," I assured her. She squeezed me tight for a moment, sniffled, and then pulled away, climbing into the back seat of the car. I climbed in the front, adjusting the seat as Leo made quick work of the keypad.

"Enzo, you scrubbing this footage?" I asked as the gate opened and Leo began climbing into the car beside me.

"Already gone," Enzo said over the speaker.

Our cars rolled through the now open gate; my fingers tightly curled around the steering wheel as I drove past unit after unit.

"Number 323," Enzo said as I turned a corner and headed down to the third row. Every unit looked the same. There wasn't anything to indicate that something strange or sinister was lurking behind these doors for us.

I pulled the car up to the unit in question, and we all got out.

"Leo, you're up again," Sal said, gesturing to the padlock keeping the unit closed. It only took three minutes for Leo to pick the lock, and then we pushed the garage door up. The first step in discovering my father's secret was done.

CHAPTER 28

ASH

I stood next to Sal, Carmen slowly approaching from the back of the other car to stop beside me. It was dark, no automatic light to fill the void of the storage space in Bernardo LaMartina's name. Leo pulled a flashlight from the pocket of his jacket and shined it around the space.

There were only a few things stored here. A cedar chest sat pushed against one wall, a closed oak armoire was in the far corner, a metal footlocker sat beside it, and a heavy metal contraption stood in the very farthest back, tucked behind a garment rack that was filled with clothes of some kind.

Leo, Adrian, and Benny all stepped into the space, Sal following shortly behind them, but Carmen seemed hesitant to go through.

"I remember this place," she whispered, her shoulders hunching as her eyes cast over the silhouetted figures of the others walking through.

"We're all here with you, Carmen," I said, reaching out my hand to her. It was still taped and a little bloody, but she took it without pause, squeezing tightly before she walked forward to join the others.

I felt oddly out of place, like I didn't belong here. This was for *them* to discover, and I just happened to be along for the ride. But with each moment I stood in the storage unit with them, Carmen clutching my hand, bringing me closer, the glances Adrian kept giving me, like he was reassuring himself I was there, and the little touches Sal gave as he looked around and passed me that let me know he was soothing me just as much as himself. They were telling me I was one of them. I was part of this. I was important.

"What is all this?" Benny asked, stepping up to the cedar chest and casting it in his cell phone's screen light.

"Not what we came here for," Adrian said as he moved over to the back corner.

Benny popped the chest open, revealing at first a few quilts, but as he lifted them, it was filled with weapons.

"Guns and knives," Benny said, glancing up to watch Adrian as he pushed the garment rack out of the way, bags of clothes swaying.

"Not surprised. I keep all sorts of things like that in mine," Sal said with a shrug.

"You have a storage unit?" Benny asked, and everyone chuckled darkly.

"Of course we do," Adrian said, touching a panel on the metal thing that had been hiding, albeit poorly, since Adrian found it right away. The panel popped up when Adrian pushed it, coming to life with his touch. "Carmen," he said, glancing up to look at her.

She walked back to the device, dragging me along with her. We looked down at the panel. There was a digital grid that had illuminated when it popped up. No instructions were on there, but it seemed like Carmen knew exactly what she was supposed to do, holding her hand up shakily and looking at Adrian, who nodded, before she pressed it to the panel.

A bar of light ran up and down her hand as soon as she put it on there, then an electronic whirling, before a black bar popped up beside the panel. Adrian grabbed it, turning it and a clunk resounded, then the top opened. He reached inside, pulling out a flash drive.

"A flash drive," Benny said, his voice mildly disappointed.

"I'm not surprised," Enzo said over Leo's speaker.

"Why?" Sal asked as he gestured for us to move back to the cars.

"Three locations. Whatever information Bernardo was keeping hidden, he went to great lengths. Using his daughter instead of himself, putting it in all these different locations. It's probably encrypted too," Ingrid said.

"It might take a while to get anything off of them," Enzo grumbled.

"Call Kia," Leo said as we all climbed back into the cars and Benny closed the garage door to the unit. There were plenty of other mysteries in that unit, I could tell, but we weren't here for that now. The LaMartinas all looked at the closed door like it wouldn't be the last time they would come there.

"Leo, I don't want to bring Kia back into this," Enzo said, now sounding irritable.

I remembered Kia from months ago when Carmen was taken. She came to Lee's Summit, and worked out in the gym a few times while she stayed. She was also at the wedding, though she stayed to herself and slipped out while Adrian and Sal were gone talking to people for over an hour. She and I had briefly commiserated about being on the outside of their strange little family bubble after having gotten away from one of the older aunts who had made comments about my hair color and how her strapless dress showed off too many tat-toos. She was one of Leo's military friends, though I didn't know much more about her.

"Three heads are better than two. She might be close and can come help us," Sal said, a little smirk on his face as he paused at the driver's side of the other car. He was clearly pleased at Enzo's distress.

"I'll call her," Ingrid said. I could practically hear her eyes rolling and I couldn't help my own smile at Enzo's expense.

"Next location?" Adrian asked as soon as we were all in the cars once more.

"Thirteenth and Prospect. Right next to I-70 East to St. Louis," Enzo said.

"We're going to see the whole city by the end of this," Carmen said, though her fingers were still laced in mine in the back seat, little shakes running through her here and there.

"Will you help me with this tape?" I asked after Adrian pulled the car back out onto the road and headed back to the Missouri side. I asked her because one, the tape was getting a little irritating, especially now that I had cooled down and I wasn't pumped with adrenaline from the fights, and two, she needed a distraction.

"Oh! I'm sorry!" she said, pulling her hand from mine and immediately going at the tape, tearing it off. "Is this your blood?"

"What?" Adrian and Sal said simultaneously, though Sal's voice was a little delayed over the phone.

"It's not. Got a little of 42's blood on me during that fight," I told them, though when the tape came off the first fist fully, Carmen gave me a sardonic look at my split knuckles.

"It's fine," I whispered. Not wanting her to draw attention to it. Both men would find out, eventually.

"Oh, you are so lucky," Ingrid said, her voice getting louder as if she had stepped out of the room and was coming back in. "Kia is in Wichita. She can be here in three hours or so."

"See?" Leo said, grinning toward the phone as if he could hear the sour face Enzo was undoubtedly making.

Adrian pulled the car over. This storage unit was clearly different than the one we had just been in, was more of warehouse flex space. There was a centralized entrance with a check-in desk that could clearly be seen through the glass front door.

"I'm not sure we can lie our way through that one, not with all of us," Leo said as he eyed the stout security guard behind the desk.

"Is there a loading dock?" I asked, more to the phone so Enzo and Ingrid could pull the information for us.

"There is. Looks like there's a guard for that area too, and it's fenced off," Ingrid murmured.

"One car will go, the other one stays and watches," Sal said over the phone. Suddenly I felt completely ill-equipped to be in this car, seeing how Carmen would have to go into the unit, and I was dead weight.

"Enzo, you in the security feeds yet?" Adrian asked as he pulled the car around toward the back.

"Almost," Enzo said.

The back was just as Ingrid had described; a long area was fenced off with one singular garage door waiting there. A much younger-looking security guard was pacing in a circle, smoking a cigarette, the cherry of which blossomed every few moments, letting us know exactly where he was.

"I'm in. I'm looping the feeds and then you should be clear to move," Enzo said as we all climbed out of the car. Carmen didn't reclaim my hand this time, opting to come right behind Leo, who slipped forward toward the locked gate, working his magic to unlock it with the keypad that sat there.

I watched that cherry brighten as the guard rounded the farthest corner again, now heading for us once more. Once he saw us, I knew it was going to be an altercation. There really wasn't cover here, just the long expanse of concrete from the gate to the loading dock area.

Just as I suspected, Leo got the gate open, and the guard seemed to catch sight of us at the same time.

"Hey!" he called as we all slipped through the opening gate.

I didn't think. I just ran at him. As I got closer, I noticed the favoring he was doing on his right side, and that he was far taller than me, but that really didn't matter. My fist went back, snapping up and forward as he got close. The momentum of his own run only served to make my punch even harder. I didn't even need the secondary blow I laid on his face with my other hand before he was on the ground, out cold.

"Oh," Leo said as I turned around and saw him aiming the gun at the now unconscious security guard. "That works. Let's get moving."

We rushed to the garage door, which had another normal-sized door beside it. Thankfully, the guard had propped it open, probably for ease, and we slipped in, finding ourselves in an open area that was about the size of a standard living room, with three branches sprouting off it, all with smaller garage doors with storage units behind them.

"What unit?" Adrian asked, Leo's phone now pressed to his ear. There was a moment of pause before he turned to us. "515."

Carmen raised an eyebrow at Adrian, her face clearly conveying something that I wasn't aware of.

"What's the last unit number?" Adrian asked and then made eye contact with Carmen, a little smirk on his face. "They are our birthdays."

"March twenty-third, Adrian. May fifteen, Benny, September thirteenth, is me," Carmen said when I looked confused.

"So sentimental," Leo grumbled, heading down the hall that held the five hundreds.

"It's kind of sweet," I offered, getting a laugh out of Adrian and Carmen.

"So sweet that our dad used our birthdays to hide something," Carmen said.

"I'm not sure my dad even remembered my birthday," I offered with a shrug as we came to a stop in front of the unit with the number painted in massive bold beside it. Adrian's arm snaked over my shoulder, his lips coming down on my head for a moment as we looked at the door. There was a silent promise there that my birthday would never be forgotten again.

This padlock was easy, took Leo no time to get into it and we quietly opened the garage door only enough to crouch under, so the sound didn't echo through the halls and alert the other guard. After a moment of Adrian fumbling around, a light switch was flipped, and the room illuminated with eerie fluorescent light.

This unit also had quite a bit of stuff in it. Trunks, more clothes, and a similar metal device that had a box on top of it labeled "pictures."

Adrian pulled the box off, setting it to the side, but not before I could see the curiosity in his eyes about the contents there. Were there pictures that were mean-ingful or images that could be useful in other ways?

We didn't have time to find out though, because as soon as Carmen pressed the panel, another pad popped up, though this time there was a button on the top. At first, she put her hand on it, nothing happening as it had before.

"I don't think it's your hand, this time," Leo said as he watched her try again with her other hand.

She glared at him for a moment before closing her eyes and taking a deep breath. She was trying to remember being in this space before. I could tell by the way her shoulders tensed, and her brows knitted together as she thought.

Her eyes popped open a moment later, recognition in her eyes, and she leaned forward, pressing her fore-head against the button. Another bar of light scanned up and down the pad now, shining in her eyes, but when it was done, and she had stepped back and away from it, watching with the rest of us, another bar popped up from the panel.

"I don't know if it's another flash drive. We hav-en't opened it yet, Benny," Adrian snapped onto the phone. He did as he had the first time, turning the bar until it unlatched the top, opening it up. When he pulled his hand back out, he held a flash drive, but also an envelope.

"We've got to go," Adrian said, closing the safe and gesturing for us to move. "Enzo said the other guard is on the move."

We climbed out, Adrian switching off the light before they closed the garage door and locked it once more. It was only when we turned the corner, almost out of the room, when a loud "Hey!" echoed off the walls of the

concrete block hallway. I turned around to see the other guard racing down the center hall right for us.

"Go!" Leo said, pushing the door open for us to leave.

I ran as fast as I could, passing the guard I'd knocked out and racing out the gate to the waiting car. Carmen was hot on my heels, climbing in behind me, and we looked back to see Adrian stopping at the gate, looking back for Leo.

"Where is he?" Carmen yelled, hands going to the door handle as if she were going to bolt out the door again.

But then Adrian turned, looking at us, the figure of Leo jogging behind him, and she relaxed.

"What the fuck was that?" she asked as soon as they were back in the car.

"Took a page out of Ash's book and made sure he took a nap with his buddy," Leo said with a grin over his shoulder at us.

"Can't have them calling the cops until we're well away," Adrian added as he pulled away from the curb and back onto the road.

"Now we're heading toward Worlds of Fun," Leo said as the phone call transferred back to the car speakers and I glanced behind us to see the headlights of the other car with Sal and Benny within.

"You might have company," Ingrid said, making my stomach drop.

CHAPTER 29

SAL

I hated this. I hated it more when I had to let Adrian, Ash, and the others go in that building without me, and then yet more when Ingrid said those words as we were getting back on the highway, headed toward Worlds of Fun.

"How many?" Leo asked from the speaker.

"Can't be certain, but I picked up on the car that Freddy was in earlier and it's headed there too," Ingrid said.

"Ahead of us or behind us?" I asked.

"They are nearly there," Enzo said.

"Cazzo!" Benny said beside me, immediately rifling through the glove compartment and grabbing the gun that was stashed there. "I should have taken more than a knife from that fucking storage unit."

"There's more in the back," I said to him, jerking my head toward the trunk.

"Carmen, grab the case back there," came Adrian's voice over the speaker.

"You know how to use one?" Carmen asked, and I realized she was asking Ash.

Why hadn't I thought to see if she knew how to use a gun? Why hadn't I considered she would be in a situation where she would *need* to use a gun, given that she was with *us*?

"I've only used one once," Ash said, a little tremble in her voice.

"Exact location, Enzo," I asked, switching lanes so I could be in front of Adrian's car. If something happened on the road, I wanted to give them a chance to keep going. I wanted Adrian and Ash to keep going, even if it was without me.

Enzo gave it, and Benny dutifully put it into the GPS so I could see which exit to take. The highways were nearly deserted by this point. Only us and a few other cars seemed to be driving in the early morning hours, but I still pushed it, nearly doubling the speed limit until we were close. Adrian's car was right behind me, keeping pace, and the conversation turned to silence as we all waited for the impending conflict we were about to face.

I saw them at a distance, watching as car after car took the exit we needed. Black SUVs and sedans. It looked to be about five or six cars all lined up, slowly heading exactly where we were.

"Take the exit before. You might be able to cut them off," Enzo said, and I whipped to the right, taking the exit far too fast, Adrian's car right behind me.

"Take a right," Enzo instructed, and we followed his directions for several minutes, going far too quickly for these streets which were mostly industrial.

"Go down this street. The next stop, take a right and the storage facility will be right there. Orange sign."

Seventy miles an hour down this stretch of road, passing semi-trucks that were taking breaks at gas stations and warehouses that were just seeing their first employees arrive. I stopped abruptly, taking the right Enzo had told us to, and I saw it, the orange sign indicating the storage area, with no fence or locking mechanism in place. You simply drove up to your unit.

"913," Carmen said, repeating the number of the unit and her birthday. I got to it, realizing we had somehow managed to beat O'Shea and his convoy to the unit, though how long we had until they arrived was hard to say.

Leo leaped out of the car before Adrian had fully come to a stop and immediately went to trying the lock. I pulled the SUV up in front of it, providing some cover for everyone.

"How long do we have?" I asked into the phone as I got out, pulling my gun from the holster at my back and watching the road we had just come from.

"Couple minutes," Enzo said, his voice full of anguish. There was no way we were going to get out of this with the information we needed without running into them.

"Got it!" Leo called, and I glanced back as they shoved the door up, opening the unit and shining their phone flashlights to illuminate the space. This one was much fuller than the first one had been.

"Fuck!" Adrian yelled, clenching his fists at his sides, clearly trying not to start throwing the shit filling the unit around.

"I'm getting on the roof," Leo said, bending down and planting a hard kiss on Carmen. "Get it and get out."

"No! I won't leave without you," Carmen said, her voice already shaking.

"You help her get it and you take her away. No matter what," Leo said, and I glanced back to see he was talking to Ash.

Ash nodded solemnly as Leo kissed Carmen one more time, then immediately jogged over to Adrian's car, climbing on the hood, before jumping up and grabbing the lip of the garage door frame and pulling himself up and over the top of the cinder block structure. He didn't have a sniper rifle, but he wasn't very noticeable where he was. It would provide some element of surprise when our enemies came.

I heard the sound of the car engines, my focus going back to the entrance where I knew O'Shea and his men would be coming.

"We're fucked," Benny said, standing next to where I was at the hood of the car, aiming his gun where the cars were pulling up.

"Help me move this," I heard Adrian say, and then the loud sound of crashing behind me. There was no time to delicately sift through Bernardo's things. We needed our hands on whatever was in that safe and then to try to make it out of this alive. And then I saw the headlights.

"They're here," I said, loud enough for everyone to hear.

The cars screeched to a halt in front of us, their headlights blinding us, but it didn't matter. I still saw the gnarled face of Freddy O'Shea in the passenger seat of the first car. Doors opened and his men began piling out.

"Not sure why you keep doing this Freddy. You know how badly it ends up for you nearly every time," I said when his door finally opened, the silhouette of his form coming around the car to stand at the front.

"Well, because it's so fun at this point, Lupo. I'll almost be sad when I don't get to see your ugly nose anymore," Freddy said with a smile in his voice.

"Funny, someone like you poking fun at anyone's appearance," Benny sneered beside me.

"Just do it," I heard Carmen whisper behind us in the unit, and then a moment later, the now familiar whirl and clunk of the safe opening.

"All this off of an overheard conversation years ago, O'Shea? Has it been worth it?" I asked when I knew Carmen had gotten it open and Adrian had his hands on the last drive.

When I could hear their soft steps move from within the unit and step toward Adrian's car, I felt a little more relieved, but only so much as Freddy stepped close enough to my car hood for me to see the terrifying smirk spreading over his mangled face.

"Whatever it was, it scared Manzo Morelli. He wanted it destroyed, but Bernardo, like any good mobster, couldn't let that juicy information go," Freddy said, pulling his gun from his back and pointing it over my head. I didn't risk a glance back behind me to see who he was aiming at, but my gun didn't waiver from where it pointed straight at his chest.

"So what? You think seventeen-year-old information will hold some weight the way it would have years ago?" I asked, trying to delay and make sure Ash and Carmen got in the car. There was enough space, if I recalled correctly, for them to back out quickly and get away.

"If it was bad enough to scare Morelli, I'm sure it would be enough to take him down. And if we can take down the Italian mob, our clan will be the most powerful in the country. We already have more connections across the pond."

"It's too bad you're not going to find out," I said, but as the words left my mouth, he shot his gun, the bullet clearly hitting metal. The sound of car doors slamming with Ash and Carmen getting in resounded, and then I shot mine.

It hit Freddy in the shoulder instead of the chest where I aimed, him having ducked down almost immediately after he shot his weapon. Adrian's car started, O'Shea's men began firing at us, and I pulled Benny down with me to hide behind the fender of the car for a moment.

I glanced over, watching as Ash looked at me from the driver's seat, her blue braids like a beacon drawing my gaze to her. Bullets ricocheted off the SUV, and she threw it in reverse, pinning three of O'Shea's men to their car, before she sped in the opposite direction of the entrance.

"Where the fuck is she going?" Adrian screamed as he ducked behind furniture in the unit, occasionally firing back.

"Get those bitches!" called the voice of none other than Marek Lewandowski, prompting one of the cars to speed off in the same direction Ash and Carmen went. The car didn't get far though. I saw the moment Leo finally brought himself into it, shooting out the tires before they even got close, before taking the men in the car out one by one as they got back out.

I popped back up, my eyes immediately falling on the brute of a guard that was Freddy's go-to, Hamish, if I remembered correctly. The large Irishman with a scar across his face was coming right to the car, presumably to try to get hold of the downed O'Shea. I aimed at him and just as my bullet hit him in the chest, another bullet from above got him in the face. I watched in awe and horror as his jaw dangled off his face, eyes wide with terror and pain, before he dropped to the ground.

Freddy may have started with a convoy of five or six cars full, but now he was down to a few men left.

"Cover me," I said to Benny as I stood back up from our spot by the fender, walking around the front of the car as I loaded my spare clip into my gun.

Freddy was still on the ground on the other side of it, which made sense as to why I hadn't been shot at for the most part and took out so many. Their leader was in the way of the target. His battered leg, which he still couldn't walk on, was stretched out, the cane too far for him to reach and his left side covered in blood from the wound I inflicted. Hamish's blood was pooling at his feet, and he stared at his fallen guard before lifting his eyes to look up at me.

"Tell them to stand down now or you're dead," I said, pressing the barrel of my gun to his head.

He didn't, instead smiling at me sinisterly, pressing his gun to my stomach in response. I didn't take a moment, not a second, not a breath, pressing my finger on the trigger and watching as it decimated his skull, leaving blood and brain matter all over the side of my car.

"Oh, fuck!" Marek screamed as I turned away from Freddy's corpse, my gun now easily popping with each new bullet I fired into the remaining men who seemed frozen in shock at witnessing their leader's demise.

Adrian ran up, standing beside me and between the four of us, with Benny and Leo behind us, the only one left standing, a spent gun now on the ground at his feet, was Marek.

"Salvatore, I am sorry—"

"His name is Sal," Adrian said, cutting him off before he promptly shot him between the eyes.

The silence that took over the storage area was eerie. Six bullet-riddled cars and a pile of dead Irish and Polish men were littered before us, and I heaved a breath into my lungs. The sound of tires screeching broke the silence, and headlights came around the corner, quickly revealing themselves to be Adrian's car with Carmen and Ash inside.

"Leo!" Ash screamed after opening the car door. "We need to go. She's shot!"

"I'll clear the car," Adrian said, opening my car and pulling all identifying information out as Leo slid down from the rooftop position he was in, going immediately to Carmen's side with Benny only a step behind.

I turned and helped Adrian, my heart racing as I grabbed the bags and my suit. We'd have to torch it, especially because I could hear the faint sound of police sirens in the distance. Tossing everything into the back of Adrian's car, I waited until they got Carmen into the back seat and Ash pulled the car toward the entrance before Adrian tore open the fuel line, gasoline spilling all over the pavement in front of his father's storage unit.

"It will still be traced back to us," I said, hearing how hollow my voice sounded as I pulled a few dollars from my pocket and my lighter.

"It will be traced back to my dead father, who had several storage units we had no idea about," Adrian said, watching me as I lit the bills on fire, tossing them at the puddle of fuel and watching it ignite. Grabbing my hand, Adrian pulled me to his waiting car, opening the trunk for us to climb into.

"Where?" was all Ash asked over the sound of Benny instructing Leo on how to hold her to stop the bleeding.

"The gym," I yelled over the commotion, and Ash pulled out of the storage lot.

CHAPTER 30

ASH

"**Y**ou and Carmen will get in the car and get out as fast as you can," Adrian said to me as Freddy's forces pulled up, illuminating the full storage unit with their headlights.

"But—" I started, but he pressed a finger to my lips, his eyes sliding over to the doorway.

"This one," Carmen said with a groan quietly, pushing a button on the panel like the other two contraptions, making a little needle pop up.

"What is it?" Adrian asked, looking at it confused.

"The prick," Carmen murmured, holding out her hand hesitantly. I understood. It was one thing to deal with blood from a fight, it was quite another to willingly make yourself bleed.

"I'll help," I said, taking her hand in mine.

"We don't have time," Adrian hissed, his attention going back to what was happening in front of the unit.

"Just do it," Carmen whispered a little louder, closing her eyes and relinquishing her hand to me. I pressed it against the needle, pulling away and watching as the blood dropped against the screen. It absorbed it somehow. Perhaps it wasn't an electric panel like the others, but it was hard to tell in the dark. After a moment, the same electric whirling happened and Adrian found the handle, practically tearing the safe open and pulling out the flash drive hidden within.

"Now go!" Adrian hissed, pulling his gun from where he had stashed it behind his back, and gesturing toward the other SUV.

Carmen grabbed my hand again, pulling me as we quietly crept through the stacks of stored items. I tried not to look at the men that were blocking us all in. I tried not to feel the familiar eyes of Marek Lewandowski catching even a brief sight of me. We only had to go a few feet, just a few feet without cover to get there, but it was a few feet too many. Bullets rang out, hitting the car as we raced to get in.

I climbed in the driver's seat, slamming the door, and looking over at Sal as he crouched a little behind the car. Those eyes told me everything. They said they loved me and they told me to run.

With Carmen beside me, I threw the car in reverse, looking back to see three of O'Shea's men coming toward us with guns raised. As if that would stop me. With tires screeching, I tried not to think about what I was doing, only that I needed to go, to make this easier on my men, to get Carmen, my best friend, to safety. I could hear the bones of the men I had just run over break, their screams still ringing in my ears, as I put the car back in drive and sped away from the unit, only realizing that I had turned toward more rows of storage units, not the road.

"Oh shit," Carmen said, her voice sounding pained and scared. I glanced over, finding with horror that blood was pouring from her shoulder.

"Fuck!" I hissed, my hands gripping tighter to the steering wheel as I pressed the brake to make a turn once we hit the end of the row. This had to go in a loop, right? I'd be able to come back around the other side?

"This is really bad," Carmen said, now slumped and leaning on the passenger door, blood now soaking everything on that side of the car.

"I'm going back around. Benny—"

"I don't know if any of us are making it out of this," Carmen said, cutting me off before I could suggest her brother could help her.

But what she said couldn't be true. They were going to make it out of that fight. They had to.

"No, they're all alive," I said, hoping I was right, trying to believe that those words would come true, especially now that the sound of gunfire had stopped, the only sound was the rev of the engine as I gunned it farther down the row.

The car's tires skidded a little as I took the next turn too fast, and we came around to see Carmen was wrong. Sal and Adrian stood beside one another on the other side of the now completely destroyed SUV, Benny still where he was on the other side of the car, and I could see the head of Leo on the roof.

"Ash? I don't think…" But Carmen didn't finish whatever she was going to say, slumping a little more against the door, her eyes fluttering closed.

"Leo!" I screamed as I rolled the window down. "We need to go. She's shot!"

My voice sounded strange to my own ears. Desperate. Scared. I felt the tears well in my eyes. I didn't cry. This didn't happen, but it was happening now.

The men moved immediately. Benny and Leo rushed over to the passenger side of the car and grabbed Carmen, while Sal and Adrian pulled things from the massacred SUV and lit it on fire. Carmen was roused by Leo's presence, or maybe it was the pain that moving her to the back seat caused, but either way, her eyes snapped open, her breathing becoming panting that could be heard loudly between the snapping comments between Leo and Benny.

Tears streamed down my cheeks. The idea that I could have lost Sal and Adrian, that I could still lose Carmen, came over me as I waited. I could give myself this. I could give myself this pain for a moment, but then I needed to get over it. I was stronger than this, and the fight wasn't over, because we still needed to get out of there, and I could hear the sound of sirens in the night air now.

I wiped the tears away, breathing slowly, and trying not to let Carmen's cries get to me when the trunk of the SUV slammed closed. Through the rearview mirror, I could see the other SUV in flames, and my men safely in the trunk now.

"Where?" I asked, not trusting myself to say any-thing else.

"The gym," Sal yelled, and I gunned it.

This drive was probably the scariest one I had ever experienced in my whole life. More frightening than when Marek forced me into the car. More gut-wrenching than when my father drove us home drunk when I was fourteen. The highway was starting to come alive in the very early hours of the morning, and I wasn't sure if Carmen was going to make it back to Lee's Summit, especially not when she went silent.

ADRIAN

"Benny! Fucking fix her!" Leo screamed in the tiny exam room at the gym. The office converted to an exam room was not really equipped to deal with this sort of thing. We could have taken Carmen to the doctor I had on retainer, but he was farther than the gym, and Carmen had passed out halfway there, from blood loss or pain. We weren't sure.

"I need the fucking pliers, Leo. Hand them the fuck over," Benny snapped, his hands somehow steady even though he was effectively operating on our little sister. "It didn't go through, or this would be easy," he said quietly after he wiped the blood away from her shoulder, which only remained clear for a moment before it started pouring out of her again.

"Fuck!" Leo said, his hands shaking as he handed the pliers to Benny and then paced back and forth.

"Let me help him, Leo," Ash said, stopping him and looking up at him with pleading eyes. She looked like she had been crying, her face paler than I had ever seen it, eyes wide with fear of her own, but she was somehow willing to step in, to be the steady hand that Benny needed to actually save Carmen's life.

Leo swallowed and nodded, letting Ash pass so she could grab things as Benny needed them. I heard Sal on the phone just outside the room instructing Enzo to get the doctor here, if nothing else with antibiotics. She would need them.

I stood watching numbly as Benny worked to get the bullet out, his hands steady, brow furrowed in concentration.

"He's coming," was all Sal said as he came back into the room and stood beside me. I reached out my hand to him, needing the contact, and he immediately laced his fingers in mine. The unsaid words between us were clear.

I couldn't lose my baby sister. I couldn't.

Thirty minutes passed, Benny got the bullet out, stitching something it had torn along the way within her before closing the wound completely. She remained motionless on the table. The only indication she was still alive was the rise and fall of her chest.

"It's the best I could do," Benny said quietly once he finished bandaging her shoulder. He slipped the sixth pair of gloves off his hands, stepping away, and falling back against the wall. "It's the best I could do," he repeated, though this time his voice shook, thick with anguish as his eyes filled with tears. Leo took Ash's place beside Carmen, kissing her face and hair, while Ash went to Benny's side.

"You did, and I think she'll be okay, Benny," Ash said, touching his now-shaking shoulder.

"Will she?" he whispered, looking up at her and letting the tears in his eyes fall.

"She will be," I said, crossing the room to him before I knew what I was doing and pulling him against me. It had been a long time since I hugged my brother like this. We may have been grown men, but he needed the comfort of my reassurance just as much as I did. "She will be, and I'm so proud of you for saving her."

Benny's sobs shook us both, and he clung to me for a long time, long enough that Dr. Drifus came in with Enzo before we parted.

"Excuse me, young man," the doctor said to Leo, trying to shoo him away from Carmen, but Leo wasn't budging.

Not that the old doctor wasn't used to that. He had dealt with quite a few gunshot wounds and overprotective, paranoid people in his days as a doctor to Salvatore Lupo. Instead of arguing about Leo's stubbornness about moving, he simply worked around him, pulling out an IV bag of saline from the large bag he had brought with him, quickly getting that placed, before checking her pupils and moving on to examine the wound.

"Whoever stitched this was a bit rusty, but it should heal well. There will be a scar," the doctor said after quite a few moments, all of us very quietly waiting for more.

"She'll have full function of her arm?" Benny asked, having pulled away from me to watch the other doctor work.

"I can't be certain, but it looks good. She should start doing some light therapy on it in about a week, about the same time she finishes these." He pulled out two bottles of antibiotics, placing them in Leo's outstretched palm before coming over to where Sal stood in the corner of the room, holding out his hand.

"I'm giving you half," Sal said, narrowing his eyes at the old man.

"You'll give me all since you're replacing me with this one," Dr. Drifus said, jerking his head in Benny's direction. Sal chuckled, pulling out a wad of cash from his pocket and handing it over to him.

"We should take her back to the moms," I heard myself saying, even though I felt like I was on another planet.

Leo, Benny, and Enzo got Carmen into Enzo's car, while Ash cleaned up the blood. She was still in her clothes from the fight, the number thirty-three still painted on her bare stomach, and I saw now that her knuckles were split on her right hand.

"What happened?" I demanded, crossing the room before I even realized it, and pulled her hand away from the exam table where she was wiping.

"It's nothing. Let me clean this so we can go with the others," she murmured, pulling her hand from me.

"Let me see it!" I screamed. The room stood still for a movement while Ash and Sal looked at me. My whole body shook, my vision blurring as my gaze went between them.

"Okay," she whispered quietly after a moment.

I took her hand, not really seeing the cuts in her flesh anymore, as I pulled it to my lips. The sob came from deep in my chest, bellowing out before I could stop it. Ash's other hand went through my hair as I fell to my knees before her. Sal was there a moment later, pulling me against him and letting my tears fall against his chest.

"She's okay," Sal whispered. "Carmen is okay. Ash is okay. We are okay."

They held me like that for a long time before we got back into my car, Sal driving us to be with the rest of them.

When we got there, it was chaos. The moms arguing with Leo about which room to take Carmen to, Enzo and Benny telling them to shut up or they'll wake Nora, while Ingrid quietly slipped away, presumably to check on her daughter. When we walked in, it seemed to go still.

"Take Carmen to Leo's room," Sal said.

"That's right across from where Nora's sleeping," Liliana protested while Leo immediately headed up the stairs carrying Carmen.

"I don't think anything will be happening across from a child, especially not in the state she's in," I said, giving the moms a pointed look.

"But—"

"Leo's not going to fuck her while she's hurt, Ma. It's fine," Sal snapped, effectively shutting Liliana up, while my mom raised her eyebrows in shock.

"Who's got 'em?" Enzo asked, talking about the flash drives. I pulled them from my pocket, handing them over to Enzo just as Ingrid came back down the stairs.

"She's still sleeping, and it sounds like Carmen woke up," she told us, settling back in her chair beside Enzo's as he looked the drives over carefully.

"I'll put on some coffee," my mom said, touching Liliana lightly on the arm to indicate she should come with.

"Let me help you," Ash said, parting from my side to move through to the back of the house where the moms were headed.

"Let's see what's on here," Enzo said, plugging the first flash drive in.

As suspected, it was encrypted.

"Do we think we plug in all three or decrypt as we go?" Ingrid pondered aloud, but Enzo was already plugging the next one in.

"How long until Kia gets here?" Sal asked.

"Probably at least another hour," Ingrid said, her eyes focused on Enzo's screen as he plugged the third one in.

"You think you'll be done with this by then?" I asked.

"Probably not, given what I'm looking at here," Enzo said with a sigh, running his hands through his hair. I glanced at the screen, seeing a bunch of letters and numbers in code that made no sense to me at all, and raised my eyebrows.

"You let us know, won't you?" Sal asked with a chuckle, before clapping his brother on the shoulder and heading to the kitchen. He wasn't going for coffee and as I followed him, I knew I needed something

stronger with everything that just transpired. The trusty little cabinet by the microwave that was far too thin to hold anything but cookie sheets and cutting boards was where Liliana had always kept her hard liquor, and it was calling our name.

"Let me clean that for you, dear," my mom said quietly to Ash, before she pulled the little first aid kit from the top of the fridge and looked back at Ash's fingers. It felt, for just a moment, like when we were kids, watching my mom and Liliana doctor whichever of us children had gotten hurt outside. The first aid kit was always there for as long as I could remember.

"Are there going to problems after this, Sal?" Liliana asked as he went to the cabinet by the microwave, pulling out a bottle of whiskey and setting it on the small kitchen table.

"There are always problems in this business, Mama, but what the O'Sheas were trying to take Carmen for is now being looked at by Enzo and Ingrid, so I don't think they'll be after Carmen anymore," Sal said, patting the seat next to where he sat and looking at me. I sat beside him, wanting nothing more than to reach over and take his hand and have Ash on my lap. Their touch was what I needed, especially now that the excitement had come to a grinding halt. Hurry up and wait.

"But they'll be after you two?" Liliana asked.

"They always are," I said tiredly.

"We just killed Colin O'Shea's only heir, so yes, I think they will still be after us," Sal told her, opening the whiskey bottle and taking a long pull.

He pushed the bottle to me, before my mom let Ash go, deeming her wounds clean enough, but instead of leaving the room, she came over and sat on my lap, the feel of her against me immediately soothing something.

The addition of Sal's hand on my leg under the table a moment later seemed to close that hole a bit more.

"Go next door, get some rest. Enzo will tell us when to get you," my mom said, watching the three of us for a moment, some uncertainty in her eyes, but more concern. I supposed we all looked rather haggard.

"Take the whiskey, *figlio*," Liliana said to Sal as Ash stood from my lap.

With kisses on our mothers' cheeks, we briefly told Enzo we were going to the other house before we trudged out the door and across the yard.

CHAPTER 31

SAL

The three of us moved silently through the empty house, Adrian leading us up to his old room, which was still filled with various personal items of his, and even some of his clothes for this very situation. There were plenty of times over the years that the place we laid our head at the end of the day was not necessarily where we thought it would be. It was always nice to make sure we had those items to make the next day run a bit more smoothly.

"Shower," he said with a grunt, pulling us to the bathroom at the top of the stairs.

"Oh, thank god," Ash said, the relief on her face mirroring how I felt. "I feel disgusting."

I didn't blame her. She had fought just hours ago, getting blood from other fighters and then Carmen splattered across her body, but there was also dust and dirt from the various storage units and Adrian reeked of gasoline. We needed to wash away the bad parts of the night and replace them with something better.

It wasn't a huge shower, just a standard tub-shower combination, but the three of us would be able to fit. We quickly stripped out of our clothes, the water hot in only a few moments, and we all got in.

There was a moment where we all simply stood in the hot spray, Adrian and I on either side of Ash, holding the three of us together, before we parted. Adrian began taking out Ash's braids as I grabbed the soap, lathering it up and starting to clean the numbers off her skin.

"I should be taking care of you two," she whispered, though her eyes were closed as Adrian's fingers ran through her hair.

"Shh," I hushed her, moving on to cleaning the sweat from her body. With each soapy swipe, she gave a little moan, Adrian's mouth now having moved to kiss her shoulder, hands sliding down from her hair to help me soap her.

I reached around her, now gently soaping and caressing Adrian as well as Ash, their hands moving to touch my skin. This was comfort. We needed this. Needed each other.

"Are we clean enough?" Adrian asked, as Ash moaned quietly, each of her arms having come around our shoulders like she was anchoring the three of us together.

"We're done," I said, reluctant to move us, but wanting to fall into bed with them, I pulled away just enough to turn the water off. Slowly we stepped from the tub, toweling each other off before walking, still naked, back to Adrian's former bedroom.

We all climbed into the double bed. There wasn't much space, but it didn't really seem to matter much to us. Ash in the middle, with Adrian spooning her, while

I pressed chest to chest against her. She looked up at me, her light eyes tired, but needy.

A lot had been asked of her that day. She had been pushed into our life, having to do things and see things she probably wished she wouldn't have, and yet she wasn't running from us. Instead, her arm was under my neck, her hand curling around so her fingers could run through my hair, while her other hand was grasping at Adrian's thigh. Adrian touched his feet to mine, his hand coming around her hip to touch me, while he continued kissing Ash's shoulder and neck.

"I love you," I said, my eyes flitting between Ash's and Adrian's, before I closed my eyes, leaning into the kiss I had been resisting giving Ash on her plush lips.

She kissed me back, fingers tightening on my hair, and I felt her hips move, pressing back against Adrian. He moaned, his hand grasping at my skin a bit more tightly, before his fingers softened, grazing across my hip until they brushed against my erection. It was hard to avoid getting hard when I was in a bed, naked with the two people I loved most in the world.

"I need you both," Ash whispered, pulling her lips from mine. I let my hand wander, caressing down her body, over her peaked nipples, feeling the way her abs clenched, then to that apex of her thighs that was already wet for us.

I felt Adrian's cock, nestled in her folds, but not inside her, already slick with her juices and pulsing at the addition of my fingers there.

"Both at the same time?" I asked, only because I wanted to be sure that's what she meant. She nodded, her hand coming to meet mine between her legs.

"Do you have lube in here, Adrian?" I asked and watched the shadowed smirk come to his lips from over her shoulder.

"The drawer next to you," he said. I pulled away only to reach into the drawer, grabbing the lube from where it sat, completely unhidden if someone were to come looking. A quick squeeze of it into my hand, and it was back to Ash's center, only this time my fingers found their way to her puckered hole, gently rubbing the entrance, and waiting until it relaxed a little to push my fingers in.

Her moan was deep, resonating in her chest and vibrating both me and Adrian. I felt Adrian's cock against my hand as I gently thrust my finger inside of her, adding another while my other hand slowly rubbed circles around her clit.

"More," she said, her voice low and heavy with desire.

I looked into her eyes again, my own breath ragged as I rubbed a bit more vigorously on her clit, making her eyes roll back, her back arching and pressing my fingers deeper within her ass.

Adrian grabbed the lube, taking a generous portion for himself, and as soon as he was done, I grabbed his cock, lining him up with where I had just opened her up.

He pressed in, my hand still there, feeling each inch as he slowly started sinking in deeper, but getting to watch Ash's face, brows up, jaw slack, breathing in little pants. I could have gotten off just watching her face while Adrian thrust in her ass. But our girl didn't just want him. She wanted us both.

Her eyes snapped open again when Adrian pushed all the way in and held there, both pulsing together and looking at me. Wanting me.

"More," Ash whispered again, her hands coming out to grasp me, urging me closer. As I shifted nearer, Adrian pulled Ash's leg over his, opening her up a bit more for us.

I lined up, pressing inside her to a collective groan from all of us. The feel of Adrian's cock in her ass, making her so tight, I knew none of us would last very long at all.

We were one in this moment, but it really meant always. The three of us made a whole. Adrian and I began moving in tandem, thrusting slowly and letting it build. The need for release, the need for this connection, the need for each other was just as overwhelming as the physical feeling of both Adrian and me being inside Ash.

One of my hands went down to rub on her bundle of nerves, her sounds becoming incoherent screams of pleasure while my other went to Adrian's hip, wanting to touch him more, feel him in this moment. And then the building fire within us began to explode: first Ash, the feel of her body contracting with her orgasm and the change in her cries being a trigger for both me and Adrian.

I saw it in Adrian's eyes as they looked at me over her shoulder. The moment his cock hardened within her, her body tightened against us both and triggered our orgasms too. To watch him, to stare into Adrian's eyes, and feel Ash as she clung to me while I came felt like it was close to heaven. Or maybe the only heaven I deserved.

We all lay there for a bit, our breathing coming back down to normal, before Adrian and I got up.

"Where are you going?" Ash asked quietly, briefly waving her hand toward us like she didn't want us to go. I grinned, leaning back down to kiss her on the lips.

"To get a washcloth for you before we all fall asleep like this," I said, gesturing to our very fluid-covered bodies. She let a little chuckle fall from her lips, and I left to find Adrian in the bathroom.

He was leaning on the counter, looking down at the sink, his body hunched, head down, like some sort of Roman sculpture before my eyes.

"You okay?" I asked, stepping a little farther in and hesitating only a moment before I let my hand touch his shoulder. He relaxed, turning his deep blue eyes to me, and a smile spread over his lips.

"We're all okay. I think we're all going to be okay," he whispered. He stood to his full height, taking my face in his hands and pressing his lips to mine. "I love you too, Sal," he said when we parted.

When we got back to the room, it was a miracle Ash was still awake, she protested for a moment when we started cleaning her off, but her tired limbs gave up quickly, and the two of us came around her as we had been before, my front to hers, Adrian spooning her from behind, and we fell asleep. It might have been the best night of sleep I ever had.

ONE MONTH LATER

Adrian and I stood in the elevator of the hotel. He had cleaned up again for this occasion, dressed in a black suit, complete with vest and tie. If we weren't heading to the most important meeting of our lives, I would be dragging him back to the room we had just left, but as it was, I had to remain focused.

"You okay?" he asked me, his hand touching mine ever so slightly as the elevator dinged, indicating we made it to the lobby.

"As much as I can be," I said, trying not to think too much about what we were about to do and more about breathing.

The past month had been strange and unsettled. Even though we got the information, it took Kia, Enzo, and Ingrid weeks to decrypt the files contained on the flash drives, it took Carmen just as long to mostly heal after her gunshot to the shoulder, and our families were still waiting for the inevitable retaliation from Colin O'Shea for his last son's death.

But this wasn't what we were dealing with today. While Leo and Enzo manned our men, Adrian and I were in New York City, walking through the lobby of a very luxurious hotel and headed out the door to the corporate office of Nova Tech, where Manzo Morelli agreed to meet us in his office.

While we dealt with smaller businesses, Morelli was on a different level. As the king of the Italian Mafia in the United States, it made sense he needed something bigger to cleanse the dirty money.

Travis and Roman were waiting with the cars, and we climbed in, silent as we made our way through the streets of New York. Adrian and I had known it was possible we would not come back from this. It was possible that Morelli would choose to shut us up permanently, rather than see this as the act of loyalty he had demanded, but it was a risk we had to take.

Any more time without the backing of the full Mafia, especially now that we had dealt an even greater insult to O'Shea, and I was certain we were headed for an all-out war against the Irish. Not only did we need Morelli's help, but we also needed the alliance with Gregor Stepanov to be solidified between him and the Mafia as a whole.

Lots of very important things to discuss, and no way to know how Morelli would react.

We made it to the building, checking in at the desk and being escorted to the elevators to the top floor, where Travis and Roman were not allowed to go.

"Breathe," I said to both myself and Adrian. In most capo's and his second's relationship, there would be no consoling, no show of weakness, but we were different. Everything about us and our families was different. I had to believe we would prevail because of that, otherwise I wouldn't be able to hold my face in this mask of stoicism and get through this.

I was raised by an evil man. I worked in a cruel field. I could be ruthless when necessary, but I was not the stone-hearted creature that my father was, even if that's what the rest of our world thought.

Adrian knew that. Adrian was beside me.

The elevator doors opened, and we stepped out onto a very lavishly decorated floor. There were ornate chairs and couches in a central waiting area, with offices lining the outer walls. I knew which one was Morelli's before we were escorted there. The double doors looked like they were imported from some ancient temple and set within this modern luxury, as if to show anyone who met him here that he could do anything he wanted, and no one could stop him.

The doors to his office opened and the man, who I assumed was his second, Victor Caruso, opened the door for us before we could knock.

"He's expecting you," Victor said, gesturing for us to come into the office. I went in first, Adrian right behind me and the door was promptly closed.

It was as if we stepped into another world as we passed the threshold of his office. Morelli sat behind a large desk. Ornate carvings decorated the exterior of it, as if it was made from a single block of wood. Oil paintings were hung on the walls, framed in gold. There were Persian rugs delineating spaces, one at the bar area in one corner, one at a seating area in the other, and a very large one that his desk sat upon. There was even a fireplace.

Morelli stood as we entered, his presence imposing, even in the opulent room.

"Ah! Salvatore and Adriano. Welcome to New York," Morelli said, though he didn't come around his desk, instead gesturing for us to take the two leather seats in front of his desk.

"Thank you for meeting with us," I said.

"When you told me you had my final request, I couldn't deny you an audience. I'll admit I am curious what show of loyalty you have for me," he said, glancing at us as if he expected us to have more. Did he think we'd bring the head of an enemy or a massive fortune?

"When Romolo told us about the request, I'll admit, it made me wonder what exactly you were looking for, but thankfully the answer seemed to fall in our lap," I said, watching as Morelli's eyebrows shot up in surprise.

"Oh? I already heard all about what happened with Colin O'Shea's son. Glad to see you've handled *part* of that little problem," Morelli said, leaning back in his chair.

"Yes, we expect some retaliation from him at some point. We'd like to know we have your backing when it comes to that, though it's more that Gregor Stepanov would want our support. I vowed to him that he would be the one to take Colin O'Shea's life," I said, keeping my face carefully blank, my voice steady.

"You keep saying 'we,' Salvatore. *You* would be the capo if what you've brought me proves to be enough. You know that, don't you?" Morelli said, his eyes shifting to look at Adrian now, a slight distrust in his gaze.

"I'm sure you know that a leader needs his second. Adrian and I have nothing to hide from one another."

Morelli forced a smile, eyes staying dead and fixed as they switched back to my face.

"I am intrigued to know what you've done to prove your loyalty to me, Salvatore," Morelli said, gesturing for me to give him whatever it was.

"Do you feel the same way about your second, Sir?" I asked, glancing to the side where Victor stood. Morelli looked confused for a moment, his head shifting as he glanced at Victor, before turning it back to me.

"Of course," Morelli said, but I could tell there was an undercurrent of uncertainty in those black shark-like eyes.

"Very well," I said, standing and pulling a disc from my pocket. "May I use your computer?"

There was a moment of hesitation as Morelli looked at me, eyes on the disc in my hand. It was as if he already knew what was going to be on it, perhaps not outright, but he could feel it in his bones.

"Victor, go to tech and get a generic laptop for us to use. I'd hate for a virus to accidentally corrupt my computer," Morelli said, glancing at his second, who seemed to stiffen at the request. There was no illusion about why Morelli would send Victor away when he could have an administrative person do that for him.

"Yes, Sir," Victor said, leaving the room a moment later, the silence persisting a beat or two longer than was comfortable.

Morelli gestured to me to come around the desk, waking up his computer monitors with the push of the button on his keyboard and gesturing for me to take over as he pushed away from his desk.

I put the disc in, following the instructions Enzo had given me, and went through the motions we had practiced. The last thing I needed was to look stupid or incompetent. There was a reason Enzo was the one who dealt with all the computers.

I opened the disc and there was the file filled with evidence of Manzo Morelli's deceptions.

Photos of him meeting with FBI agents and his file from the FBI as an informant on the previous leader of the Mafia. But it got worse from there. There was footage from security cameras of Morelli killing the former boss and his closest men, even photos of his trip to Italy where he seduced the wife of the second of the Costa Nostra, gaining ties to the Boss directly after she killed him.

Bernardo LaMartina knew all of this because Morelli had entrusted *him* with this information. Bernardo had been Morelli's ally during all of this. The only man Morelli hadn't killed who knew the truth of his rise to power and yet, Bernardo hadn't destroyed it all as he was supposed to. He kept it, hid it away for only his children to find, and now here I was with Bernardo LaMartina's oldest son, showing Morelli exactly what he wanted gone forever.

If Colin O'Shea had gotten his hands on this, especially with the alliance he was building with the mainland Italian boss overseas, Morelli would be dispatched, the Mafia on US soil a mess, and it would be so easy for O'Shea to take the reins on all the underground dealings Morelli controlled.

"What is it that you want?" Morelli hissed, shoving me away from the computer and ejecting the disc. He immediately broke it, throwing it to the ground and breathing heavily as he glared at me.

"The fact that we do not go to anyone with this is your act of loyalty. We could do so much with this information, don't you think?" I asked, raising an eyebrow as I came to stand by Adrian, my hand on his shoulder this time more for my comfort than for his.

"You want me to believe you won't use this?" Morelli asked, an angry vein bulging by his temple, and his face turned red with rage.

"As long as we have the backing we need, as long as our people are safe, I don't see any reason to use any of it," I told him.

"And what about him?" Morelli asked, pointing a finger at Adrian.

"As long as our people are safe, Morelli, I wouldn't use it, even if it's my birthright to do so," Adrian said, standing to his full height and looking down at the much smaller man before us. Morelli's larger-than-life presence seemed to have diminished since revealing what we knew to him. I could now see him just as he really was, a small Italian man, age creeping up and frailty beginning to show. His power was in his wealth and influence, yes, but also in the impression he left people. That illusion was now lost on me.

Morelli looked between us, his eyes shifting quickly, sweat beading on his forehead. He took in a deep breath, smoothing back his hair and adjusting his suit, before walking over to us. The vein was still prominent, his face still flushed, but he held out a hand to me.

"It will be a pleasure to serve as Capo," I said, taking it, only a faint smile on my lips. I pulled him forward a little, catching him off guard as I did so and putting my mouth close to his ear. "And I will serve, but know that if anything happens to anyone we care about and we find out there are ties to you, all of this will be revealed."

With that, I released him, turning and walking out the door with Adrian on my heels. When we made it to the elevator, Victor was coming out with a laptop, but he didn't seem surprised at us leaving.

Silence persisted between me and Adrian all the way back to the hotel where we packed our things, Ash waiting for us there, her eyes alight as soon as we walked through the door.

"Well?" she asked, but neither of us knew what to say. Adrian nodded his head, smiling faintly and she jumped up, kissing him and then me. "Tell me?"

Adrian turned to me, cupping my cheek with one hand as he slid his hand around Ash's back, the three of us locked together.

"Sal, you did it," he whispered. The reality of what had just happened struck me then. We had the backing and support we needed. We had secured my position, secured our families' lives, which had been held in balance since my father's death. Until the day that Morelli died, we were guaranteed our place.

"*We* did it," I said, pulling him forward and kissing him with all the relief and passion I felt in this moment. There were no other two people I would ever want to share this victory with.

EPILOGUE

ASH

The familiar scent of sweat, blood, cigarettes, and booze surrounded me, my vision still slightly dazed and I could taste the blood on my tongue from where Hurricane slammed me on the mat just a round before. That didn't mean I was going to back down. I only had to win this round, and the victory was mine. I knew it and she knew it, which was why she was so thoroughly pissed that I was back up again after that move.

"Kick her ass, Ash!" came Carmen's voice from the sideline. She had made herself my unofficial coach, much to Leo's disdain, but he could rest easy that there was always at least one person in attendance for my fights that would watch out for both of us.

Tonight, we were graced with two.

I could feel the sets of blue and brown eyes watching my every move. Somehow, it didn't make me nervous, it emboldened me.

One fight per month. That's all I really needed, and thankfully I got the hook up from two people in charge of such events. This one just so happened to land on the night we were going back to the Kansas City house. We had been staying in Sal's old apartment in Lee's Summit while additional security was being installed at the house, and I found I actually liked it in the smaller and less garish space much better, but the men needed to be in the thick of everything happening in the city, and I resigned myself to moving back into my opulent bedroom, if only because I knew I wouldn't be sleeping there most of the time.

I spit the blood from my mouth and grinned at Hurricane with red teeth before I ran at her. I had already hurt her leg, her wrist had been twisted when she slammed me to the ground, and I suspected she had a pulled muscle from something else before we even began, based on the way she was moving.

She stumbled back as I surged forward, my foot coming out to knock out that injured leg, using the momentum of her own fall to aim a solid punch right to her face.

Everyone seemed to go silent for a moment, and time stood still as I watched her eyes roll back in her head. I didn't need to throw another; she was out cold from that blow alone.

I was still watching her when I felt the ref pulling my arm up, the muffled sound of, "Winner!" being shouted close to my ear.

Shit, maybe I did get a concussion.

I managed to get down out of the ring and make it to the doors that lead back to the locker room before Carmen caught up to me.

"You're hurt," she said with hands on her hips as she looked down at where I sat on the bench.

"Maybe?"

"Shit! Adrian's going to kill us," she grumbled, squatting down to help me with my finger tape.

"It's already dissipating," I said, and that was true, my vision was already back to normal, and I could hear just fine, a fact that I honestly wasn't too pleased about, because Vallo chose this moment to break out in an aria, his not-quite tenor voice echoing loudly. That was probably how he provoked people into punching him to push his fights to later in the evening. Made sense. I wanted to punch him too.

The doors burst open and there were my men. They walked through the room, their faces looked like they could kill any man who crossed them, and they were headed right for us. Unfortunately, those looks in my direction didn't have the effect that they were often going for, especially since my panties immediately soaked at the prospect of what I was in for later.

"You're hurt." It wasn't a question. Adrian took my face in his hand, turning it so he could inspect for injuries, while Sal crossed his arms over his chest.

"It's nothing," I said, but Adrian caught my lip with his thumb and pulled it down to reveal my still bloody mouth.

"You're fucking bleeding!" he practically growled, turning to look at Sal, whose scowl only got deeper.

"Jesus, she's fine!" Carmen snapped. Her glare aimed at her brother.

I smirked when both men's eyes snapped to her, but she didn't back down, her green eyes narrowing. She may have been small, like me, but Carmen was formidable, and all the Lupo and LaMartina men knew it.

"You ready?" Sal snapped, his focus coming back to me.

Was I ready to go home and have them show me exactly how much me getting hurt in a fight angered them? Absolutely.

"I'll meet you in the car," I said, gesturing to my shoes and my bag.

"Not a chance," Adrian said, turning to look around the locker room, their intimidating glares making some of the toughest men cower.

I took my time changing into my regular shoes and slipping my various supplies back in my bag, Carmen happily sitting and watching. She loved being petty against them just as much as I did. We made a great team.

When we finally made it to the car, I sat in the back seat, and surprisingly Adrian sat beside me, leaving shotgun to Carmen.

"Don't forget about shopping tomorrow," Carmen said when she climbed out of the car.

"Shopping?" I asked, having completely forgotten. Ingrid was finally getting married to Enzo. They had discussed it for nearly six months before she finally said she'd consider it. Then Enzo, ever the charmer, did the biggest gesture. Ingrid couldn't say no. So of course, I was obligated to go shopping for dresses with the ladies.

"You better not try to get out of it, Ash," Carmen said, aiming those fiery green eyes at me this time.

"I'm not!" I insisted, cowing a little as she shot me one more fierce look before closing the door and heading up to her apartment.

The air in the car changed almost immediately after she got into the building. Adrian's hand, which had been holding my thigh, slipped upward, the pressure increasing.

"You're lucky we have a surprise for you," Sal said, his dark eyes watching from the rearview mirror.

"A surprise?" I asked, trying to lock in on that, since Adrian's mouth was now on my neck, seeming utterly unfazed by my sweaty skin.

"Mhm, otherwise you'd be in big trouble for getting hurt," Adrian said, his voice a rumble in my ear.

The idea of being in *trouble* with these two was tantalizing, especially coupled with the wandering fingers that had traveled from my upper thigh to blatantly between my legs, stroking me through my yoga shorts.

The drive from Carmen and Leo's apartment wasn't long, only a few minutes and we were pulling into the garage, but that had been plenty of time for Adrian to get my heart rate spiking and my breath coming out as pants. Sal practically tore his keys from the car, climbing out and opening the back door. He groaned when he looked at us, Adrian having let his hand find its way under my sports bra, pinching my nipple while he kissed my neck.

"We have to go in," Sal managed to grunt out, his hand going to his tenting pants and squeezing his erection.

"You're right," Adrian said, giving a sharp tap to my now throbbing core, my juices having soaked through my shorts. "Let's show you the surprise."

I didn't care at all about any sort of surprise. I wanted to crawl out of my clothes and onto their skin.

Adrian ushered me out of the car into Sal's arms. He took the opportunity to press me close to his chest, breathing in my scent from the top of my head while his hands wandered down to greedily grasp my ass. This surprise better have been worth the wait, because the fact that they were stopping themselves from doing what we all wanted was a feat.

We entered through the kitchen, and I was guided through to the dining room instead of going up the kitchen stairs. The lust-filled haze I had been in disappeared the moment my brain registered the fact that this room was different. *Very* different. Gone was the long rectangular table with overly decorated chairs, the curtains were no longer the busy, gold-plated flowering things they had been, instead there was a large round table with beautiful inlaid wood designs on the top, the curtain exchanged for a more subtle design that still accentuated the colors of the space.

"This is so much better," I said, reaching out to touch the tabletop with my fingers.

I had been told this was all lavishly decorated for Salvatore to show off his wealth. This change seemed to signify something for Sal and Adrian. This was much more their style. Much more *our* style. Simple, but elegant. Comfortable.

"We thought you might like it," Sal said.

"It was clear on your face how much you hated the décor," Adrian said with a chuckle.

"I wasn't going to say anything," I said, giving them both a glare that I couldn't hold as I turned back around to them. "So this is the surprise?"

"Just part of it," Sal said, taking my hand and leading me through the main hall to the stairs.

There were more changes here. Some of the paintings were gone. In their place were beautiful photos of the family. Some from the wedding, but many more from the past. There were even two photos of all six of the Lupo and LaMartina kids. The first one was when they were all very young, Carmen looked to be about six, one of her teeth had fallen out and an adorable gap was there, Benny and Leo were grinning with mischief as they held bunny ears up behind her mass of curls. Enzo was lying in front of them all, laughing, that dimple in his cheek peeking through as it did to this day. And standing behind all of them, were Adrian and Sal. They looked to be about eleven and twelve, arms over each other's shoulders and grinning into the camera.

The second one was at the wedding. All six of them were standing side by side.

My heart felt full, tears springing to my eyes, knowing what everyone went through and that we had all made it out in the end, happier.

"Come on," Adrian murmured, wiping the tear that had escaped and trickled down my cheek with his thumb.

We made our way upstairs and down the hall to a door I hadn't been in before. There were too many rooms in this house and even though I had spent a week here with nothing better to do than explore, I felt weird looking around places I wasn't invited to. I had told myself that would change when we came back, because if I was living here now, I was going to know this place inside and out.

Apparently, my men had similar ideas. Sal opened the door, and the room was revealed. There was a massive custom-sized bed with large wooden posts. Simple designs were carved into the surface of the wood. A leather couch sat by the windows and several dressers that matched the wood of the bed were sitting on either side of two doors. The room was painted a soothing blue, a blue that was very much the color that I gravitated toward, and I noticed several photos framed on one wall.

I went to them, seeing they were pictures of *us*. One from the wedding. Someone must have taken it while we were sitting during Carmen and Leo's cake-cutting. I felt my cheeks heat at the idea that anyone would have been paying attention to what was happening in that moment. My eyes were closed, face serene while Sal's nose was nearly touching my shoulder. Adrian on my other side, looking at me and Sal with a look that could only be described as feral with need. This picture, while not explicit, was incredibly sexy. The other photos were from more recent times. Family dinners at the moms', where all of us were laughing together.

These were good. These were what we really were. There wasn't a plot to take one of us away. There wasn't an immediate impending threat. This was just a family together.

I had a family now.

I turned around, a wave of appreciation filling me as I took in my men. Sal looked his normal stoic self, waiting until he was certain of how I was feeling to react, while Adrian was grinning.

"I love you," I said, my voice thick with emotion as I looked at them both.

They came toward me, engulfing me in their arms, whispering how they felt about me, and I silently thanked the universe that I allowed myself to let them in, because this was where I was meant to be.

BOOK CLUB QUESTIONS

1. Ash is a strong, independent woman. Why do you think she felt like her fate was sealed when she knew the Lupos and LaMartinas would help her?

2. Who were your favorite and least favorite characters in this book? Were there any from previous books you wished had been more prominent?

3. Why do you think it took Sal and Adrian so long to realize their feelings for one another when their feelings for Ash were so apparent to them?

4. How do you think the conflict will go with the Irish, now that Freddy is dead and Colin O'Shea no longer has heirs?

5. Sal has essentially threatened Manzo Morelli. What kind of blowback, if any, do you think they will likely see in the future?

6. We got a little glimpse of how Liliana felt about the throuple situation between Ash, Adrian, and Sal. How did you think the final reveal of their relationship would go with the family?

AUTHOR BIO

Chelsea Burton Dunn is a Kansas City native—the Missouri side, not the Kansas side. That matters to locals. Where is that you might ask? Right, smack-dab in the middle of the country. She has two beautiful children and is married to a superb partner, but let's not forget their snuggly cat and eager-eater of a dog.

Having always been a little strange herself, she instantly fell in love with paranormal, supernatural, and fantasy books, movies, and TV shows as a child. Did everyone think it was a phase? Absolutely. Was it? Absolutely not. Being weird is a blessing, not a curse. She's always embraced that part of herself and those around her.

She started writing from a very early age, initially starting and completing one of the *Dead Man's Hand* books in high school. She is a lover of music, having her other love and talent be for singing. She performed on main stage operas in the children's chorus from grade school to high school.

Chelsea loves to delve into the difficulties of life, love, and loss while spicing it up with a little magic and monsters. As she liked to say when she was younger, "The monsters in my head need to come out to play every once in a while," so giving them life on the page seemed appropriate.

You can see more about Chelsea, her projects, and find her social medias by going to www.chelseaburtondunn.com

Discover more at
4HorsemenPublications.com

10% off using HORSEMEN10

* 9 7 9 8 8 2 3 2 0 9 6 9 4 *